Zane Radcliffe was born in Bangor, Northern Ireland in 1969, the year the Troubles started. The day he moved to London in 1994, the IRA declared a ceasefire. Typical.

He graduated from Queen's University Belfast and was editor of the student newspaper. After a brief stint as a music journalist he became an advertising copywriter. He has received a British Television Advertising Award and has passed both his Cycling Proficiency Test and Trumpet (Grade 3). He recently relocated to Edinburgh. His second novel, *Big Jessie* is also published by Black Swan.

www.booksattransworld.co.uk

Also by Zane Radcliffe

BIG JESSIE

and published by Black Swan

LONDON IRISH

Zane Radcliffe

BLACK SWAN

LONDON IRISH
A BLACK SWAN BOOK : 0 552 77095 7

First publication in Great Britain

PRINTING HISTORY
Black Swan edition published 2002

7 9 10 8 6

Set in 11/14 pt Melior by
Phoenix Typesetting, Burley-in-Wharfdale, West Yorkshire.

Black Swan Books are published by Transworld Publishers,
61–63 Uxbridge Road, London W5 5SA,
a division of The Random House Group Ltd,
in Australia by Random House Australia (Pty) Ltd,
20 Alfred Street, Milsons Point, Sydney, NSW 2061, Australia,
in New Zealand by Random House New Zealand Ltd,
18 Poland Road, Glenfield, Auckland 10, New Zealand
and in South Africa by Random House (Pty) Ltd,
Endulini, 5a Jubilee Road, Parktown 2193, South Africa.

Printed and bound in Great Britain by
Cox & Wyman Ltd, Reading, Berkshire.

Papers used by Transworld Publishers are natural, recyclable products
made from wood grown in sustainable forests. The manufacturing processes
conform to the environmental regulations of the country of origin.

For my parents, Peter and Pat Radcliffe.
You know who you are.

CHEERS

Natalie – for love, encouragement and chicken pesto. Mike Oughton – for seven of the best. My agent, Jonny Geller – for reading the typescript on a windswept Cornish beach. My editor, Simon Taylor – for the seven-figure advance. Steven Emerson, Stuart Dodds, Darren McKinney and the 'Non Iron' lot – for unending laughter. Liane and Liesel – for if I don't, they'll kill me. And huge thanks to all at Transworld.

26th June, 1982

You needed to pee but you didn't want your da to stop.

You jammed your knees together in anticipation of the next bump. They walloped the car like big concrete waves on these coast roads. Your da said that drumlins made the bumps and when you asked him what drumlins were he explained that they were Irish goblins.

Another concrete wave slipped under the windscreen and *whumph*, your tuppence tickled.

'Boun-seeeeeeeeeeeeee!' you screamed.

'These roads are getting worse,' your mammy said.

But you knew they just got better. She probably got a bouncy too because girls have tuppences and your mammy was a girl. You dug your hands into your skirt pockets to hold your pee in.

'How far now, Da?'

'Not long now, Roach.'

'Her name's Roisin,' said your mammy. 'We

christened her Roisin Mary Jocepta McKay and that's how she'll be referred to.'

Your mammy never called you Roach. That was just between you and your da.

'OK then. Would you like another bouncy, Roisin Mary Jocepta Toyota Sultana Banana Havana Anaglypta McKay?'

'Aye Da,' you laughed.

'Roisin, would you stop bending your father's ears when his eyes are on the road.'

'Ach leave the wee girl alone, Dympna.'

You liked it when your da took your side. He pointed out the window: 'Look. See what's up ahead, Petal?'

And it was great when he called you Petal. He never called your three big brothers Petal. He sometimes called them the Three Stooges but you didn't know what that meant.

You rested your chin on the hot grey plastic of the passenger seat. It sort of burned so you sat forward and nuzzled into your mammy's shoulder. Her jumper tickled. She wore an identical jumper to the one she'd knitted for your fifth birthday, only bigger. Your mammy could make wool go far.

'Well, do you see it, Petal?'

'It's a archway,' you offered.

'*An* archway,' said your mammy. She was always correcting you like that.

You scratched your chin. The rocky arch spilled out of the mountain to your left and fell over the road in front of you like a big hooked finger. Northern Ireland had a hooked finger on the map. This must be it, you thought. A shadow ripped through the car as you sped under its bony knuckle and on along the Antrim coast.

'Who built the archway, Da?'

Your da said that the sea built it and you laughed because he surely meant the man in the sea, with the coral crown and the big fork. The man in the sea was tall and silvery-green and you had seen him fight Sinbad on telly at Christmas.

The road became less bumpy but you could still hear the tent poles clanking on the roof rack. You had already bagsied the foot-pump and appointed yourself to the position of Chief Lilo Filler. Your tongue tensed as you imagined licking the nozzle and the short sharp shot of air if you jumped on the pump with both feet. The air would taste of ground sheets, packet bacon and gas.

You went camping every summer. You camped at the best place in the world: Gaeltacht. The people that lived in Gaeltacht spoke Irish and you had to pretend you understood them, even when you couldn't. It didn't matter anyway because you got to do Irish dancing in your new dress that your mammy had made. Everybody understood Irish dancing, so that was OK. Your brothers stayed back on the farm because your da said they could barely speak English, never mind Irish.

'And what's that, Roach?' Your da was doing his pointing thing again.

'It's a horsey.'

'No, it's not a horsey,' said your ma.

Well it had a long nose and a mane and you were sure your mammy was mad.

'*Ta se an capall*,' she said. 'Say it Roisin, *an capall*.'

'A crapper.'

Your da nearly burst himself laughing and you knew

you'd said the Irish all wrong. Just wait till I show him my dancing, you thought, angry with yourself.

'Ah Jeez, that's priceless that is. *A crapper*. She's her daddy's girl, aren't you Roach?'

'Daddy, sing the non-iron song.'

They had been playing the non-iron song all day on the car radio. That was because last night, Northern Ireland had beaten Spain at football to win the World Cup. Your da had allowed you to stay up and watch it.

'OK love, the non-iron song it is.'

Your da slapped the steering wheel as he sang: 'When yer man gets the ball, Non Iron beat them all –'

'Michael, stop acting the goat and keep your hands on the wheel. Any more of that carry-on and we'll be fish food.'

Your mammy was afraid that the car could easily topple off the edge of Northern Ireland, down through the circling gulls and into the sea.

You weren't scared. You would have been had you looked down to your right. The car skirted another bend on the steep coast road. You pressed your lips to the window and puffed out your cheeks. The glass tasted of coins. The car turned inland, where the rocks became hedges and the sea, fields.

You slid along the plastic seat and a sunny patch scalded your legs. That was your mammy's fault. She had told you to wear a skirt because it was hot and trousers would only bring on your heat rash. Sweat creased the backs of your knees. Your da was sweating too, but that was OK because when Georgie Best Superstar was in your toilet he had dark red sweat patches under his arms. It meant you were cool. Your

12

mammy didn't like your da having a picture of Georgie Best in her toilet. She took it down and replaced it with a picture of the baby Jesus. Your da said the Son of God didn't look as good as his father and put 'Our Lord Georgie' back up again.

'How far now Da?' You felt tired. Your eyes were going.

'Half as far as the last time you asked.'

'How far was it the last time I asked?'

'Twice as far as it is now.'

'You're dead clever, Da. Mammy, isn't Da clever?'

'Your father isn't dead anything, darling, but he will be if he keeps driving like an eejit.'

'Sure I must be clever, Roach. I married your mammy, didn't I.'

Your da put his hand on your mammy's knee. She kept her eyes on her map.

Your da *was* dead clever. He could make his thumb come apart and put it back together again. He could play tunes on a blade of grass, any tune, just by blowing on it. If you asked him how he did it, he would grab you and rub his beard in your face. Your cheeks would sting but it would be a good sting. It was worse when he was just starting a beard. Your mammy didn't like him with a beard. She said it made his head look upside down. That was because your da was bald. She said he was bald because of something called *hairheadity* and this meant that your brothers would go bald too.

You examined his head, with its eyes on the road and its ears bent. It looked like a hunk of Coleraine Cheddar, beading in the heat.

You peeled your legs off the seat and turned round to

13

look out the back window, balancing on your knees. This way you could see where you'd been. The parched road whizzed out from under you and split the fields in two. Cows just stood, dumb and baking in the sun. That's why some meat you buy is ready-cooked, you thought.

Sunlight splintered off the chrome window frame onto the tartan rug that was draped across the boot. You were worried the rug might catch fire, like a beetle under a magnifying glass. Your brothers had taught you how to do that. They said that if you sunbathed wearing your glasses, your eyelashes would catch fire.

Your brothers were dirty wee liars.

The air *whumphed* in through the small windows either side of you. It sucked at your ears and your hair did an Irish dance. You weren't getting any cooler. You could fry an egg in here, you thought, but you couldn't fry eggs. You once made your ma a wee cuppa tea with hot water and milk. Just hot water and milk. Well, you were only five, how were you to know?

'Hold on tight Roach, here comes another bump. Bounseee—'

At first you just felt your knees buckle a little. Then your head whacked against one of the small windows and your left ear filled up with something very warm. That's the biggest bouncy ever, you thought, as the car flipped upside down and your da's severed head landed on the tartan rug.

Like when you sometimes woke up in the tent to find that your lilo had gone down during the night. That's

14

how you felt with your cheek biting on the tarmac. Dust was hanging in your nostrils. Your pants and legs were soaking wet.

The car wasn't car-shaped any more. It was on its side. That's what bombs did to Ulsterbuses on UTV, you thought.

You managed to stand upright. You were almost as tall as the car was wide. The door above your head was heavier this way, but somehow you managed to push it open. You stood a leg on your mammy's shoulder. Even though she was dead, she gave you a foot-up and you climbed out into the sunshine. Your other leg wasn't working too well.

You lay down on the side of the car. It was difficult to get comfortable. The petrol cap was sticking into your back. You felt like the princess who slept on the pea.

You closed your eyes, but the horror wouldn't go away. The explosion replayed itself on the back of your eyelids in frightening technicolor. You opened them again and let the sun boil the salt from your tears.

The car was hot. You could smell petrol. It had soaked into your skirt. You knew you could catch fire. You thought of those beetles again, the ones under your magnifying glass. You knew you had to move, but it was a big drop down to the road. You turned onto your tummy and edged your legs over the side of the car. You held onto the rear wheel and slowly lowered your hips, then your chest, until you were hanging and kicking and calling for your da to scoop you up in his big hairy arms. You let go. But he wasn't there to catch you.

Your legs gave way and the road took the skin from

15

your knees. You didn't have time to cry. You had to get away from the car.

You saw a dead horse by the side of the road and you decided to go over and lie against it instead. The wee girl beside it didn't mind. She was dead too.

One

Only one hundred and fifty-seven shopping days till the new millennium.

That's if you excluded Sundays. I didn't like to exclude Sundays. Sunday was my busiest day on Greenwich market. The punters came religiously.

I ripped some kitchen roll and wiped the grease from my hotplates. I had sold a lot of crêpes, considering the weather. The last week of June and it was raining. Fucking Wimbledon weather, it was. But it seems there's nothing like a hot crêpe on a cold wet day and the punters they came, from all walks of life and all corners of the globe (if, indeed, a globe has corners).

I was approached by some gum-chewin', breeze-shootin', God-fearin' Yanks, all loud-mouthed, leather-faced and dressed for golf. They looked like they had strayed into the market in search of some spectacularly wayward tee shot. In truth, they were after a pair of Diana, Queen of Hearts oven gloves. I pointed them in the right direction. They asked if I wanted a pair. They had noticed that my hands were pocked with burns from my hotplate.

I served the obligatory French school party, easily distinguished by their uniform: twenty of them, all with hair sprayed an identical fluorescent green. If punk wasn't dead, they were killing it.

Next up, a German couple. They were over in London, sizing the place up. London could have been theirs. Judging by their sauerkraut expressions, it was a case of what they didn't have, they didn't miss. And anyway, Hitler would have a job on his hands trying to ethnically cleanse the London of 1999. One, because it was too cosmopolitan. And two, because Hitler was dead.

A Sunday morning in Greenwich market afforded a microcosm of the capital.

I watched a swarm of WASPs buzzing round the stalls, snapping up handmade furniture and home-made jam to take back to their wholesome Hampstead homes. I saw a crustie lugging a bag of chickpeas so large, I assumed it was destined to be dropped over some Third World dictatorship enduring severe trading sanctions. I noted pushchair children with lollipop-sticky faces; young couples enacting the farewell formalities of one-night stands; old couples enacting the farewell formalities of existence; up-all-night Aussies navigating their way back home (Earl's Court); and the post-church saved souls washing down the Body of Christ with quick cream teas. I watched fairweather footie fans congregate in the Greenwich Tavern to genuflect in the light of that shifting stained-glass window that is *Sky Sports Super Sunday*. And I took no pity on the middle-aged philanderer in his last night's dancing trousers as he desperately bought up fistfuls of carnations, terrified that his wife might have woken up before he had a chance to slip back unnoticed into his cold half of the conjugal bed.

All human life is in Greenwich market and, if you don't believe me, several thousand Japanese tourists already have it captured on quality-grade home video.

As I scraped the charred remnants of a bygone crêpe, I spotted one of London's most familiar creatures, a species already named and classified:

The Common *Big Issue* Salesperson
bigissu vendor

Habitat: confined to major cities, principally London. Enjoys tube exits, shop doorways and supermarket car parks.
Concentration: very little.
Markings: yellow ochre index fingers.
Call: *'gishoo gishoo'.*

In my six years working the market, I have built my *Observer's Book of London Man* (ed. Anthony Bickmore) into a comprehensive and useful little volume: over 480 pages, 134 colour plates. *'Indispensable . . .'* David Attenborough would write of it. That's if I stuck a gun in his mouth, a pen in his hand, and asked him to in my best Belfast brogue (though, having spent half of my twenty-eight years living in Scotland, my native Ulster accent has crept north-west and now resides in some mucky field outside Stranraer).

It's not that I feel some overwhelming need to classify every person I lay eyes on. Hey, none of us likes to be put in a box. Ask a corpse. My mental cataloguing of people is an involuntary pursuit. I can't help it. How can I, when I'm confronted with people every day. There are loads of the bastards. They're on the tube, on the telly, on the moon. People drill holes in my teeth. People put final demands through my door. People say stupid things to me like *I hope we can still be friends*.

People are everywhere. Look to your immediate left . . . see. And what box have you just put them in, I wonder. We all do it whether we like it or not. And if, like me, you have grown up with your father's veterinary textbooks as preferred reading to the *Beano*, it becomes second nature to dissect, annotate, cross-reference and classify anything with a pulse. All in the blink of an eye. A reflex index.

If I've learnt one thing about people, it's that you can't trust them.

Londoners baulk at the statistic that at any given time, at any given place in the Big particulate-riddled Smoke, they are never more than twenty feet from a rat. As they recoil in disgust, sardined under some merchant banker's armpit in a metal cage, in a dark tube tunnel beneath London's sewers, they would do well to remember their dangerous proximity to humans. There are seven million of the bastards running round their city and in my experience they're a damn sight more harmful than rats. Rats don't start wars, increase the basic rate of taxation, or read over your shoulder on the train. London is overrun by people. They're a bloody plague.

Three good reasons not to trust people:

(1) They drive.

(2) They cook your food.

(3) They say *trust me*.

Let's put that last one to bed. As soon as someone says *trust me*, in that treacly way they invariably do, tear up their words, swallow them, digest them, incinerate the resulting stool and scatter the ashes at sea. When they say *trust me* – the words swirling off their tongue and into your ear like syrup from a spoon – it is because they want you to confide in them some information you'd rather not share, or they want you to conspire with them in an event you'd rather not be a party to. If you succumb, you become someone less than you were. They will now have something on you, see. They will know your secrets, your peccadilloes, all your little mistakes. And before you know it, so will the rest of the world. But you'll only have yourself to blame. This person merely said *trust me* – molasses! molasses! – and by doing so, you invested them with the power to embarrass you, blackmail you, screw you, throw something back in your face, stitch you up like a kipper, shit upon you from a great height and generally make you dance to their tune. They said *trust me* and now they're the bloody Puppet Master.

People drive. Half a tonne of glass and metal travelling at speeds of up to 140 mph, often in opposing directions, and piloted by probably the most fallible machine known to man: Man. Just think about that the next time you're cruising happily up the inside lane of the North Circular. It's not a thought that compels you to up the volume on Heart 106.4 FM and, with your elbow out the window and the wind in your hair, burst into a rousing chorus of 'Convoy'.

Yet on you go, driving along with that badly secured IKEA futon hanging out the arse of your hatchback. Until some stressed-out City boy doing eighty on autopilot in his company S-Class – ear glued to his mobile, Big Mac in his lap – gets word he's been sacked, *oh and can we have the Merc back?* And before he's even depressed the small red phone-shaped icon on his Nokia, he decides *fuck it* and swerves, power-assisted, into the oncoming traffic. Into you.

You put the same trust in people at tube stations. As you watch the *****Stand Back Train Approaching***** scroll across, what's to stop some care-in-the-community day tripper from pushing you onto the track, just to see what would happen? Yet, every day, millions of us stand on platforms inches away from an unimaginable horror. Imagine it.

And people cook your food. That is to say, you *let* them cook your food. There you go, trusting people again. Example: you are in a restaurant and you ask the waiter to fetch you a clean spoon. While he's at it, he gobs in your tiramisu. He just *didn't like you*. There are over nine thousand restaurants in Greater London. There's a whole lot of trust going on.

Trust isn't an issue with the humble crêpe (plug, plug). On a busy day I'll make four hundred, easy, and with every one of them it's all cards on the table. I make them right here, right now, right in front of your piggy little eyes. I put in them what you want in them. I leave out what you don't. There are no bodily fluids in one of my crêpes. That's if you discount the blood, sweat and tears.

See, there's an art to making a crêpe. The choreography begins when I squirt a little oil from a recycled Jif lemon into a ball of kitchen roll. I use it to grease the hotplate in big shiny circles. I wait until the hotplate speaks to me before pouring the batter on. It hisses and spits and sends up smoke signals to tell me it's ready. A good batter should be a viscous oyster-beige. I let it fall in folds from the jug onto the hotplate. It mustn't run, nor must it be helped out. Then I twirl a drumstick through it 360 degrees, like I'm putting the clock back one hour. I spread it nice and thin, to the size of an LP. This is the Critical Point. If you haven't got the right balance of egg, flour, salt and milk, you're screwed. You only learn by trial and error (my epitaph). Too much flour and at the Critical Point you'll have a pancake: thick and clumsy, a bit like yourself. Too little and you'll be left with something translucent, resembling rice paper or the skin on an old lady's hand.

The secret of a good crêpe is its ability to sustain fillings without overpowering them. There's art in that.

I don't charge much for my crêpes, not when you consider that Londoners willingly pay fifteen quid for a pizza (cheese on toast) or a bowl of pasta (water and flour, it's glue for Christ's sake).

And I like the smell of my job. How many of us can claim that? Not those orange women who man the toiletries counters in large stores. They are surrounded by some of the most expensive smells the world has to offer, yet it's like chemical warfare in there. Don't go in without a caged canary. If you were responsible for putting the caps on Magic Markers you'd enjoy the smell of your job. I'm sure working in an oil factory has its olfactory perks. And the groundsman at Stamford Bridge, I imagine, relishes the scent of his labour: all that cut grass and Deep Heat.

But you can't beat the smell of a good crêpe.

I forked some butter onto the hotplate and watched the little yellow bricks fizzle and complain. I inhaled deeply – burnt popcorn. As the sweet smell subsided, the air seemed to ionize. It became electric, thick and damp and highly charged. A dark sky had thrown itself over the market like a heavy duffel. Across the river, lightning snapped at Canary Wharf with the urgency of a paparazzo's flashgun. It was just as impertinent.

Resolution Number One: I had to get out of London, now and for good.

I had decided to make my New Year's resolutions early this year, just in case the millennium bug bit and the globe imploded. The end of the world could be nigh. I didn't actually believe it was nigh – I wasn't entirely sure what nigh meant (isn't it Northern Irish for *now*?) – but I had to get out of this city before it destroyed me. I figured that the threat of impending apocalypse was a good reason to do it sooner rather than later.

So, as my butter spat and separated and Canary Wharf blinked and cowered, I made four New Millennium's resolutions:

(1) I had to get out of London. Now and for good.
(2) I had to stop screwing other men's wives.
(3) I had to start talking to my father again (a

24

resolution I had made and broken every year since I was fifteen).

(4) I had to stop trusting people.

I consider myself a man of strong will, and proved it by sticking faithfully to Resolution Number Four for all of two minutes and twelve seconds. For that was the time it took Joe Carlin to approach my stall, light his fag and deliver a proposal that ended in the words: *trust me.*

You see, if I had stuck to Resolution Number Four, things would never have got so complicated. If I had only stuck to Resolution Number Four, I would not have become the most feared man in Britain, with fourteen murders to my name.

Two

'Bic, I'm in a bit of fix. I need you to do a job for me. There's good money in it.' Joe's lighter refused to co-operate in the rain. He had the shakes. Joe always had the shakes.

Joe Carlin ran the markets. He was a mess of a man. His face was a complex relief map of lines and creases. His complexion was fag-filter brown. He looked like a spent tea bag. Joe would smoke a cigarette from tip to butt without once removing it from his lips. The frames of his glasses were held together by a nicotine patch. His chest burbled when he spoke.

'Joe, you really should quit smoking. Listen to your lungs,' I said.

'Sod lungs. You can't take them with you. Honestly, people get so hung up on material things,' he burbled.

'So what's this job you're talking about?' I asked.

Smoke flew out of his nose as the words flew out of

his mouth. In a couple weeks, he said, the tenth of July to be precise, the annual Cutty Sark Tall Ships Regatta would start from Greenwich pier. The race day would be a Saturday, but Joe had been ordered by the Met to shut the market down for security reasons. Apparently all the top nobs would be attending: the Queen's Admiral, the Government, the local council, that bird off *Countdown*, everyone. Joe knew that us stallholders wouldn't take the closure too well. We would be missing out on a lot of business. Thousands of people were expected to descend on the market to watch the regatta. As a trade-off, Joe had negotiated the contract to organize all the catering for the day. He had since put out the feelers. He had called every catering firm and party organizer in London. For the sort of money they were asking, he could have bought Charlton a decent bloody striker, or so he claimed.

Joe was tight.

And that's where I came in. Joe wanted me to handle all the catering.

'No way,' I said.

'Come on Bic, it'll be the biggest pay day of your life. Five numbers and the bonus ball. You're hardly rolling in it. Your backside wouldn't be hanging out your jeans if you were flush.'

'I'll need to hire staff. I'll have to quadruple my stock.'

'I'll help you get whatever you need.'

Joe had never been this accommodating. He must have been desperate. I realized then that I should do the decent thing and help him out of his tight spot.

'I'm sorry, Joe. You'll have to find someone else.'

I didn't like Joe Carlin.

'OK, Bic. What if I reduce your rent?'

'It's not a question of money. It just isn't possible. Not for that many people. Not on that scale.'

'You'll manage.'

'No, Joe.'

'Trust me,' he said.

The rain got bored being drizzle so it decided to pelt instead. It would have pissed if it had had the energy.

It was six by the time I closed up. I clacked the shutters together, so the words *Life's* and *Crêpe* were adjacent. It's a corny name, but it brings in the punters. They never tire of having their photograph taken standing underneath the legend, always smiling and always clutching an obscene amount of piping hot, bought-and-paid-for crêpe.

The cold gnawed at my knuckles. My key struggled to sink its teeth into the padlock. I stretched the corners of my mouth with thumb and finger, folded my tongue back and blew out a loud whistle. I counted elephants: *one elephant, two elephant, three elephant, four elephant, five elephant, six elephant, seven elephant, eight elephant, nine elephant, ten elephant, eleven elephant, tweeelph*— two wet paws thrust themselves at some velocity into my groin.

I bent down, knees cracking, and opened out my palm. Dunc's hot pink tongue lapped up the cast-off I had saved for him. I was going to have to stop feeding my dog leftover crêpes. He was clearly losing fitness. In normal health he would have crushed my testicles on the tenth elephant.

I had rescued Duncan from a bin-liner bobbing on the

Thames. I had watched someone drop him in. Hence, Dunc. He was so small back then, maybe a day old, and pinky-orange in colour. I was relieved that he had grown into a red setter. For a nervous first few days I thought I had rescued a baby orang-utan. I felt like Clint bleedin' Eastwood.

The city is no place for a dog, least of all London and least of all a red setter. From the moment they are born red setters are clinically deranged (source: Dad's text-books again). Some might say that being mad from birth is less of a disadvantage and more of a prerequisite for living in London. And sure enough, Duncan had adjusted to the city better than I had. He had a way of conning my fellow stallholders out of food. Gingerbread men, sunflower-seed brownies, carrot cake and Bombay mix he often washed down with Tea Tree aromatherapy oil (Dunc's preferred tipple). Then he worked it off in Greenwich Park.

He licked the last oily fleck from my palm.

'Good boy.' I tickled him on the chin and thought, strange, dogs don't have chins. He took this as the signal to rear up on his hind legs and spar with my testicles once more.

In return for the stallholders' philanthropy, Dunc cheered them up. Not by doing anything extravagant like jumping through flaming hoops or saying 'shaushagesh'. He cheered them up by his sheer presence. Rather like those dogs the Japanese employ in high-rise offices, whose job it is to patrol the corridors and lick a few executive faces, reducing stress and increasing the life expectancy of your average Osaka suit by a dog year or two. Dunc had the same effect on my colleagues.

He followed me along Nelson Walk into the High Road and on towards the overground station. The mouth of the station spewed out hunched heads and bags shouldered from the rain. Londoners were flooding back into the city from their weekends away. That's what you do in London. You get out of it at every available opportunity.

The road was jammed with impatient traffic. The wet tarmac wobbled in reflected red and orange from tail lights. A group of drunks had taken up temporary address outside the off-licence. Their coats hung about them, heavy mats in the rain. This was one of the few occasions when water touched their faces. One of them was dancing. He looked very young, or would have, had most of his hair not fallen out. I caught a glint of gold in his hand: Tuborg Gold. The young, old man punctuated his jig with deep glugs. His knotted beard dripped the stuff when he danced. He seemed very happy. The weekenders studiously avoided him. They didn't seem so happy.

The rain now considered pelting a touch passé and instead opted to lash. I ducked under the canopy of a grocer's. A bucketful of wind caught it like a clarinet reed and it emitted a long melancholic drone. It hadn't been a bad day for business, however, and my takings were burning a hole in my bumbag. I treated myself to a couple of baking potatoes. Later, at my flat, I would dance the hot bakers from hand to hand, like the drunk's jig, before splitting them with a wedge of Irish cheddar. My tongue would be scorched.

God it was cold. Though, being God, he didn't need

me to tell him. I pocketed my change and weaved out through the angry faces only to be met by an incurably beaming one.

'Bic. How's about you big man.'

It was my cousin, Jambo.

Jambo and I had grown up together in Stranraer, from the time I was dumped there to live with my Aunt Sylvia, his mother. He was the closest thing I had to a sibling. We had come down to London in '94 to look for work. He had been christened Jambo by the lads at school. Given that his full name was Jamie Jameson and he was the only Hearts fan in Stranraer, it was hardly a lateral leap. The lads put little imagination into nicknames. Since I wasn't marked out by any obvious physical defect – a strawberry birthmark covering half my face, or a third nipple – the lads had trouble giving me a nickname. So they 'nicked' my name. Bickmore was pruned to Bic.

Without looking up I knew it was Jambo. The Scots and the Northern Irish are the only heterosexual males who can ask *how's about you big man* and walk away with their jaw, or their arse, intact.

'I'm foundered,' I replied.

'I was hopin' tae catch you. Come wi' me. We're goin' tae get our baps whacked.'

'We're what?'

'We're goin' for a heercut. You look like you could do wi' a chop.'

Jambo was covered in mud. He worked for the construction firm building the Millennium Dome. He looked like he'd been dug up.

'Jambo, I'm heading back to the flat. I'm going to put my feet up and I'm going to fall asleep halfway through a baked potato. Come on, Dunc.'

'Ach bollocks. This is London, you tit. You're not supposed tae stay in. Do you no read *Time Out*? Let's gan on a bender.'

'A bender? Since when did having a haircut on a Sunday evening constitute going on a bender? I hadn't realized that *Time Out* were listing Barbers between Arts and Clubs.'

'There's no need fae sarcasm. Look, one o' the guys down the Dome site says his missus runs a salon in the East End. *Curl Up and Dye* it's called. I think that's some sort ay heerdressing joke. Anyways, she's havin' a trainees' night th'night. We can gan along and get ourselves a free bap whack. Gratis, like.'

'Free?'

'Aye. And they might even gi' your dog a clipping while they're at it.'

'So, let's get this straight. You want me to drop everything and come along with you to some salon I've never heard of, where I'm to let someone who's never cut hair cut my hair, despite it not needing a cut?'

'Trust me.'

I had heard those words earlier from Joe Carlin. They sounded even less convincing from Jambo's mouth. I had found myself agreeing to help Joe with his catering but I wasn't going to make the same mistake twice.

'I'm going home,' I said.

'Jesus Bic, your dog's eatin' my heer.'

Jambo sat to my right with his head in a sink. He was

32

having his scalp soaped by a young girl, she couldn't have been fifteen. I kicked Dunc away from the little stack of ginger hair, copper filings, under his chair.

'I can't believe I agreed to this,' I said.

'Quit your gurning, big man. Jeeeeez—' The girl yanked Jambo's head out of the sink. She towelled it dry with a force that belied her years.

'Mind my ears, darlin'. I've only got two ay them,' he pleaded.

Such attention had not been lavished on me. I had been sitting for twenty unattended minutes staring into the vast mirror in front of us. The plastic cape that was tucked under my collar made me look like I was ready for an all-day banquet. I perused the racks of Dax wax, the gels and mousses, the creams and hot oils, the wall-mounted tongs, blades, clippers, diffusers and other instruments of torture. Even the big gas-suspended chair felt like a tool of execution, with its footplate and its taut leather arms. I expected the attached dome of the dryer to lower itself onto my head and dispense several thousand volts into my temples, electricity splitting my ends. I was unable to move. I could only sit and stare at myself in the mirror. I saw a man without life insurance.

'I think they've forgotten about me. By the time they remember, I'll need a beard trim as well.'

'Relax, Bic. I'm havin' my heer streaked. It takes longer. They have tae give me a wee cut and wash first. They'll get tae you in a mo. Keep your heer on.' Jambo nudged the young girl and laughed at his own joke.

'Very good. But Jambo, do you not think you're a bit old and a bit *male* to be getting blond highlights?'

'They're no highlights. They're lowlights.'

'All right, lowlights. Hardly appropriate for a self-styled hardman of the Tynecastle terraces. The blokes down the Dome site may want a piece of your Scottish ass.'

'Shut it. If you were ginger you'd understand.'

'That's another thing. I didn't think you could dye ginger hair.'

'You can't,' chirped the young girl. I had forgotten she was there. 'But you can bleach it,' she said. 'Mr Jameson's hair won't hold colour very well, but we can remove its natural pigment.'

'She's no wrong, Bic. You can bleach red heer. Look at Ginger Spice.'

'But Ginger Spice is a natural brunette.' Having been an avid chronicler of her early career as a 'glamour' model, I said it with some confidence.

'Aye, well— Christ almighty, it's a fuckin' deed jellyfish.'

The young girl had produced a rubber streaking cap. Jambo's eyes widened as she suckered it onto his wet head.

'Ma ears. Mind ma ears.'

Finally my girl appeared. Or rather, her tummy appeared. In the mirror. It was flat and tanned, like a lovingly sanded piece of wood. She had a metal ring through her navel. Skewered on the ring was a solitary yellowish orb of brushed metal, a petrified drop of gold. I stared at the crop-topped girl standing behind me. She wasn't much older than Jambo's, seventeen at a guess. Her hair was a controlled explosion of thin plaits. She spoke grudgingly, addressing her words to my reflection.

34

'What can I do for you?'

I hadn't thought what haircut I wanted, a fatal error when you're already sitting in a salon with scissors hovering round your head.

'Um, I don't want much off. Nothing really. You could tidy it up a little I suppose.'

My trainee swapped her grudging look for a frown. She cocked a comb in her hand. The same hand she threw onto her hip. 'Great,' she said. 'I wait months to get in on one of these trainees' nights, with a chance to impress Debbie and land myself a job. And what do I get – *yuy cud tidy it op a liddle Iyspose.*'

It was quite a passable take on my Ulsterscots, for an English lass. She wasn't finished. 'All the other girls are doing demi-waves, hair extensions, Jennifer Anistons, even blond sodding streaks.'

'Shucks, you noticed,' said Jambo. His streaking cap was secured and individual strands of crocheted hair fountained out of his rubber scalp. He looked like a doll; a doll that was recovering from chemotherapy.

'Sorry,' was all I could offer her.

'S'all right,' she sniffed. She pumped my chair up. She rolled out her little tool belt of implements. She turned her back on me and I heard a buzz as she calmly oiled her clippers. She straightened my head and added, 'If Debbie doesn't pick me, she doesn't pick me. No big deal.'

I sensed her disappointment. I don't know why I said it, the words just tumbled out. 'Actually, I'd like a number four all over with the Heart of Midlothian crest shaved into it.'

Before Jambo picked my request up on his impressive

35

array of ginger aerials, I had swiped his biker jacket off its hook and unpinned his enamel Hearts badge from the lapel. I presented it to my trainee.

'I'm sorry, I don't know your name,' I said.

'Samantha Gold . . . Sam.'

Sam chatted as she assessed my head. She was Jewish. She lived out towards Walthamstow, a place where a teenage girl had three career options: she could become a hairdresser, a checkout operative, or Peter Stringfellow's latest squeeze. Since she didn't fancy the latter and because all the checkout jobs went to minorities (they discouraged applications from people with severe adding abilities), Sam had taken up her scissors and tongs.

She studied the badge. She walked behind me again and I felt her hands on both sides of my neck. 'Hold still,' she scolded. Her fingers probed my scalp. 'Hmmm,' she pondered. She probed and prodded some more. 'Oh dear,' she said.

'Oh dear, what?'

'You've got a big lump there, a couple inches below the crown.'

'Oh, that'll be the horse.'

'A horse kicked you in the head?'

'No. I fell off one. Is it a problem?'

'I'm sure it was at the time,' she said.

'Well, it was for the horse.'

'How do you mean?'

'My dad shot it,' I said.

'That's terrible.' She seemed genuinely horrified.

'I know. He should have tortured it first.'

'How can you say that? You're an animal lover. I mean, I assume that's your dog over there.'

Duncan stood in the waiting area, where he had attracted a little harem of enthusiastic young women.

'Duncan! Give the lady her handbag back.'

Dunc cowered under a chair.

'You like dogs, but you don't like horses,' said Sam.

'Dogs don't throw you over hedges.'

Sam studied my head some more. She tutted. It didn't look good.

'That's a nasty lump,' she said. 'It'll be tough to shave a true line over it. Almost impossible, I'd say.'

Great, I thought. A get-out clause.

'Yep, almost impossible. I'll give it a go.' Sam let her electric clippers loose on me.

I panicked. 'The badge, have you memorized the design?'

'No.'

'No?'

'No. I pinned it to the back of your collar, where I can see it.'

'Ah.'

'It's going to look wicked.' She pushed my head forward and added, 'Trust me.'

This was the third time in a matter of hours that I had broken Resolution Number Four. I sat with my jaw glued to my chest like you do at a sermon. I prayed. I was stuck like that for what seemed an eternity. The clippers buzzed and rattled my brain. The smell of perming fluid made my nose hair curl.

Resolution Number Five: I must never again have a Hearts badge carved into my skull.

'Hey Bic,' said Jambo. 'Why are you gettin' a pair o' tits shaved intae your heer?'

'What?'

'Shit, don't move,' barked Sam.

Her clippers hit the floor.

'Oh no.' Sam whipped some tissues out of a box. She pressed them onto the back of my head.

'What's up?' I asked.

'Shit, shit, shit, shit, shit,' was the emphatic reply.

'What's going on down there?' Debbie, the salon owner, clicked along the tiled floor towards us. Her slingbacks came into my restricted view. 'What have you done to this man, you stupid girl?'

'It was an accident,' said Sam.

'An accident?' choked Debbie. 'We're in the business of cutting hair here. We don't mutilate people.'

'I'm sure it's not that bad,' I offered. What I meant to say was *please tell me it's not that bad*.

Sam was pleading, 'He moved his head and the clippers slipped. I think the blade's faulty.'

'Enough,' said Debbie. She snatched the tool belt from Sam. 'I don't employ thick little Yiddo girls, even if they can cut hair. Go on, get out of my salon.' She grabbed Sam's top and dragged her towards the door.

That was when everything changed.

Debbie might have confiscated the tool belt, but Sam still had one implement in her hand. In a move straight out of *Edward Scissorhands*, Sam cut Debbie's earlobe off.

'Jesus. I'm bleeding. She cut me.'

The bloody scissors hit the tiles and Sam legged it.

'Dunc, stay here.' Once again, I don't know why I did it but I ran out the door after Sam.

I had forgotten how cold it was. The condensation on

38

the inside of the salon windows should have served to remind me. But I hadn't anticipated snow. Not in the last week of June. The climate was fucked. Greenhouse gases, CFCs – I made a mental note to confiscate all the hairspray when I got back to the salon.

I chased Sam through a gaggle of kids. One of them shouted, 'Oi, Superman. You're supposed to wear your underpants on the outside of your trousers.'

Shit, I had forgotten about the plastic cape. It remained fastened to my collar by a Hearts badge. The kids broke into a chorus of the Superman theme as they chased after me. I tried to unpin the cape as I ran, a manoeuvre that would have caused Houdini to tweak a tricep. I gave up and concentrated on pulling away from the baying pack and catching up with Sam.

She raced along Bethnal Green Road and peeled off into the unfamiliar side streets. This slowed her progress. I managed to collar her in an insignificant cul-de-sac to the rear of an old church.

'Sam, whawus thalolla bou . . . shit.' My lungs were still being chased by kids on Bethnal Green Road. 'Chrice I'm unfi –' I hacked and spat. I tried to shake off the long guy-rope of saliva that connected my mouth to the pavement.

'Here.' Sam handed me a tissue, one without my blood on it.

I cleaned myself up and we fell back, panting, against the church wall. Snowflakes phutted into our faces. We stayed like that for a few minutes, until I was sure that I could breathe life back into my words.

'Sam. What did you do that for?'

'You heard her. I won't be treated like that.'

'I know. But chopping her ear off . . . shit.'

'Racist bitch.'

'Exactly. She wasn't worth working for. You're better than that. In fact, you should be glad you fucked my hair up.'

Sam laughed. It might have been a nervous laugh, the realization hitting her that she could now be facing an assault charge. Perhaps it was just the vision of a red-faced and scalped caped crusader that she found so laughable. Whatever, I was happy to see her big white teeth stand at ease in her wide smile.

'Let me undo that for you.' Sam unpinned my cape and handed me Jambo's badge.

'I have a confession, Sam. I don't even support Hearts. I'm not even Scottish. I'm a Bangor FC man. Irish league.'

'Then why ask me to shave it into your hair?'

'I suppose I felt sorry for you.'

'Listen, whatever your name is –'

'Bic.'

'Bic?'

'It's my pen name.' This was a line I used often.

'Listen, mate. I don't need anyone's pity. I need a job. I make jewellery. In order to sell jewellery, I need to set myself up – a little shop, a stall, anything. And in order to do that I need money. Dosh. Wonga. *Capisce?*'

'You could work for me,' I offered.

'You run a salon?'

'Sort of. I run a crêpe stall.'

'What's a crêpe?'

OK, so this is not one of the questions you ask the interview panel when you're on a shortlist of one for the position of Assistant Crêpe Chef. But there was something about Sam that made me offer her the job. My pity had been replaced by a genuine admiration for her. She was only a kid, but she had a game plan, she knew where she wanted to be. I respected that. So I offered her the job on the spot. The fact that the Tall Ships regatta was only a fortnight away, and that I needed all the help I could get, had almost nothing to do with it.

'They're fancy pancakes,' I elaborated.

'Go on,' she said.

'I sell them at Greenwich market. It can get hectic with all the tourists and that. I'm run off my feet most days. I could use the help. The work's dead easy. I'll teach you. And there are a lot of good people on the stalls. If you don't like them, you can cut their ears off. Seriously, the craic's great. It's right on the river and . . .'

'Cut the crap. How much?'

'Eh?'

'Dosh?'

'Oh, right. A fiver an hour?'

She threw me a look. One that said: '   .'

'OK then. What about siiiixxxxxseven pou—'

'   .'

'– ounds fifty an hour?'

'Greenwich, you said?'

'Uhuh.'

'When?' she asked.

'As soon as.'

'You're on, Berk.'

'Bic.'

'Bic it is.' She smiled that smile.

The streetlights had come on. I pushed myself off the

wall and bathed in their sodium glow. They had turned the snow orange. A car reversed over a dead animal, a cat or a rat, I couldn't tell what it was. Its squashed body became one with the slush.

'So, Sam. What sort of jewellery do you make?'

'This sort.'

She reached into her jacket and pulled out the most exquisite teardrop earring with polished amber inlay, the whole ensemble set beautifully into a severed earlobe.

Three

The hot July air tasted of raspberries.

A wasp landed on the sticky lip of a jam jar that I kept three-quarters full with water. He rubbed himself all over in the pink goo. By the time he fell into the water, raspberry jam was already hardening around his wings. He couldn't swim, nor could he fly away. He bobbed in the water, trying to buoy himself on a drowned colleague. But it looked like hard work and it wasn't long before he became just another wasp statistic.

I had always been fascinated by the way food could be used to kill. I decimated the Greenwich wasp population with raspberry jam and water. I annihilated slugs with lines of salt traced along the foot of my kitchen door. I bludgeoned mice in traps loaded with raw bacon and peanut butter. And as a kid I believed I could blow a seagull to smithereens using a sardine primed with baking soda.

I even fantasized about taking my own life with black-currant jelly. I would throw hundreds of gummy cubes into my bath and fill it to overflowing with boiling water. I would remove my clothes and immerse myself face down in the molten mix, drowning as it set. My body would be found suspended in purple aspic. I even considered tossing in a few tins of pineapple chunks, to create a stellar effect around my corpse.

But imagining one's own suicide isn't terribly P C, not when your mother has taken her own life. So I kept my terminal jelly fantasies to myself.

I was also alive to the deadly capabilities of my crêpes. I was obliged to write a warning on my menu board to accompany my Chocolate and Hazelnut Crêpe. As a quirk of law, and for the benefit of both the fatally allergic and the terminally stupid, I was forced to add the words *Warning – May Contain Nuts.*

I emptied the water out of my jam jar, filling the bin with wasp husks.

'I wish you wouldn't do that,' said Sam.

'It's summer, they're a nuisance,' I said.

'It's unhygienic.'

'Would you rather I let the bastards crawl all over our food?'

'Well no, but I'm sure wasps have feelings too,' said Sam.

'Yeah right, as if wa— Duncan!'

I pulled Dunc's red head out of the bin. He looked at me like he'd done nothing wrong. A little black and yellow wasp arse mooned out from the corner of his mouth. He licked it in with his tongue, swallowing the evidence.

'You're a bad boy.'

'I wonder who he takes after,' said Sam.

She had only been working for me one week, but already she was giving me cheek. I had given her a job, I had convinced that Debbie woman not to press charges and Sam repaid me with insults. I tried to suppress a smile all the same.

Sam was crushing hazelnuts under a sheet of cling film. An elderly American gentleman flashed his transatlantic smile at her. She abandoned her rolling pin and wiped her hands on the Queen Mother's face – a commemorative tea towel.

'Yes sir, what can I get you?' she asked, the personification of politeness.

'I want a big old pancake with heaps of chocolate. Hold the hazelnuts,' he said.

'Heaps of chocolate. You got it.' Sam flipped an already bubbling crêpe.

'You're a pretty young lady. Do you have a name?' he asked.

'Angel,' said Sam.

'An-gel.' He made it sound like two words.

'Angel Islington,' said Sam.

'Well Miss Islington, have you ever been to Florida?'

'No. I hear it's a bit Mickey Mouse.' She used her tea towel to lever the top off a reluctant jar of chocolate spread.

I grated cheese and watched as she conducted an entire conversation without ever once looking up at the Yank. His round face with its sickly tan was split by a thick white smile. He reminded me of a picked-at orange.

'Angel, what do you say I fly you back to my beach house in the Keys?'

'Sorry. I'm allergic to sand.'

The jar exhaled as the lid finally came loose in Sam's hands.

'Remember to spread it on good and thick,' said the Yank. He leaned over the hotplate. 'You know, Angel, they say that chocolate gives you the same feeling as being in love.'

'Is that a fact,' said Sam. 'I eat a lot of chocolate, but it's never made me feel paranoid, jealous and over-protective. That'll be one pound eighty.'

The Yank produced a wallet the size of a small boat. He popped it open, exposing its leather gills. They were clogged in plastic: MasterCard, Diner's Club, American Excuse, Golf City Gold Card, and one of those platinum 'priority flier' cards that only twenty-five people on the planet own, entitling the bearer to hold any plane, anywhere, at any time, to allow them on board. This was a wealthy man. I considered asking him if that beach house was still on offer.

Sam cupped his crêpe and jabbed a plastic fork into it. He accepted it and pressed a note into her hand. A big, scarlet note. A fifty-pound note.

'Do you not have anything smaller?' asked Sam.

'Yeah, an apartment on Central Park. Look me up if you're in the area. The name's James O'Connell.'

With that, the Irish-American saddled up and rode off into the big blue yonder. Actually, he just shuffled off, probably on his way to the Observatory. In the afternoon he was gonna do 'Scotch Land'.

'What am I going to do with this?' asked Sam. She

46

held the note up to the sun. It was kosher. The paper burned a deep cadmium red and she withdrew it from the light as though it might catch fire.

I told her to keep it. She knew the rules. I paid her an hourly rate and she kept all her tips.

'But fifty pounds,' she said. 'You don't think he made a mistake, you know, him being unfamiliar with the currency?'

'If he has made a mistake it'll hardly bankrupt him. Anyway, he'll probably write it off on expenses,' I said.

'But he didn't ask for a receipt.'

'Well, he can sellotape a greasy, chocolatey fork to his expense form. Why should you care, you're trying to save money aren't you?'

'Fifty pounds.' She was incredulous. 'The most I've ever held before is a twenty. Except when I used to play Monopoly with my brother. I would change all the money up into the five-hundred-pound notes. You know, the pink ones. I thought I was the richest girl in the world.'

'So you've always hoarded money. Isn't that part of your religion?'

'Yeah, yeah. It's funny though, with all those five-hundreds I could've bought the Strand, Mayfair, the whole of London. Now I can't even afford a bleedin' broom cupboard to flog my jewellery out of.'

Sam reckoned it would take a year to raise a deposit and secure herself a stall on the market. She wanted to set up directly opposite me so she could *slag* me. Her words. Of course, I hadn't known Sam long, but if I was to lose her services on my stall it would be nice not to lose her altogether. The idea of taking up the stall opposite was a good one in theory and, once she raised the deposit, might even have been possible in practice, but one person stood in her way – Loz.

Loz owned the stall immediately across from mine. He had done so since Sam was in nappies. He was going to be difficult to shift, like a stubborn stain, even at July's high temperatures. I had already told Sam that Loz wouldn't sell. She remained undeterred. She was nice to him, brought him tea, said if she was twenty years older and all that. Like a crêpe, she buttered him up and kept him sweet. Loz clearly revelled in the attentions of such a pretty young thing. He kept Sam eager on the promise that he might soon jack in his stall and perhaps he would sign the lease over to her for a fraction of the asking.

I knew Loz would never budge. He was a permanent fixture on the market. He would be sitting at his stall, blowing flecks of rolling tobacco off his Jamaica football shirt, well into the next millennium. Loz always wore that shirt. He hadn't changed out of it since Jamaica lost 5–0 to Argentina in the previous summer's World Cup. He had taken that defeat as badly as any of his fellow countrymen back home in the Caribbean. On the final whistle he threw his arms in the air and wailed: 'Five–Love, Five–Love, let's get together and feel all right'. Of course, if he'd been English he would have taken to the streets, searching in vain for any car with an Argentinian number plate, before ignorantly trashing the nearest available tapas bar.

Loz wore dreadlocks pulled through the open toe of a green and yellow sock, to keep them off his face. His dreads had turned grey. Each one resembled an unsmoked cigarette that had been left to burn.

Loz sold all manner of useless paraphernalia. Or rather, he didn't sell all manner of useless paraphernalia. There wasn't exactly a huge gap in the market for past-their-sell-by bottles of cough linctus and witch hazel that had long since separated. The demand for faded Fifties postcards of an idyllic, toy-town England-that-never-was seemed unsurprisingly low. Perhaps because they had already been written on and posted. Nor was Richard Branson's Virgin empire seriously imperilled by Loz selling assorted bootleg tapes of obscure indie bands playing even more obscure venues: *Swimgear, live at the Camden Phonebox*, or *Slaughterpig's sell-out at the Water Closet, Brixton*.

In the preceding week Loz had made one sale, a Rolf Harris seven-inch. Sam and I had organized a whip-round and presented him with a tin of fizzy wine to toast the happy event.

It was widely known that Loz only kept his stall going as a front for selling copious quantities of home-grown weed. It was widely known, but rarely discussed. If Joe Carlin had got wind of it, Loz would be out on his ragged Rastafarian rear end. Of course, this would suit Sam. His stall would come up for tender. Problem was, I actually liked Loz. Pardon the pun, but I wasn't about to grass him up.

'Don't look now, but I think Loz has a customer,' said Sam. Her slim arms juddered as she scraped the hotplate.

I looked across and, sure enough, Loz was in animated conversation with a man. A man dressed in a white lab coat. I knew that Loz dealt dope, but I hadn't

49

realized he was branching into pharmaceuticals. The two of them appeared to be haggling. Labcoat handed Loz a bundle of cash. Loz made it disappear into his bumbag. This was pushing it, I thought. Dealing in broad daylight.

Labcoat disappeared. Loz smoked the last of his roly and flicked it into the air. He removed a few stray strands of tobacco from his tongue (Loz was the only black man I knew with yellow fingers).

He raised his hand and beckoned a green transit van towards him: 'Come on, man. Back a bit. You have loads of room, man. Back a bit. Back a bit. Back a— whoa. Easy, man.'

The transit reversed to a halt. Labcoat stepped out of it and opened up the rear doors. He then proceeded to transfer the entire contents of Loz's stall into the back of his van: old *Bunty* annuals, cigarette cards, assorted shoes (left feet only), he took everything.

'The taste police have finally caught up with Loz,' I said. 'They're impounding the lot.'

Sam and I stood in the sun, not believing what we were seeing. In a little under five minutes the last item, a black Rubik's cube (all its stickers removed), was tossed into the van.

Loz offered Labcoat his hand. Labcoat declined to take it. It was about the only thing he hadn't taken. Labcoat wanted to talk some more. All Loz had left was the knackered armchair that he sat in, and two empty trestle tables. Oh, and the shirt on his back. Surely Labcoat wasn't after that as well. The armchair was full of holes and highly flammable foam erupted from every orifice. Loz's Jamaica shirt was even less desirable.

Suddenly Labcoat didn't look so happy. He was shouting a lot and slapping his palms on the table, like a science master who's just caught you thumbing a mucky mag at the back of his class. My radio was tuned to Capital FM, so Labcoat's rant was overdubbed by Chris Tarrant. Whatever he was shouting about, Loz seemed to find it funny. That is, he found it amusing right up to the point where Labcoat kicked the support out from under one of the tables. It pinned Loz to his chair. By the time he had prised himself free, Labcoat was off in his van.

I shouted across, 'Loz, did I just see you make the sale of the century, or have I been out in the sun too long?'

'Bic, man. He was me lucky millionth customer.' Loz laughed a deep, cavernous laugh. It was a smoker's laugh, somewhere between a laugh and a cough.

He bounced over to us clutching a small tin. He placed it on my worktop. The tin had a toadstool painted on it. Loz opened it, revealing a lighter, some liquorice Rizlas and a lump of waxy brown resin that simply dwarfed the rolled-up pouch of Golden Virginia wedged in beside it.

'Loz, you're not smoking that stuff on my patch. There's food here.'

'Man, you'd sell a lot more of your food if people smoked this stuff,' he replied.

'Come on. It's a bit early to be skinning up,' I said.

'Take a chill pill, man. I have no intention of smoking it. To smoke it would not do justice to this occasion.

Sam, I would like one of your finest cheese and mushroom crêpes.'

Sam responded by grabbing a more than generous handful of grated cheese. Anything for Loz.

'You see, Bic. This occasion demands that smoke will not be smoked.' Loz moulded the tacky lump of resin between thumb and finger. He struck his lighter and let the flame taste banned substance. As soggy mushrooms slipped under a quicksand of melted cheese, Loz raised the smoking brown marble over the hotplate and crumbled dope into his crêpe.

'I am going to cane this delicious food,' he said. 'Then I am going over to the pub to put some of this behind the bar.' He unzipped his bumbag a fraction, enough to give us a teasing peak at what he was now worth. 'Once there, I will get myself a rum 'n' Coke, without the Coke, and I will retire to the back bar. You righteous people are welcome to join me for spiritual enlightenment, any time between now and closing.'

Loz wolfed his crêpe and disappeared into the Seagull's Arms.

Four

The Seagull's Arms was our local. It had perched itself on the riverbank in 1837, though in those days it acted as a stock house where trade ships from every continent would offload their wares – silk, maize, bananas, sugar, spices and all things nices. Now the only food available was the slice of lime in your Gordon's. The landlord, the alopecially named Dan Duff, didn't believe in mixing food and drink. Dan was an old-school, real-ale kinda guy. You came to his pub to drink, and drink you did. If you wanted a club sandwich, a boil-in-the-bag lasagne, or even a packet of sodding peanuts, Dan would tell you to piss off to one of the many poncey bistros or licensed cafés that were popping up all over Greenwich. After a night's drinking in the Seagull's Arms, grown men had been known to tear limbs off each other just to get at the plump, juicy worm at the bottom of Dan's tequila bottle.

Sam and I locked up. We made our way to the pub via the Bosun's Yard and past the *Cutty Sark*.

Copper clouds had stuck themselves to the early evening sky like well-chewed toffees. The market was dead. The summer hum of car stereos, distant lawn-mowers and idle local banter now occupied the spaces where tourists had been. An air of resignation hung about the stalls. They looked, and probably were, exhausted.

We entered the bar.

'Evening, Bic. Evening, Sam. I'm to get you both what-ever you fancy and I won't hear a word otherwise. Loz is running a tab.' Dan hadn't finished greeting us before he was filling a pint glass with a creamy ribbon of stout, like he'd read my thirsty mind.

'Duncan, get those paws off the bar.'

'Leave him, Bic lad.' Dan produced a swizzle stick and let Dunc take one end in his jaws. This was a tra-dition. They played out their usual tug of war in which Dunc was the victor. Dan always let Dunc win. The dog skulked off to hide the swizzle stick in some far-flung corner of the bar.

'Are you still getting grief from the council over the dog?' asked Dan.

'It's nothing.'

'Because I'll start a petition, keep it at the bar for folks to sign. Dunc's one of our most popular customers.'

'Cheers, Dan. Best just ignore them though.'

'They're not welcome in here, I can tell you. One of their cronies came in last Tuesday, asked if they can use my beer garden for this bloody regatta.'

When Dan referred to his beer garden it never ceased

54

to amuse me. The only flora that grew in it were the weeds that stitched together the eighty square feet of concrete flagstones. The small clutch of wooden tables and benches may have been trees in a previous life, but Eden this wasn't. Indeed, the tables were so close to the river that if you sat at them you were in serious danger of contracting Weil's disease.

'What has your beer garden got to do with the Tall Ships race?' I asked.

'Well apparently they're getting the Queen's cousin, that Admiral Sutherland fella, to fire the starting gun from the *Cutty Sark*. Then he's doing a bit of a walk-about, kissing babies, healing the blind, the usual bollocks. Once he finishes with the plebs, they're going to throw a garden party for him. All the top brass will be there. And get this, they wanted me to do the food – canapés, hors d'oeuvres, all sorts of French shite.'

'And you advised this councillor on the relative demerits of the Seagull's Arms as caterers to Her Majesty's Navy?'

'No. I told him to go piss up a rope.'

Dan left my Guinness to stand.

'But they're still using the garden,' I said.

'How did you know?'

'I know because I'm doing the catering. Joe Carlin came to me in a blind panic a couple of Sundays back. He said Greenwich Council had his balls in a vice. He owes ground rent on the market. I don't know how, because all us stallholders pay our rent on time. He's probably squandered it all on nicotine gum. Anyway, they were threatening to run him out unless he provided a caterer at short notice. So I got the contract.

It's a lot of money for one day's work. Your loss, Dan.'

Dan looked embarrassed. 'Not quite, Bic. With the money the council are paying me for the use of the beer garden, I can afford to tear up the concrete and lay grass from Old Trafford.'

'Everyone has their price,' I conceded.

The conversation lasted as long as it takes for a pint of the black stuff to settle. Dan topped it up.

'One more thing, Bic. Can you ask that dog of yours to quit hiding stuff in my bar? Maureen was hoovering this morning and she found a chewed-up condom behind the fruit machine, dog slabber all over it.'

'Had the condom been used?' I asked.

'Aye.'

'Well, think of the poor dog then. It must have been like biting into a Locket.'

I removed myself to the back bar, otherwise referred to as the snug. Given that you could only fit six adults in it at any one time and that it now contained Loz, Sam, Dunc and two students playing Jenga at the only other table, it was snug all right. There was barely enough room for the two bookshelves swelled in paperbacks, all with well-worn, variegated spines. It was so cosy there seemed little need for the small coal fire that burned both illegally and incongruously into the hot summer evening outside.

I took a seat and drew sustenance from a glass three-quarters black with stout. But not before Sam jabbed her finger into its creamy head. She traced a shamrock into it.

'Don't you hate it when they do that?' she asked.

She knew I did. Shamrocks drawn in Guinness was

number one on my list of pet hates. It's not as if it ever looks like a shamrock. Most barmen hand you a Guinness with a crudely graffitied cock on it.

'Do they do that in Ireland?' she asked.

'All the time,' I said. 'And the Guinness is green. And the pubs stay open all night. And you don't get in unless you can play an instrument. And we all carry pigs under our arms.'

'Fuck the pigs, man.'

'Sorry, Loz?'

'Them pigs tried to bang me up, man.' Loz knocked back his rum. A punch-drunk and weary slice of lemon dropped onto his nostrils. He reeled the yellow crescent into his mouth and made pig noises through a mock citrus smile. He slammed his glass down beside a bottle of Captain Morgan.

'Level with me Loz, you've been drinking, haven't you?'

'The rum's gone to me head, man.'

'Well, they say nature abhors a vacuum.'

Loz refilled his glass. He attempted to stand on his stool, which was difficult at the best of times, the snug's ceiling falling some way short of seven feet high. He proudly offered me the bottle and by way of introduction announced: 'Bic, the Captain, the Captain, Bic.' The stool wobbled. Loz straightened, sending his head up into the propellers of a fan that hung from the ceiling. His dreads became entangled in the mechanism.

'Man, me head's stuck.'

'What the hell's going on?' Dan was collecting glasses.

'The shit's hit the fan,' said Sam.

Loz was clearly in some pain. The fan was making

57

strange honking noises. Dan ran to the bar and switched it off.

'Sam, you'll have to untangle him,' I said.

'Why me?'

'You're good with hair.'

'Will you ever let me forget,' she said.

Sam retrieved a metal comb from her bag. She extricated Loz by using its teeth to saw off a couple of dreadlocks. The two students seemed oblivious to our commotion. Obviously the art of removing small wooden blocks from a tall stack of small wooden blocks was far more engrossing than the art of removing a pissed Rastafarian from a ceiling fan.

'Me hair's gone, man.'

Loz was pretty shaken. He was on his third spliff before he calmed down. A trail of smoke reached up from between his legs and threw its arms over the table. Loz bent his head to the jay and secretly sucked it. He kept it between his knees like he was feeding Dunc some illicit scrap under the table. Dan didn't tolerate drugs in his pub. No food, no darts, no pool, no drugs – it was a wonder we were allowed to drink in the place.

'So Loz, what are you going to do with your new-found wealth?'

Loz closed his eyes. He sat like that for a few seconds. Then he said, 'I'm going to get me a big boat.'

'What would you do with a boat? You live in Camberwell, in a block of flats.'

'Not any more, man. I'm going to sail all the way back to the motherland. Back home to Jamaica.' Loz still hadn't opened his eyes. He had smoked so much plant life, he was slowly assuming the characteristics of a vegetable. I'm not saying he was on another planet, I just wasn't convinced he was aware that man had landed on the moon.

Loz lived in London, but his heart remained in Chapeltown, Jamaica. He had bunked over to France as a teenager to escape some trouble back home. Someone had tried to shoot him. From Marseilles, he had made his way to London in the late Seventies. He hadn't always been a market trader. His curriculum vitae listed more jobs than a Wednesday's *Evening Standard*. He had started out as a street cleaner. He was sacked when he stabbed a down-and-out with a litter fork. Loz claimed that the tramp had attacked him, until it emerged she was a housewife from the Home Counties sleeping rough outside Dixon's in readiness for their January sale. He got a job driving the buses. He was dismissed for taking his Archway-bound 134 on a detour to Primrose Hill, parking it, and making thirty commuters wait outside his dealer's while he popped in for some gear. He once got a job writing stings for Capital Radio. He was sacked after a bust-up with the controller of programming, who had rejected Loz's proposal for the world's first topless radio show. He became a sales rep for a South London glazing firm. He was dismissed when he tried to advertise them by wrapping their flyers round bricks and throwing them through windows. As an unlicensed hotdog vendor, Loz was thrown in jail for laying out an entire Dutch school party with campylobacter poisoning. Nor did he last long as a lifeguard on the Docklands ferry, when it emerged that Loz couldn't swim.

Loz wasn't alone in wanting to return to his home-land. My own thoughts had become increasingly occupied with Northern Ireland. I had been dumped in Scotland at the age of ten to live with my aunt and Jambo. But my days on the family farm just outside Bangor on North Down's Gold Coast were more happily remembered than those days when I mitched off Stranraer Boys to suck menthol cigarettes in the shadows of rusty ferries. (I had naively thought that the word menthol meant they must be good for you, when in fact it meant that two drags and your face turned the colour of mint.)

I had toyed many times with the idea of jacking in the stall and returning to the land of my birth. I had made serious enquiries about the cost and feasibility of setting up an ostrich farm somewhere in the province. Ostrich farms were big business in Scotland. As far as I knew, there were no such farms in Northern Ireland. There was a gap in the market. I was going to make ostrich meat a necessary addition to the traditional Ulster Fry. It would be easy to raise the capital. I had squirrelled away quite a bit in my six years selling crêpes. The Tall Ships regatta would top it up nicely. Financially, there was nothing to stop me from hanging up my spatula and buying an incubator, some fencing and a plot of Irish land.

I had spent my childhood being moved from pillar to post. I needed to put down some roots. I had decided that London was not the place (Resolution Number One). As unformed as Loz's dream was, I understood it. Haven't we all dreamt of filling a shoulder bag, tipping up at an airport and grabbing the first flight to Whoknowswhere? London does that to you.

Sure, it's the coolest city in the world. The thing that binds you to London is the notion that, at any given time, you can do any given thing. In London you can view half a cow suspended in formaldehyde, you can eat Mongolian food, you can pee standing next to a soap star, and you can dress up as a rhinoceros and run its bloody marathon. You rarely do it. But you *could*.

One in ten people in Greater London are first- or second-generation Irish. I was part of the largest ethnic minority in the capital, but I didn't feel like I belonged. The Scots twang to my accent didn't help matters. I was constantly being tarred with the pejorative 'plastic paddy', like being born in Ireland wasn't enough. I had come to resent the way I spoke. I felt like an alien. I felt like tartan made in Tyrone.

Nor could I assimilate myself into the ethnic vacuum that is Britishness. Even the Scots have to stand through a national anthem that includes the line: *rebellious Scots to crush*. Was it any wonder they devolved? The Northern Irish Assembly, devolution in Scotland and Wales – the British goose was well and truly cooked. The grass had to be greener back home, back in my own motherland. But until I got out of London, I was stuck in a rut. Betwixt and between.

A couple of hours slipped by and Loz's bar tab moved into three figures, like the speedometer on that first fantastic spin in a new sports car. Time flies when you're having run.

Loz stroked his missing dreads in the way an amputee strokes a phantom limb. He left all the conversation to Sam and me.

'Could Barbara not prise herself away from the husband and kids tonight, Bic?' asked Sam.

She was just trying to stir. She thought I deserved better than Barbara, a thirty-nine-year-old married mother of four. Some people would term those credentials 'baggage', but my relationship with Barbara was pretty free and easy. At least, that's how I saw it. But then, I wasn't the one having to invent evening classes twice a week in order to escape my husband and shag me.

Adulterous women are, ironically, more honest. Pick up any single girl in a bar and she'll invent any history that suits her. But have an affair with a married woman and all her energies are so devoted to concealing it from her husband and kids that, by the time she gets to you, she has neither the industry nor the inclination to lie. Within fifteen minutes of my meeting Barbara she had said: *'I'll be forty in November, my husband will forget to buy me a card, my two eldest – Daniel and Susan – will serve me breakfast in bed, but I'll already be up, packing Rowena's lunchbox and bathing my three-year-old. Still want to fuck me?'* That's honesty.

'Just because I occasionally see Barbara, it doesn't stop me from seeing other women,' I asserted. 'If I wanted monogamy, I'd be dating a swan.'

'Bic, you're twenty-eight. You'll be left on the shelf.' Sam had a way of saying *twenty-eight* that made it sound like forty-eight. Probably because she spoke it from an eighteen-year-old mouth.

'What's so wrong with being left on the shelf?' I asked.

'The highest instances of madness occur in single men over forty,' said Sam. 'Just look at Loz.'

It was no accident that I chose to date only married women. I knew that nothing could ever come of these relationships, and that was the way it needed to be. I had resolved to leave London sooner rather than later. Now was not the time to be starting a deep and meaningful relationship. Barbara was neither deep nor meaningful. Barbara was simply convenient. But Sam was right (though I didn't like the suggestion that I'd end up a lonely drug-addled Rastafarian). I would end up *on the shelf*. Maybe it wasn't such a bad place to be. Trophies end up on shelves. Then again, trophies also end up in attic boxes, tarnished and forgotten.

Resolution Number Two: I had to stop screwing other men's wives.

Dan pulled me up from the black waters.

'Right folks, drink up.'

'I'm not ready to leave, man.' Loz waved his bottle at Dan.

'All right, but you'll have to settle your tab now. The till is time-coded, so I can't ring anything through after eleven,' said Dan. He said we could stay until one, or until he restocked the bar, whichever came sooner. He wanted cash in hand. He went to the bar and came back with a till receipt so long it was practically a short story. He gave it to Loz. It might as well have been written in Sanskrit for all the sense Loz could make of it. I grabbed it off him and looked at the total.

'One hundred and seventeen pounds and seven pence? Jesus, Dan, did we break a window?'

But Dan was over the other side of the bar turning a stool upside down, like he was emptying a child's pockets of change. He had the bar cleared and the door locked in no time. Dan never had to raise his voice to get people to vacate the bar. One sight of his six-foot-three frame hulking towards you and you'd happily leave your fresh pint, your coat and your girlfriend, to beat the curfew and escape the landlord's wrath.

The only bad thing about these lock-ins was that you were often confronted with the vision that confronted us then: Dan's wife, Maureen. In her nightie. *Sans* make-up.

A posthumous tribute to all the laboratory rabbits who have had powders and creams rubbed into their broken skin in order to help test the make-up that normally hid this woman's face – you did not die in vain. I would gladly let the men from Max Factor squirt foundation into my eyes if it ultimately led to the concealment of Maureen's bake. Indeed, when you set eyes on her they tended to react as though foundation had just been squirted into them.

Nor did her nightie conceal much. Maureen had more spare tyres than a crash barrier at Silverstone. Ulster's loyalists were preparing to celebrate the Twelfth of July, and had Maureen been living in Belfast, not Greenwich, they'd have chucked her on an 'Eleventh Night' bonfire.

Maureen attended to our needs while Dan was in the cellar checking barrels. She waddled over to our table. She resembled one of Rubens's large ladies, had Rubens painted with a toilet brush and a migraine.

'That's a beautiful nightie, Maureen. You look like a million lire.'

'Thank you Anthony, love.' She ruffled my hair and added, 'My suitcase is packed. You only have to give me the word.'

Everything about this woman made me feel uncomfortable. Not least that she used my real name. The only other people that referred to me as Anthony were my dad, my Aunt Sylvia, and the HSBC Bank. (I had tried 'Bic' with the bank but their highly intelligent computerized applications system couldn't cope with a single, stand-alone name. Unless the First Name and Surname sections were both filled, the system crashed. Pele, Prince and Fish from Marillion clearly did not bank with HSBC.)

What absolutely terrified me about Maureen was this jocular pretence that she was about to leave Dan and run off with me. She knew I was dating an older woman, and I was sure that in some dark boudoir in her brain she actually believed that I fancied her. Rumour had it that Dan and Maureen were swingers and that they often organized lock-ins of an altogether more salacious nature. Joe Carlin had already testified to waking up in the Seagull's Arms and going for a pee, only to find Maureen's fuchsia lipstick all over his cock.

Thankfully Dunc halted her advances. He jumped up at the window in a mad fit of barking, grey haloes of condensation expanding and contracting on the pane. Pressed against the other side of the glass was Jambo's flattened face. He pointed Maureen towards the front door and ran round the building to be let in. She opened the latch.

'What are you doing, coming here at this ungodly hour?' she asked.

'How's about you, Mo. Room fae one more in your house ay ill repute?'

'Get in then. Pint of McEwan's, isn't it?'

'Aye. You're a darlin'.' Jambo kissed her hand.

'Don't push it, Jamie.'

I wasn't the only one she was on first-name terms with.

'Shuftie up, will youse.' Jambo joined us in the snug. He was in his work clothes. His overalls and boots were caked in clay. The Dome was behind schedule and they had Jambo working nights. It was construction by flood-light.

'Well, this is an unexpected surprise,' I said.

'Have youse not heard? As of tonight all work on the Millennium Dome has been stopped. We've all been suspended on full pay, fae the time being.'

'What's happened?'

This was news. We were all ears, and Jambo was never more at home than with a pint of McEwie's in one hand and a captive audience eating out of the other.

'It's all because ay a couple o' birds,' he said. 'The environmentalists got wind we had a couple o' rare birds nesting in the Dome. Black redwings.'

'Black redstarts,' I corrected. I knew my birds.

'Aye, whitever. Anyways, they're a protected species. Apparently there's some auld law that says these birds cannie be disturbed. Bloke on the news says there's only twenty pairs in Britain. The tree-huggers are all camped out at the site tae make sure no construction takes place. Which is fine wi' me.' He toasted his good fortune with a glug of my stout.

'Bomb birds,' I said.

'What?'

'Black redstarts. They're also known as bomb birds. During the Second World War, bombs weren't the only things that exploded in London. There was also a boom in the black redstart population. Apparently they like nothing better than a good bomb site in which to build their nests.'

This was a problem of mine. I was a bit of a jackdaw for bird trivia.

'Well I'm glad some good came of the apocalyptic nightmare of World War Two,' said Jambo. 'Londoners must ay been chuffed. Never mind that you had your roof blown off by a Nazi bomber, at least you could wake up with the sun on your face, tae hear the call o' the black redstart ringing in your ears.'

'Well you're not complaining, are you. No work and full pay.'

'Aye, and for the foreseeable future. At least until these birds rear a couple o' bairns.'

Maureen approached Jambo. 'The tab's closed, Jamie. Two twenty for the pint.'

'I'm getting these Jambo, man. Me came into some money.' Loz ripped a fresh twenty from his purple wad.

'Jeez, Loz, where'd that come from? Did you sell a kidney?'

Loz related his good fortune to Jambo, albeit a more incoherent version of events than that told earlier to Sam and me. The bloke in the lab coat was in the business of collecting curios for a themed restaurant that he was opening. He had paid Loz one thousand pounds in cash to take all his wares. Once he'd loaded the junk into his van, he made Loz another offer. He wanted to buy his stall, another thousand to sign over the lease. When a lease came up for tender, or when it expired, there was a waiting list. This process wasn't strictly official, more of an unwritten agreement among the market traders. Sam was first on the list to get Loz's patch. Loz had refused to sell to Labcoat, but not out of some unwritten obligation towards Sam. He had simply figured that if someone was prepared to give him one thousand pounds in cash for a vanload of used wigs, mouldy pencil cases and illustrated bibles (with the pictures cut out of them), then they'd be prepared to give him ten times that for a prime trading post. Loz had got greedy and Labcoat hadn't been too happy about it.

Sam found her second wind as Loz told his tale. She saw her chance.

'So Loz, you now have a stall, but you've nothing to sell,' she said.

'That is right, young lady.'

'Well, what about it? You and I could set up as partners. I'll flog my jewellery on your stall, you pay the rent and we'll split all profits. At least for six months, until the lease comes up for renewal. Then I can take sole control, and you can sail that big boat back to Jamaica.'

'And how would we split the profits?' asked Loz. He had become suddenly lucid.

Sam sat forward. He had bitten. Now all she had to do was reel him in. Don't be too greedy, she thought. Make it forty sixty in his favour. But it would be her jewellery they'd be selling. She would be doing all the hard work. She didn't want him to say no, though. Fifty fifty? Best not price herself out of the deal. Keep a level head, Sam. It would only be for six months, then she could take up the lease. Loz would be miles away on his boat, dodging the Jamaican port authorities.

'Forty sixty,' she offered.

'Seventy thirty,' countered Loz.

'You're getting greedy again, Loz,' I said.

'OK, Sam girl. Sixty forty my way. And I'm still running my little sideline. I have certain clientele who rely on me to furnish them with the finest herbal remedy this side of the river.'

'Done,' said Sam, before he changed his mind. She would have shaken on it, but Loz's hands were engaged in the familiar origami of rolling a joint. Nevertheless, she had closed the deal.

'One condition, Sam. You do nothing until after the regatta. I need you,' I said.

'No problem, boss.' Sam stood up with renewed enthusiasm and threw her arms into the sleeves of her jacket like a bird trying on a new set of wings.

Loz, in contrast to his new business partner, seemed almost blasé about the deal. He popped the thin end of the jay into his mouth and searched his pockets for his lighter. No joy. And Jambo had used up his last eight matches constructing a Millennium Dome on my Guinness, jabbing them at angles into the thick, curved head. Loz bent his head down to the fire and leaned forward, pressing the fat end of the jay onto a white coal. He sucked the heat out of it. He brought his head back up. The end of the jay was now burning brightly. As was Loz's fringe.

Sam reacted first. She threw the last of her drink over him.

'Easy, girl. I thought we had a deal.'

'Loz, your hair was on fire.'

'Aw, man.' He slapped his frazzled dreads. The smell of singed dreadlock wrestled with the sweet smell of cannabis. It won.

Sam produced her mobile and instinctively pressed the last-number recall. 'I'm off,' she said. 'Dad should be coming off his shift. He'll pick me up in his cab.'

'What time is it?' asked Jambo.

'Gone two – hi Dad, it's Sam.'

'I'll cadge a lift wi' you, Sam. I'm out your way,' said Jambo.

Sam nodded. 'Seagull's Arms, Dad. Five minutes. Great,' she said.

'Ach stay, Jambo. Have another drink. It's not as if you have to get up for work tomorrow,' I said.

'Don't think it's a good idea, Bic. I think we're about tae get kicked out. Maureen's stood at the bar wi' a face like a busted guttie.'

'She always has a face like a busted guttie.'

'Aye, but now it's got shite on the sole.'

Maureen switched off the lounge lights, leaving only the snug illuminated. Jambo and Sam took the hint and left.

Loz and I finished off his bottle. Dan joined us for a nightcap, while Maureen went upstairs to visit the Land of Nod (having seen her passport photo, I was surprised they let her in).

I had to be up early to get the stall open. Accepting the contract to cater at the Tall Ships regatta meant I had to buy in more supplies. A dozen barrels of your regular cash'n'carry batter would be delivered to my stall at six a.m. That gave me just over three hours. It was an hour each way to my flat in Crouch End. That only left me one hour's kip. This clearly was not enough for any sane being. Except, famously, Maggie Thatcher. I rest my case.

I said goodbye to Loz at the *Cutty Sark* and walked in the opposite direction.

If I hadn't been so pissed, I might have been able to remember the last words he said to me. I would come to rue that when the police interrogated me on the matter.

Five

Barbara had contrived to stay at my flat for the whole of the previous weekend. She had told her husband she was on an Information Technology field trip. It was the weekend after the fire. Stupid eejit in one of the flats below me had come in drunk and stuck a chip pan on the hob. He left the fat to heat while he went to the bathroom. He fell asleep on the toilet. When they recovered his body his arse was welded to the molten plastic seat.

In an effort to get rid of the smell of charred neighbour, I had to get rid of my carpets. Barbara had offered to lend a hand. She dumped the kids with their grandparents. Her husband couldn't look after them. He worked lates.

We spent the entire weekend sanding and staining the bare floorboards a deep Jacobean Oak.

One week on and I was still waking up to the smell of wood stain.

My clothes smelt of rum'n'smoke. I had slept in them. I cheered myself with the thought that at this moment Loz was probably feeling a whole lot worse than I did. Two bottles of Captain Morgan and a cheese, mushroom and cannabis crêpe – I wouldn't like to be cleaning out his cage.

My eyelids ungummed themselves and I became immediately aware of the vagaries of the British summer. The previous pink summer's evening had given way to a grey slab of early morning sky that hurtled towards me through the skylight above my bed. This was accompanied by the *tick-tock-tick-tock* of heavy, metronomic raindrops on the windowpane.

Red sky at night, shepherds talk shite.

As dawn's cobalt brightness invaded the room I understood better what those soap-powder housewives meant by 'bluey whiteness'. I sat up and caught my reflection in the newly glossed fire surround. The black paint had bubbled and distorted my features like B-movie horror. I felt like I looked.

I pulled my socks from my feet, a snake shedding skin. I jammed a finger between two toes and rubbed hard, arousing black maggots of dirt. The thought that I needed a bath was immediately negated by the chilling realization that I never set the water heater to come on this early. A bath was out of the question. I should at least wash my face. My skin felt like the cracked bedroom walls – rough stucco plaster falling away like icing to expose a damp marzipan of brickwork underneath.

I needed Alka-Seltzer.

I found the kitchen. Dunc was asking to go to the

73

toilet. I let him out onto the fire escape. I had trained him to walk down two flights and crap on the steps outside the flat below. The couple in Flat A deserved it. Newly-weds. Leslie and Charley. A bloke with a girl's name and a girl with a bloke's name. They worked together, from home, as a freelance advertising team. They wrote ads for white goods, yellow fats, blue chips and red tops. They appealed to the green consumer and chased the pink pound. It's a colourful business, but you had to question the wisdom of people who live together, work together and who work where they live. They had no escape, that's if you discounted the one my dog was crapping on.

Their 24/7 ran something like this: five days arguing loudly about the most single-minded way to sell bottles of own-brand supermarket vodka (usually ending in them throwing the things at each other); followed by one day of tense but blissful silence; then one long day of boisterous, unrepentant sex, climaxing in a knock at my door. I would open it and they'd be standing there all coy and holding hands, like in their wedding photo-graph. They would invite me down for a meal – *Charley's cooked her special couscous* – like they felt sorry for me, living on my own and all. I was the one with the emotional independence (they were married), the financial independence (they depended on free-lance), and the view of Alexandra Palace (you could see sod all from the downstairs flats). And *they* felt sorry for *me*.

Dunc asked to be let back in.

'Good boy.'

I decided to reward him for ablutions well performed.

I opened a can of Pedigree Chum with rabbit's liver. Actually, I used a tin-opener. Big mistake. There is nothing more likely to resurrect technicolor memories of the drunken night before than a whiff of Pedigree Chum with rabbit's liver. I unsuckered the dog food from the tin and into the dog bowl, without stopping to mash it up. Dunc didn't know what to make of it. He just stared at the wobbling, tin-shaped jelly of reeking meat, while I redecorated the sink.

I went downstairs to check the post. The banister fell down the stairs, twisted and black as a spent match. It wasn't safe. I put my finger to the wall and traced my name into the soot. The letters burned out of the black in the bright tangerine of some bygone wallpaper. The fire had torched several layers of the stuff. I wondered if I could age the building by counting them, like the rings in a tree.

I emptied my postbox of a fortnight's mail: three bills, one blue airmail envelope and a free sample of leg wax addressed to a Ms Anthea Bickmore.

It was then I heard a buzzing sound from within Flat B, the burnt-out flat. Jesus, it had only been two weeks since the fire and already squatters had moved in. Squatters with hairdryers, by the sound of it.

I approached what was left of the door, speculating all the time as to what lay behind it. Whoever they were I hoped they weren't large or violent. I wasn't exactly well equipped to defend myself – *One false move, punk, and I'll pump you so full of leg wax you'll wish you hadn't been hirsute.*

The buzzing banged, buzzed, banged, then reverted to buzzing uninterrupted by bangs. It sounded like these squatters were hoovering. At five in the morning? A better class of squatter, perhaps.

As I opened the door a new fear gripped me – what if there's a struggle and my dick falls out of my boxers?

Buzz, buzz, bang, buzz, bang, buzz, buzz –

I steeled myself behind the half-open door. My arm snagged on a band of yellow police tape, designed, no doubt, to keep out squatters and their Hoovers. The whole place looked very black and very wet. Long tributaries of water trickled down the charred walls, forming cold, tarry pools around my sockless feet. The fire had been heavily doused. The flat resembled one of London's many leaking tube tunnels, victims of a rapidly rising water table.

The air was thick with soot. I brought my jumper over my nose.

Buzz, buzz, bang, buzz, bang, buzz, buzz –

I didn't dare lean in any further for fear of being seen. The element of surprise was all I had. I wasn't about to forfeit my one weapon that easily. That would be a bit like David saying to Goliath: 'Hey mate, you wouldn't hold this sling for me, while I go and get me some stones.'

Buzz, bang, bang, buzz, buzz, bang –

Right, I had to make my move. I ripped off a length of the plastic police tape and wound the ends round my hands to form a garrotte. I performed one last check to ensure my boxers were securely buttoned. This was it. If I'd had a partner I would have said something macho and portentous like, *If I'm not back out of here in twenty minutes, look after Mary and the kids for me.* But I was all on my own. And I didn't know anyone called Mary.

I pulled the yellow garrotte in my hands. It snapped.

Great. I had just failed my audition to be the next Bond.

Buzz, bang, buzz.

The noise stopped and with it, my breathing. I edged forward just enough to see a hunched figure filling a bag. Looters. I considered running upstairs to phone the police. But by the time the duty sergeants finished devouring their cream horns and stuck those ridiculous tits on their heads, the thieves would be long gone. It was now or never. Before I had time to deduce that never was the more attractive of the two options, I had hurled myself headlong at the hunched figure, knocking him to the wet black floor.

The element of surprise must have worked, for he let out a terrified high-pitched yelp, his vocal cords distorting to produce a female falsetto. I turned him onto his back and put my hands round his throat.

She begged me not to kill her.

Her bag burst, showering us in black soot and dust – funeral confetti. It wasn't a bag of loot at all. It was a Hoover bag. In the chrome of the vacuum cleaner I caught a reflection of myself in my boxer shorts, sitting astride a middle-aged woman with my hands round her throat. If a stranger had walked in at that moment and seen the state of the flat, perhaps they would have forgiven me for throttling the cleaning lady. They might even have joined in. But this wasn't the cleaning lady.

'I'm his mother,' she gurgled.

I helped her to her feet.

'I am so, so sorry. I thought you were a burglar. We get a lot of burglaries in this area, Mrs . . . ?'

'Fitzgerald. Bernie Fitzgerald. Kyle's mother.'

Irish.

'Who's Kyle?'

'My boy lived in this flat.'

'Oh, you mean Kyyyyyle.' Truth was I never knew the stupid bugger's name. 'Poor Kyle. Tragic business. He was a good friend,' I said, trying to console her. Don't ask me what he looked like.

'You two were close?'

'Me and Kylo were like that.' I raised two fingers and wrapped them round each other. 'We had so much in common. I'm from Ireland too. Kyle and I . . . we had great craic.' I knew I was overdoing it, but I wanted to make her feel better, to make up in some way for my attempt on her life.

'I bought my Kyle his first train set when he was four. He always said he wanted to be a train driver,' she said.

'And he was the best, Mrs Fitzgerald. Nobody drove a train like Kyle drove a train.'

'Yes, he always wanted to be a train driver, but he was too short-sighted.'

'Short-sighted? Ah yes, sure wasn't he always losing his glasses,' I said.

'Of course, he got rid of his specs at primary school once his glandular fever cleared up. His eyesight had corrected itself by then.'

'His *sun*glasses. Always losing them. A real sun-worshipper was Kylo. In summer we'd nip down to the lido on Park Road, have a swim, catch some rays. Kyle was a real charmer with the ladies.'

'That's odd,' said his mother. 'When Kyle came out, told me he was gay, he never mentioned that he'd learnt to swim. He must have thought I'd be shocked at the idea and disown him.'

I held my hands up. It was a fair cop.

'You didn't know him, did you,' she said.

'No.' I felt awful.

'Don't fret, son. Kyle was always a bit of a loner. I blame myself. He was my only child. I smothered him.'

I had seen women like Bernie Fitzgerald before. The long-suffering mother who talked so glibly about the death of a son, like there was some great inevitability about it. Who talked like it was all her fault. Such women were to be seen often in Ulster's news bulletins.

'I should've been there to make him his chips. He always said his mum's chips were the best. Silly boy. He *was* only a boy. Do you know, I could only identify him by the watch on his wrist. I gave it to him last year, on his sixteenth. It's all melted now. It stopped at half past nine. He was born at half past nine on 25th June 1982. I remember because Gerry Armstrong had just scored his goal, and the ward sister switched the television off because my blood pressure had gone through the roof.'

Her clothes were soaked so that it seemed as if her mascara was streaming down her cheeks, seeping into her cardigan, and dripping from the cuffs and pockets into the black puddle at our feet. It was only then that I realized the utter madness of running an electric Hoover over a wet floor. I unplugged the thing.

'Come on, Mrs Fitzgerald. It isn't safe in here.'

I put my arm round her and tried to motion her to the door. She was having none of it.

'I just want to make the place respectable. I always told Kyle to leave things the way he found them.'

She lifted a mop that was propped against the sofa. It

79

didn't look much like a sofa any more. It was a rogue sculpture of black springs and coils, like the seats on a petrol-bombed bus. She mopped up the black water.

What could I do? I could hardly kick her out of her dead son's flat. I went to the hallway and switched off the mains to Flat B.

As I said my goodbyes, she stopped me.

'Son,' she said. 'Six o'clock. The cuckoo's popped out.'

I looked down and discreetly lifted my penis back into my boxers.

I had to get my skates on.

I needed to be in Greenwich to meet the delivery from my wholesaler. One dozen twenty-pound barrels of glutinous batter. The thought did nothing for my hangover.

I ran my feet under the showerhead to get rid of the soot. I dressed. I returned to the kitchen and fixed myself an impossibly strong, high-octane, No Milk Allowed coffee. I ripped open the blue airmail envelope, knowing full well what was inside. I received one of these envelopes, with its South African postmark, every month. They were from my dad. This was the only contact we had. I never wrote back.

Resolution Number Three: I had to start talking to my father again.

Each month he would enclose a one-page letter and a blank cheque to cover my studies at the University of London. My dad thought I had been studying Botany all these years and that I was now in the final year of my doctorate. I often thought about writing back to him and telling him the truth, that I ran a crêpe stall and that I had never even been to a gig at the University of London, never mind a lecture theatre. My Aunt Sylvia was in on the deception and kept him informed of my 'progress'. We had even faked a graduation photograph.

The charade suited them both. Dad could content himself that his son was making something of his life, that I had an aptitude for the natural sciences inherited from him. And Sylvia would do anything to ensure her brother was happy. She said he'd had enough pain in his life (as if I hadn't suffered when Mum died). Dad could be proud of me and proud of himself for bringing me up 'proper'. Fact was, he probably still pictured me as a spotty fifteen-year-old, for that was the last time he had seen me. My dad's idea of parenting now amounted to nothing more than a short letter and a blank cheque.

I didn't want his money. I had my own business. I was proud like that. But I had to make sure he thought I was spending it on my 'studies'. So I regularly made out the cheques for eight hundred quid and cashed them. I gave all the money to Battersea Dogs' Home. I gave it in his name. Kenneth Bickmore was one of their most generous benefactors.

If he knew he'd be furious, and not just because the money wasn't going on my education. My father is a distinguished vet. Distinguished by the fact that he hates dogs. He hates them almost as much as I hate horses. Perhaps phobia is another thing that runs in the Bickmore blood. Dad was bitten by a stray early on in his career. It made him very sick. From that moment he chose to specialize in livestock. For years he gained a solid reputation working the farms round County

Down. He developed particular expertise in equine medicine. Word spread, and it wasn't long before he found himself working for all the big-name horse trainers the length and breadth of Ireland. He was in demand, and did quite nicely out of it thank you very much. He bought several acres down the coast from Bangor and asked my mother to marry him.

My mum loved the farm, it had stables and everything. She couldn't ride her horses when she first moved in. She was pregnant with me.

My first memories relate to that farm. My first memories are all good ones: the proud hills dressed in canary gorse; the petulant breeze off Belfast Lough making tunes in the tall grasses; and the overgrown field beyond the farm's boundary. I loved that field. I was lured into it like a rat after the Piper. I would lose myself in it, teasing bees and gauging the depth of foxholes with a grubby young arm. I was fascinated by anything that moved. My dad would say, if it moves it's biology, if it smells it's chemistry, and if it doesn't work, it's physics. But he didn't like me spending so much time with only myself for company. Why aren't you getting into trouble with other children, with *normal* children, he would say.

He banned me from going into the field, like I was some sort of kid. But to a child there is no stronger drug than prohibition and when Dad's back was turned, I'd be climbing under our barbed-wire boundary once again.

In that field, I could balance ladybirds on grass blades which, in adult scale, was like balancing a halved orange on a pencil. The world was a different scale back then, bigger and boundless. I would try to catch crickets, tuning into their rasp. I would approach slowly, with my hands cupped, ready to pounce. Then, clap! and each time I uncupped my hands, gradually allowing the light back in, I'd be utterly convinced that I'd caught one. But my hands would always be empty. I was never too disappointed because I'd hear another rasp and I knew I could always try again. Life was all about second, third and fourth chances.

My father's whole demeanour started to change one particular summer. Mum and I had been getting used to him leaving the farm for days at a time. But, that summer, the days became weeks and we rarely saw him at all. And whenever he did come home, he might as well have been down in Cork treating a crocked gelding, he was just as detached and remote.

The strain was showing on Mum. I remember trailing a jam jar through a bog and collecting a conserve of frog-spawn and tadpoles (currants with tails). I presented the thick broth of spawn to my mother and she presented me with a thick ear. Mum had never hit me before that day. She hanged herself two days later and for months I thought it was because I had brought filthy frogspawn into her clean house. My dad never told me otherwise.

After Mum died, Dad sold up and moved the two of us away from Northern Ireland to Wales, where he took up a resident post at a stable in Llanstumdwy, not far from Aintree. Llanstumdwy – named by someone who'd stood on a typewriter. Or someone suffering

83

from Irritable Vowel Syndrome. If only it were that interesting. The place was dull beyond belief, a complete culture shock. The world was closing in on me and I didn't like it one bit. I endured a soul-destroying Welsh winter while my dad endured a soul-destroying breakdown. He got fired. We upped sticks again and headed for Stranraer where Dad sought sanctuary with his sister, Sylvia.

Sylvia brought me up 'proper'. She ran a guest house overlooking the ferry port. One of her guests back then was a wealthy South African landowner. He had a ranch in the Drakensberg mountain range on the border with Lesotho. You didn't need to be well off to acquire land in the region at that time. With the white muscle of the South African government firmly behind you, you could just steal the land from the Zulu. This man got talking to my dad and offered him a job. He wanted him to run a flying animal hospital on his ranch at Cathedral Peak. Aside from an assurance that there were no dogs, Dad didn't take much persuading.

Dad thought I'd be better off staying in Scotland with my Aunt Sylvia. I could play with my older cousin, Jamie. I had my school. There would be no place for me on an untamed African mountain.

I crumpled up the thin blue letter and made Dunc beg before letting him eat it. I stuck my red bills into the mouth of an ornamental frog on the microwave. I had a train to catch.

Rather, I had a bus, two tubes and a train to catch. W7 from Crouch End to Finsbury Park – Victoria line to Euston – Northern Line to Charing Cross – Dartford BR as far as Greenwich. I had done the route so often I could probably do it in my sleep. In fact, I often did.

I was on the point of nodding off, somewhere between Warren Street and Goodge Street, when I found myself sharing the tube carriage with an air hostess who had showered in Chanel No 5, a young man whose bottom betrayed at regular intervals his love for hot and aromatic curry, two Italian backpackers with ever-increasing circles of sweat under their armpits, and a busker with halitosis doing neither himself nor anyone else any favours by blowing enthusiastically through his didgeridoo. I felt like I had gatecrashed a meeting of Malodorous Anonymous.

By the time I arrived at the market I was criminally late. Luckily Geoff, my wholesaler, had waited.

'Sorry Geoff, I was on a bit of a large one last night. Cheers for waiting. You're a star.'

'Fuck up asshole and help me unload these barrels,' he said. Geoff was a gracious soul. He was fat and forty with a featureless face. Geoff was easy to draw.

We stacked the barrels in a pyramid formation against the back wall of the stall. Geoff's hands were more used to lifting than mine. His fingers resembled two bunches of pricked beef sausages.

'I mean it, Geoff, thanks for waiting. I thought I'd missed you.'

'You nearly did. I was about to piss off, when I saw that pantomime going on over there.' Geoff sucked his fag's last and flicked the butt in the direction of the *Cutty Sark*. A ring of squad cars had surrounded the ship. It looked like the police were performing a dawn raid on some pirates.

'Shit. What's going on?'

'Not sure,' he huffed. 'But they've put a tent over the deck and they ain't scouts.' He flared another fag into life.

We watched for some minutes as drones of officers marched into the blue tent and then marched back out again, all carrying plastic bags, like ants stealing from campers. They all wore protective clothing.

A WPC made her way towards us.

'Good morning. I wonder if I could ask you gentlemen how long you've been here,' she said.

'I've only just arrived, but Geoff here's been hanging about for, how long Geoff?'

''Bout half an hour.' He blew the smoke from a lit Camel straight into her face.

'*Khrrroum. Khum.* Sir, *kyeogh*, have you seen anything strange?'

'I've seen a lot of strange things, love. I once saw a man inhale milk up his nose and squirt it out his eyes,' he said.

The policewoman's eyes were watering. She was still coughing.

'No, *khoum*, I meant have you seen anything out of the ordinary this *khrur* morning.'

'Yes I have,' said Geoff.

The policewoman took a small notebook from her breast pocket and became the first person I had seen, outside the movies, to pointlessly lick the end of a pencil in preparation to jot something down.

'So what was out of the ordinary . . . can I call you Geoff?'

'You just did. There's been some strange goings-on.

86

First, all these people showed up on that ship over there.'

The WPC jotted furiously. From the illegible characters that erupted like barbed wire across her pad, I guessed she was proficient in either shorthand or Gujarati. The Met were continually espousing their commitment to fighting institutionalized racism within the force, so I could be forgiven for favouring the latter. So she scribbled Gujarati while Geoff talked Shite.

'There was a struggle . . .'

'Yes.' *Scribble, scribble.*

'. . . as these guys wrestled . . .'

'Wressss-tllled.' *Scribble, scribble.*

'. . . a blue tarpaulin onto the deck, forming a tent.'

The woman snapped her notebook shut, like a castanet. It made the same curt sound, a fitting accompaniment to her expression.

'Very funny, Geoff. You are, of course, referring to my fellow officers who are at present investigating a suspicious death on the *Cutty Sark*. And because I'm a woman, you think it's OK to take the piss.'

'It's not because you're a woman, love. It's because you're a rozzer,' said Geoff. He was talking his way into a cell.

'May I remind you that I have the power to arrest you for wasting a *rozzer's* time.'

'Steady on, love. I'm only having a laugh.'

'Having a laugh, are you? Follow me.' The WPC escorted Geoff over to an ambulance parked at the dry dock. I followed, protesting his innocence.

Two paramedics were attending to a casualty on a stretcher, but all attempts at resuscitation seemed futile

– he was already inside a body bag.

The WPC unzipped it and rounded on Geoff. 'Does this gentleman look like he's having a laugh?'

I looked into the body bag and saw Loz. His face was encased in a cracked glaze of congealed blood. He stared up at me like a toffee apple.

Six

Loz was buried in Charlton Cemetery in a plot over-looking Ha Ha Road. I guess you could say he was having the last laugh. The funeral was a joke.

It was an uncomfortable affair, not because there was only one mourner other than myself, but because I was forced to wear a shirt and tie. Jambo's shirt and tie. The tight collar etching a red Plimsoll line round my neck was marginally less irritating than the tie securing it. The only tie Jambo owned was somewhat inappropri-ately covered in a wacky race of Hanna-Barbera cartoon characters. As Loz's coffin was lowered into the earth I swear I could hear Muttley's wheezy chuckle.

The Revd Nathaniel Devenny either knew Loz much better than I did, or, by gauging the size of the congre-gation, he had deduced that little was known about the deceased and even less was cared. The eulogy he de-livered rivalled God for powers of creation. He managed to summon a whole history from nothing. The history of Lawrence Edward Chick Burton.

The morning breeze toyed with my tie. I stood with Yogi Bear slapping me in the face and did my best to look respectful. I listened as the Reverend Devenny spoke about Loz's *selfless service to the community* (Loz served them hash). How, when anything bad happened, Loz was *always there, ready and willing to help* (yeah, to help the police with their enquiries). How, in all Loz's years in the market, he *never had an unhappy customer* (the Reverend had clearly smoked Loz's wears). He praised Loz for his active involvement in *community drugs programmes* (Loz was Director of Programming). And, bizarrely, he described Loz as a *man of many talents* (he had died jumping off the mast of the *Cutty Sark* so, presumably, flying wasn't one of them).

The Reverend concluded by reading out a couple of stock passages from the Gospels, you know, Matthew 5:14, John 16:20, a funeral by numbers. He snapped his bible closed and I allowed him just enough time to check his watch to see when the next stiff was being wheeled in, before I asked him where he had got all his information.

'A Mr Joseph Carlin, from the market,' he said. 'Nice man. Brown teeth.'

Joe Carlin, I thought. That figures. Joe has fed the Reverend all manner of bullshit about our dearly departed Loz. The last thing Joe wants is the police sniffing round one of his licensed stalls, particularly when that stall was selling unlicensed herbs. The council would have Joe out on his ear, which wouldn't have been entirely a bad thing.

Joe had been screwing the stallholders for rent for twenty-five years. He'd been screwing me for the last six. In some ways I couldn't blame him. The Greenwich market, originally just a fruit 'n' veg market, was reopened in the early Seventies and became colonized by a ragbag of artists, King's-Road-reject fashion designers, and dubious craftspeople doing all manner of things with offcuts of leather and pieces of string. It was a decade of free spirits and free expression that would later give way to free love. Those early free-range Greenwich marketeers didn't bother with unions. Unions weren't 'cool'. So, for twenty-five years, they allowed themselves to be screwed by the guy that held their leases – Joe Carlin. Like the girls in the length of skirt fashionable at the time, some said they were asking for it.

Not any more, though. By the time I started selling glorified pancakes south of the river, my fellow stallholders had formed Greenwich 27, a formidable alliance of all twenty-seven concerns. Actually, it was more of a fortnightly pub lunch attended by only nine of us – eight now that Loz was dead (though, to be fair, the only demand Loz ever made at our meetings was for someone to pass him the Branston pickle).

The wind dropped some invisible coins, bent down and lifted up the Reverend's funeral robes, exposing a teasing glimpse of cassock underneath. He fought with his skirts, a not too convincing impersonation of Marilyn Monroe on an air vent. He recovered long

91

enough to tell me that Loz had no known family and that it was nice of Joe Carlin to pay for the headstone.

Greenwich 27 had paid for the headstone. We had paid for the whole burial. We were going to have Loz cremated, only we feared the smoke would send all the residents of Greenwich and Woolwich as high as kites.

The Reverend said I was welcome to visit Loz's graveside any time. 'Mine is a progressive ministry that welcomes all souls, even be they homosexual souls.'

Great. He thought I was Loz's lover. Had Joe Carlin made him believe that too?

The Reverend Monroe grabbed one of my hands, shook it with both of his, and then wafted his flapping skirts past a couple of salivating gargoyles into the church.

That left one other mourner at the graveside. One tearful mourner. I knew he couldn't be a relative. The Reverend had said that Loz had no known relatives. There was one other clue that led me to deduce that the mourner wasn't family. He was an albino. Loz, on the other hand, was as black as bereavement on a small Hebridean island. Although, it would not have been altogether impossible for them to be related. It only took one crazy, mixed-up gene somewhere in Loz's family. I felt sure there were plenty of those.

The albino had cried himself out, making his pink eyes even pinker, if that were possible. Why was he crying? Had Loz been his dealer? Did he not realize there were other places to buy weed? I knew Loz dealt good shit, but shit, it must have been legendary the way this guy was greetin'. Still, I thought it touching that Loz at least had a few genuine tears spilt on his grave. I offered the albino my unopened packet of tissues. I had brought them to the funeral as a precaution, in case my eyes started to stream. My hay fever had got worse since I moved to London.

I extended my condolences.

'You must have been close,' I said.

'The closest.' The albino dabbed at his eyes. 'That's what makes it so hard to take.'

'So were you Loz's friend?' I asked.

'Me? No.'

'A relative?'

'No, I'm no relative.'

'But you said you were close?'

'The closest. I put Mr Burton in the body bag. I could see the brain hanging out of his skull.'

Fitting, I thought. Loz was always out of his skull.

The young copper broke down again. So, I thought, the Met are recruiting gays, lesbians, blacks, Pakis and albinos. If they're not careful, they'll be employing paddies next.

'The sarge said I should come along today. He gave me the morning off. He said it would be therapeutic. It's the first dead body I've seen.'

You've obviously never met Maureen at the Seagull's Arms, I thought.

I had to remind myself I was at Loz's funeral. I shouldn't have been making light of it, but I had never been comfortable with public displays of grief. When my mother would cry during the Sunday matinee I'd feel compelled to crack a joke. Either that or I'd simply get up and go to my room. In fact, the former was often followed by my mother's urgent instruction to do the latter.

'Have you got any closer to finding out what happened?' I asked. 'I mean, I was probably the last person to see Loz alive and he was far from depressed. I can't believe he'd take his own life.'

'The autopsy turned up certain chemicals in Mr Burton's blood.'

'Aaaaah. Drugs. That makes sense. He was celebrating. He'd just come into some money. Let me guess – he got wasted, thought he was Captain Birdseye and decided to sail the *Cutty Sark* out of dock, oblivious to the fact it's welded to it. Loz always fancied himself as a sailor. I reckon he climbed up the mast to check his bearings, only he lost them and fell to the deck. Death by misadventure.'

'Misadventure?' The albino blanched. 'There were enough chemicals in his body to kill a small horse.'

'Now there's an idea,' I said. (The only horse race I ever bet on is the Grand National. On how many will be shot.)

'What a waste,' said the albino.

'Indeed.'

I walked back to the market via Charlton Park and Shooter's Hill, through Greenwich Deer Park, past the Old Royal Observatory, and emerged from Circus Gate looking like a right clown in Jambo's interview suit and cartoon tie.

I had told Sam I would be back at the stall by twelve, in time for the lunchtime rush. I had lied. It was gone one by the time I found her juggling crêpes like a plate-spinner, and cursing like a *bad* plate-spinner. Without looking up, she hurled an apron at me.

'Get fucking cooking. One cheese 'n' mushroom, one cheese 'n' ham, and one ham 'n' ham.'

'Ham 'n' ham?'

'It's your new lunchtime special. Two fillings for two quid. This guy wants ham twice.'

In my absence the stall had burst into flower. Bouquets of fluorescent handwritten cardboard signs now blossomed all about it, announcing a new season of 'Lunchtime Specials', 'Two for Ones', and 'Free Breakfast Coffees'. Sam had been busy.

'Free coffee? I don't sell coffee, never mind give it away for free.'

'You do now. Check it out.'

Sure enough, Sam pointed to a coffee percolator burping and seething on the worktop. Its plastic handle had melted, giving it a curious Dali-esque appearance.

'Where did you get that?'

'I found it in a box behind Loz's old chair. Seems he didn't totally sell up the other day.'

'Jesus, is it hygienic?' I asked.

'Well, no-one's died this morning. In fact, judging by the rush on breakfast, these free coffees are going to be a nice little earner.'

'And the Lunchtime Specials? Two quid's a bit cheap.'

'You're cheap, you mean. Look at the size of the queue. We're gonna get through eighty to ninety people between one and two.'

'Sam, I appreciate all this, but I liked running things the way they were – there you go, love, cheese 'n' ham.'

'Bic, you need to broaden your horizons. Expand a little. Where's your ambition?'

'Well, I once wrote to *Jim'll Fix It* asking Jim'll if he'd help me realize my ambition to play synth with The Human League. I still live in hope.'

'Your ambition for this place, I mean. Where is it going? Where do you want to be in five years' time?' she asked.

'You sound like my dad now. Any more, Sam, and I may have to run upstairs, slam a door and lock myself in my bedroom.'

Sam's mind was working overtime, but I wasn't going to pay her for it.

'See, I was thinking,' she said, 'you could put a few tables out front here, so people can sit and eat. I don't mind doing waitress service. And the breakfast coffee's only the start. We could invest in the proper equipment and start doing cappuccinos and mochas. And what about more adventurous fillings like Thai Chicken, or Duck and Plum Sauce?'

'Whoa there. What next, our own chain of Fusion Crêpe Gastrodomes?'

'Why not?' she asked.

'Because, I –'

'Go on. One good reason why not?'

'OK, I'll give you two reasons. One, I don't know what a Gastrodome is. And two, I can't be arsed. I like to keep things simple. Manageable. I'm happy with things the way they are.'

I didn't want her to know that I would soon be selling up and moving into ostriches. It would only upset her.

After the salon incident, it would be the second time in a month that I did her out of a job.

'The way you can't be arsed to finish with your middle-aged married girlfriend?' she asked. 'The way you can't be arsed to move from that burnt-out shit-hole of a flat? The way you can't be arsed to give me a pay rise?'

'Sam, if all this is you wanting a rise, you could have just asked me. Here.' I opened the till. Fair play to Sam, I had never seen my till so full. It had never before held every denomination of note and coin all at once. There was even a rogue quarter in with the ten pees. I pulled out a tenner and handed it to her.

'Call it a bonus, for your extra work this morning.'

'You *are* cheap!'

Sam swapped the ten for a twenty and threw the dregs of some batter into the bin.

I felt suddenly sad. Sadder than an albino at a funeral. Sad because I was about to lose her. Sam didn't know it yet, but I intended to see Joe when we closed up. I wanted to secure Loz's stall for her, before it went out to tender. I wanted to set her up in business before I sold up my own. Sam couldn't have my stall. I needed to sell the equipment to finance my ostrich farm and Sam couldn't afford it, not on top of the lease. But Loz's stall was just a couple of empty trestle tables, well within her means. Especially as I intended to buy the lease for her once the money from the regatta came in. I felt bad about leaving her and hoped it would in some way compensate. Joe would sell me the lease for buttons. I would tell him that I had seen Loz and Sam shake on it.

The last will of a dead man and all that. It would be a formality.

But I wouldn't tell Sam that. No, I'd have to tell her it took long negotiation, harsh words, a struggle or, even better, a bribe, to secure her a jewellery stall, the first step to her building some International House of Gems. She'd be forever in my debt. She might even make me a nose ring. Heck, I might even get it pierced.

Sam and I got on with serving lunch to the great Greenwich public. I succeeded in burning myself twice. I was having one of those days. I wasn't used to people dying.

My mother hadn't died, she had committed suicide. That was an altogether different thing. Suicide is planned and premeditated. Suicide has its logic, however skewed (in Mum's case 'acute depression' shaped her logic). Suicide is preventable, if caught in time. Death, however, is a more unpredictable beast. Death just happens.

My first experience of death happened long before Mum chose to depart this mortal coil. I had found a dead greenfinch in the field beyond our farm. Like a cat, I brought the bird back to the house. My mother threw it in the bin. I don't know why, but this upset me more than finding the bird dead in the first place. She shooed me out of her kitchen, but I sneaked in a little later when she was in the living room not speaking to Dad. I retrieved the greenfinch from the bin and set about burying it in the garden. I dug out its grave with a broken Sodastream bottle and gave it a fine send-off, singing 'Tit Willow' to it, the way my Grandpa Charlie used to sing me to sleep. Weeks passed and each day I stopped by the little brown scuff in the wide green lawn to pay my respects. Well, somebody had to, and I alone knew that the greenfinch was buried there. But that strange morbid curiosity that only young boys seem to possess finally got the better of me and I decided that I should exhume the body. This time I used the proper tools for the job. I pinched my dad's best silver veterinary forceps from his leather bag. I tore and tore at the earth until, slowly, the bird's skeleton revealed itself, like a tiny dinosaur. But it wasn't dead any more. It was twitching and squirming. It was alive with maggots. I have only once been more terrified.

'I can't be arsed dying,' I said.

Sam and I had shut up shop and repaired to the pub. Not the Seagull's Arms. We needed food.

'I didn't mean what I said, Bic, about you not being arsed to do anything with the business. At least you've *got* your own business, it's more than I have.' Sam prodded a reluctant slice of cold lasagne.

I struggled manfully with an impressive club sandwich that was more of a Scooby snack. 'No, Sam, you were right. I can't be arsed finishing with Barbara. I can't be arsed moving the business on. I don't like change, you see. I had too much of that growing up. Sometimes you need familiarity, a routine. You need to know where you stand.'

'But you are your own boss. You can do what you want. Think of the possibilities.'

'That's right. I've got the best boss in the world – me. I won't sack me. If I'm ill, I don't have to phone me to say I won't be in. I won't give me a pay cut or change my hours. I won't suddenly change my company culture. I won't change anything. I've got the ultimate in job security. I know where I stand. But something's missing. It's doing my head in, Sam. This place is doing my head in. I feel like I could swing for somebody.' I opened my mouth wide, like a kid feigning horror, but the sandwich didn't fit. It wasn't my size.

'So change things,' she said.

'Things are already changing. This morning I buried a friend and branched out into free coffee. This afternoon I'll telephone Barbara and end it. Who knows, by this evening I'll have met the woman of my dreams and we'll up sticks for the auld homeland to raise our two children, Chlamydia and Fellatio. Stranger things have happened.'

'Have they?' laughed Sam.

'Yes. Take those bees, for example.'

'What bees?'

'The ones in the hives that yer man kept, you know, in the strawberry field. It was on the news. Only his bees didn't make honey, they made strawberry jam,' I said.

'Really?'

I couldn't keep a straight face.

'You're cruel,' said Sam.

I loved Sam's gullibility. Loz had convinced her that he used to be the black guy in Showaddywaddy, and that he'd turned to drugs when the hits had dried up. Priceless.

'I'll tell you another strange thing,' I said.

'Stop it, Bic.'

'No seriously, listen to this one. There was a man called Bic who went to see a man called Joe. Bic asked Joe if a girl he knew by the name of Sam could lease a recently vacated stall for the purposes of retailing bracelets, necklaces, and all manner of accoutrements.'

'Get off! Seriously?'

'Well, I haven't actually asked him yet. But as soon as we finish this I'm over there. He can't say no. I mean, Loz promised. You two had a deal. I witnessed it.'

'Aw Bic, I love ya!' Sam lunged at me, wrapping her breasts around my ears and kissing the top of my head. There are worse places to be.

'Aw Bic! Bic! You're a diamond.'

'Calm down. The stall won't be available for a wee while. Joe will want to sort out the paperwork and anyway, I need you for the regatta. It's going to be a big day, we'll need to be up at the crack.'

'No problem. Whatever you say, boss. Aw! I'm really going to make a go of it. Wait till I tell Dad. Yessssss!'

'Come on now. Remember, this only came about because of Loz's unfortunate demise. Let's show a little respect.'

'Respect my arse.'

'I do, Sam. I have the utmost regard for your bottom – Jeeeeethuth!'

'Bic?'

'My thandwich. There'th a thodding cocktail thtick in it.' I grabbed a serviette and pressed it onto my bleeding tongue.

Sam tried not to laugh as I pulled a Japanese flag from my mouth. She failed.

We stopped at a chemist on the way back. Actually, it was an 'apothecary', not a chemist. Like most businesses around Greenwich market, the establishment

101

had imbued itself with a faux Olde Worlde 'charm'. Its interior was dominated by a cumbersome wooden drugs cabinet from the eighteen hundreds. This brought to mind stories of strychnine and wiry killers in top hats lurking on London's foggy, cobbled streets. Its shelves displayed a cornucopia of potions, phials, salts, oils and tinctures. I needed something for my tongue and feared that the man in the starched white coat might prescribe leeches, so I pre-empted him.

'I need thome clove oil, pleath.'

Sam had convinced me this would numb the pain. The guy looked less than convinced. He spoke with an Irish accent.

'Toothache, sir?'

'Thongue acthually. Aaaaaaaaah.' I opened my mouth wide, the way I used to when fork aeroplanes carrying their cargoes of champ, mince, and baked beans came in to land.

'Nasty. You'll be wanting some TCP,' he said.

'Thee Thee Pee?'

I could have gone to Boots for that. I took an instant dislike to the guy.

The apothecarist, or whatever you called him, wrapped the slim brown bottle and I paid. I had gauged the age of his till and expected to be billed in shillings. He handed me my change and gave me a peculiar look, like he was marking my card.

'I'm thorry, do I know you?' I asked.

'No. No, I don't think you do.'

As we exited I looked back through the window. He was punching a number into his mobile and staring right back at me.

We walked through the covered side of the market, under the arcade, and past the dais that had now been erected near the *Cutty Sark*. The Boys Brigade were rehearsing some peculiar sort of dance, more hosepipe than hornpipe, in preparation for the weekend's naval festivities.

I had just located my stall keys in the last of my suit's many unfamiliar pockets when Sam went berserk.

'Bic! Bic, look. No. What's she doing?'

A young woman. Jet black hair. Lifting small parcels out of polystyrene boxes. Carefully unwrapping them. Each containing a small object in glass, metal or stone, which she positioned on plinths. On green and purple drapes. On Loz's trestle table.

'Bathtard.'

I found Joe tallying cheques in his dingy, nicotine-stained office in the old boathouse by the river. His office furniture amounted to no more than a desk made from a sanded door set astride the broken upturned halves of a single-scull rowing boat and the rotating barstool on which he was sitting. The boathouse was hot. It reeked of linseed oil. I approached Joe from behind. He didn't turn round. A damp patch of sweat spread across the back of his shirt, a silhouette of the ace of clubs.

'You bathtard. He'th thtill warm and you've leathed hith thtall.'

Joe spun round, as if to say *I've been expecting you, Mr Bickmore.*

'Fuck, it's Bonnie Langford,' was what he actually said. 'What are you gonna do Bic, thcweam and thcweam until you're thick?'

Joe licked the rubber thimbles on his thumb and fore-finger and returned to his wad of cheques, flicking through them, occasionally stopping to pull a betting-shop biro from behind his ear so that he could ink another four-figure sum into his rent book.

'You knew, Joe. You knew I had Tham down to take the thtall. Thooner or later we both knew that Loth wouldn't have the rent, or he'd get arrethted.'

'Or die,' said Joe.

'Whatever. The fact ith, Tham and Loth had an unwritten agreement. I thaw them thake on it.'

'You and your unwritten agreements, Bic. You know that I have to advertise any vacancy. That's the law. I stuck an ad in the arcade this morning.'

'Jethuth, could you not even wait till the poor thod wath buried?'

'No, I couldn't. I've got overheads.'

'Loth hath got thixth feet of overheadth. Joe, he wanted Tham to take over.'

'I'm as sorry as you are about Loz.'

'Rubbith. You've been waiting yearth to get rid of him, but thomehow he alwayth found the rent for you.'

Joe removed the rubber thimbles, revealing black nails bitten to the quick. He lit another fag, the bikini slowly falling off the girl on his lighter.

'I think we know how Loz found the rent, Bic. I think the police knew how he found the rent, they just couldn't pin anything on him. Which is just as well for all of us. *All* of us. Think about it. If I lose the licence on this market, who takes it over and what do they do with the place? Flatten it and build more yuppie river-side apartments? Worse still, build a fucking great dome or something? Be thankful for small mercies. I've got your interests at heart.'

'Bollockth. You're only interethted in thoth chequeth in your hand.'

'I advertised as I was entitled, no, *obliged* to do. If either you or Sam had given me a month's rent up front, I would gladly have given you the stall.'

'You know Tham hathn't got that kind of money yet. All her cath goeth into making her jewellery.'

'You could have subbed her, Bic.'

'Joe, I've just thunk a lot of cath into provithionth for thith bloody regatta. I could have given you two, three, four months' rent up front if you'd held the thtall until after it. Could you not even wait one week?'

'As it happens, no. Someone came in here yesterday, enquiring about the stall. I explained to them that I had to advertise it, but they were at my door first thing this morning with the money.'

'That girl with the black hair? I mean, how inthen-thitive can you be, Joe? Among other thingth, she'th thelling jewellery for fuck'th thake. How do you think that maketh Tham feel?'

Joe sat back, smug and ugly. He picked at his head, grey hair turning yellow like someone had pissed on it.

'Bic, I don't give a shit what she's selling, as long as it's legal,' he said.

My eyes felt hot just looking at him. I kicked the rowing boat out from under his desk, sending cheques, banknotes and empty fag packets into the air.

'You're a bathtard Carlin. I'll get you back, d'you hear,' I said.

'Oh, so you're the big paddy man now, eh? Don't tell

me, you're gonna get the paramilitary wing of the Greenwich 27 to do my knees.'

Joe stood up. Bits of paper were still flitting round him like sycamore seeds.

'I'll get you back Carlin,' I said. 'That'th a promith.'

Seven

Loz didn't know that there had already been a suicide on the Cutty Sark. *He had never heard the sad tale of Captain J.S. Wallace, who took his life on a voyage from Anjer to Yokohama. Nor did Loz know that the magnificent tea clipper, the last of her kind, had also transported coal and wool in her time: 4,638 bales from Sydney to London in eighty-five days. Even as he stood looking up at the Old Lady, her salt-stiffened ropes rattling like bones on the night breeze, he didn't know that her lower masts had once been shortened nine feet six inches, seven feet off her lower yards, and that the rest of her spars had been shortened in proportion. He only knew that he was standing beside a big boat and he needed to throw up.*

He leaned over the dry dock and dry-heaved. It had been nine hours since he'd last eaten – a cheese 'n' mushroom 'n' dope crêpe – but all that came up was

107

rum 'n' bile. He heaved again, any harder and his eyeballs were out.

'Feeling seasick?' A voice from behind him.

'Bic. It's the fresh air, man.' Loz turned round and propped himself against a crowd barrier. 'Fresh air makin' me dizzy, ma—'

Loz started. He wiped his mouth with his sleeve and focused on the strange man. 'Where's Bic?' he said.

'Who's Bic?'

'Man, you talk funny. Like Bic. I thought you were Bic.'

'You see, in Ireland we'd say that you talked funny. And looked funny. We don't get many blacks in Antrim. Is that puke on your shirt?'

'Piss off, man.'

'Is that how you talk to all your customers? You're very drunk, aren't you. Do you not have a home to go to?'

'Fuck off, man. I ain't no bum. I don't need no charity.' Loz turned his back on the stranger.

'See, that's not what you said when I handed you a grand in cash this afternoon. I seem to recall you couldn't believe your luck.'

'So you're not one of them Christians? No . . . you're the man with the restaurant.'

'Ah, yes, my themed restaurant. And what theme would that be – retro chic? More like retro shit, with the junk you sold me.'

'Look, you got all my stuff man, now piss off.' Loz waved Labcoat away.

'I haven't got your stuff. I incinerated it. Surely you didn't believe I actually had a use for all that rubbish?'

Loz tried to focus better on the man. Sometimes he

was two men, identical men, wearing matching white lab coats that glowed orange under the streetlights. Both were holding identical plastic toolboxes in their left hands. Loz groped for his bumbag.

'You're not getting your money back. A deal's a deal, man.'

'I'm not after your money you fuckin' eejit. You know what I'm after.'

'Leave me alone,' said Loz.

'I'm after your little spot in the market. It's just so perfectly situated, exactly what we're after.'

'Ten grand for my stall or fuck off.'

'Oh, I don't want to buy it off you.' Labcoat walked towards Loz. 'Why would I be wanting to do a crazy thing like that?'

He knelt down and flipped open his toolbox. It contained no screwdrivers, Stanley knives, nuts, bolts or drill-bits. As far as Loz could make out, this guy did his DIY with plasters, swabs and syringes.

'What the fuck are you peddlin', man? I only do weed, I ain't buying none of your shit.'

Labcoat lifted the top tray out of his box and removed a large roll of cotton wool. He held the furry cylinder in one hand and unravelled it with the other, adopting the very deliberate, nothing-up-my-sleeves posturing of a magician. As if by magic, he whipped the cotton away and conjured a gun. It sat heavy in his open palm. He aimed it at Loz.

'Turn round.'

'What the fuck man. OK, OK. Take it then.' Loz desperately ripped big purple notes from his bumbag. 'Take it all.'

'Turn round and shut up. We're going on a wee voyage.'

Labcoat kicked over one of the long metal crowd barriers that flanked the tall ship. 'Grab a hold of that end,' he ordered.

Loz did as he was told and lifted one end of the barrier. Labcoat hoisted the other end with one hand, keeping his gun trained on the Jamaican. A wave of his barrel indicated that he wanted the barrier carried across to the edge of the dry dock. To the edge of a sixteen-foot drop.

'Now I want you to hoist your end up, get it to stand tall.'

Loz immediately dropped it.

'Hey man, I've an idea. The stall. It's yours,' he offered.

'Don't be an eejit. Pick it up and do as I say.'

Loz stood the barrier on its end, a ladder into the night sky, a stairway to heaven. Obediently, he tipped it forward and, with a crack and a buckle, it righted itself against the hull of the Cutty Sark. It formed a bridge.

'Walk the gangplank,' said Labcoat.

'What?'

'Climb up onto the ship.'

Labcoat wedged the bottom end of the barrier against a concrete bollard and checked that it was steady. He followed directly behind Loz. They negotiated the makeshift ladder on all fours.

'It's gonna fall, man,' said Loz.

'Shut up, or there's a very real chance that from this angle, I'll be sending a bullet up your arse.'

Loz kept quiet until he felt the reassurance of solid

teak deckboards under his feet. He only spoke when told to climb again.

'Right, I want you to climb up the main mast,' said Labcoat.

'Man, I hate heights.'

'Do you prefer guns?' Labcoat raised his revolver ninety degrees to his body, two centimetres from Loz's forehead. A longitude without much latitude.

'Seriously man, I got vertigo.'

'And I've got Psycho, now get climbing.'

The rungs felt cold. Loz couldn't remember the last time he'd felt the cold. July had brought the sun with it, and this was a typically balmy night. He remembered these sorts of balmy nights back home. He remembered how there were more stars in the southern hemisphere sky. It was a sky peppered with stars, like bullet-holes in a big black curtain. Brilliant bright bullet-holes, letting light through.

Loz remembered where he was. He steadied his legs and looked down at the man on the deck. He saw an ant pointing a gun at him.

'I can't go any higher, man.'

The ant shouted back, 'I don't want you any higher. What's it like up there?'

'I don't like it, man.'

'What can you see?'

'Is this some big joke? Are you a friend of Bic?'

'Oi, you'll be coming down quicker than a clay pigeon if you don't quit gurning. I'm losing my patience down here. Now what can you see?'

'Um . . . the Dome?'

'Good. Anything else?'

111

'St Paul's,' said Loz. He felt his way round the mast. 'Big Ben. The Millennium Wheel.'

'Can you see the Palace?'

'Wait.' Loz stood on tiptoes. 'No man, not the Palace.'

'Never mind. Sure we're better off without it. Fuck the lot of them.'

'Can I come down now, man?'

'Yes,' said Labcoat.

Loz pressed his head against the wooden mast. Relief oozed out of his pores like sap. He lowered one foot, beginning a cautious descent.

'Whoa. Where do you think you're going?' shouted Labcoat.

'You said I could come down.'

'Yes, but I want you to jump down.'

'Jump? I'll die if I jump,' said Loz.

'You're not as stupid as you look.'

'No way am I jumping, man.'

'You either jump down or I shoot you down.'

Loz sized it up. He needed a smoke. His black knuckles turned pink the harder he gripped. It occurred to him that his hands were no longer capable of rolling a joint even if they were free to do so. A little smoke and a little rum and he'd be ready to jump. A long, cool toke and he'd be ready to fly.

'At least if you jump, you've got a chance of surviving this,' shouted Labcoat.

Loz checked the position of the moon and shifted his back around the mast again, so that he faced due south. That's it, man. You're migrating. You're just flying south for winter. Back home, where it's all nice and warm. Go on, let the thermals carry you. Let your instincts navigate. You'll be cruising, man. You'll be home in no time. Go on. Shut your eyes.

Loz closed his eyes, set his wings and flew off into the big black curtain.

'Holy Mary Mother of God.'

His starched lab coat was spattered in the Rasta's blood. Black spots bloomed on the orange-lit material, turning it into a leopard-skin. He cursed himself for not standing further back.

He removed the coat and stuffed it into his first-aid box. One more thing to be incinerated, he thought.

He found a syringe. He filled its chamber from a squat bottle. He rolled up one of the Rasta's trouser legs, exposing a black calf flecked with grey hairs. He inserted the needle in that crease behind the knee that anatomists have yet to award a name. He slowly administered the injection. Perfectamundo. He ripped out the needle and returned both it and the empty chamber to his plastic box. He rolled the Rasta's trouser down again and, grabbing both feet, he raised the dead man's broken legs as high as he could, to force some circulation.

He abandoned ship.

Eight

I set my stall out.

I opened the shutters, grated the cheese, crushed the hazelnuts, diced the ham, sliced the mushrooms, greased the hotplate and judged the batter. And I percolated the coffee. My new routine.

I loved the early morning market, especially in summer. Up at the crack and out with the lark. I loved the puffy-eyed *good mornings* exchanged between the stallholders. I loved the sigh of tarpaulin and the rasp of shutters when stalls are opened up. I loved the conspiratorial *psst* of air brakes and the clack of trays as lorryloads of supplies are delivered. I loved that first gulp of tea, so hot and strong it clamps your knees together. I loved the smell of fresh vegetables, fresh bagels, leather, patchouli, handmade soap, pine furniture, old books, new books, and dead people's clothes – previously loved clothes. I loved the smell of the

Thames and I loved the fact that every morning was exactly the same.

Maybe London wasn't so bad.

The heat had already begun to dredge the river of its peculiar pungency – imagine seaweed pesto. Even at this early hour, a brass ensemble in full regalia was parping away on the temporary dockside stage. Six days to go until they did it for real. Six days until Greenwich officially launched the Tall Ships and announced itself to the world as *the* centre of all things millennial.

Of course, they faced stiff competition. A group of Wiccan druids in the Lake District had already challenged Greenwich's self-appointed position at the epicentre of Time. They believed they had located the real prime meridian some sixty miles north-east of Carlisle, at the foot of Sighty Crag. This had been determined, they claimed, through a long process of ancient detective work and spiritual divinity (with a little mumbo-jumbo and a smidgen of guesswork thrown in, no doubt).

More worrying for Greenwich Borough Council and indeed the British government, was the strong challenge being mounted by a small and charming community of grass-skirt wearers on the South Pacific island of Toketau. It had been calculated that the first sunrise of the year 2000 would be seen from this remote little vantage point, one hundred and sixty miles west of the Cook Islands. Toketau was the place to be. This was not without irony. The proprietors of the Royal Maritime Museum, who were hosting an exhibition on Cook as part of the Greenwich celebrations, were probably cursing the captain for ever having charted

Toketau on his map. And why did he have to go and stick it so close to the International Date Line, they'd complain.

Regardless, the Greenwich Brass Ensemble parped on with the enthusiasm of people who had never heard of Cumbrian druids or South Sea islanders.

'It's a bit early for that,' I said to my first customer of the day. I handed him a bacon and egg crêpe.

'Then why do you call it a morning special?' he asked.

'Eh?'

'You call this a morning special, yet you say eight thirty's a bit early for it.'

'No. It's a bit early for that racket over on the stage. I mean, don't the people in the flats complain?' I raised my spatula and pointed him in the direction of the stage and the tatty block of flats overlooking it.

Yolk wept from the corners of his mouth as he spoke. 'Most of the residents in those flats are genetically programmed to stay in bed until two in the afternoon. Except on Wednesdays.'

'Why Wednesdays?'

'They have to get up and cash their giros.'

'Well, whatever, I still wouldn't like to be woken by a brass band this early.'

'Folks over there could sleep through a gun battle. Many of them do so on a regular basis. Anyway, where's your bulldog spirit, they're playing a military tattoo.'

'Yeah, a particularly embarrassing tattoo, one that seems impossible to remove,' I said.

'Weirdo.' He walked off, patting his thigh in time to the band.

Half eight. Where was Sam? I called her mobile. No

answer. It was going to be a scorcher. The market would be busy. Jambo, I thought. He'd be doing nothing. That's if the black redstarts hadn't flown their nest.

I knew birds and I knew that these black redstarts wouldn't be leaving for a couple of months, not until mid-September, early October. The two birds had become front-page news since they had occupied the Dome. They were national heroes. Never mind the fact that millions of pounds of our money were being used to finance the Dome, and that this figure was increasing proportionally every day the birds were in residence, the great British public still took them to their hearts. The *Daily Mail* was the only dissenting voice, claiming that the birds were now enjoying the most expensive accommodation in Britain at the taxpayer's expense, something that would not be allowed to happen under the Conservatives. They dismissed our feathered friends with the same editorial venom they usually reserved for Bosnian asylum seekers drawing the dole in Margate.

You could even watch the bomb birds twenty-four hours a day on a live Internet feed. Not that Jambo would be doing that. He'd be at home, on full pay, watching Aussie soaps. Or he'd be down Clapham Snooker Hall. For someone who had misspent his entire youth knocking coloured balls round green baize, Jambo was remarkably bad at the sport. He spent so much time in the chair, I feared he would become the first snooker player to suffer a deep-vein thrombosis.

I called him. No answer. You can't get a reception in Clapham Snooker Hall.

Thankfully the morning rush never materialized. I

used the time to work out a menu for the regatta. It was so quiet I even markered a 'Back in 10 mins' sign and took Dunc for a quick walk in the park. By the time I returned, the new girl had set up her stall opposite. The girl with the jet black hair. It would have been easy to resent her for taking Sam's spot, but she wasn't to know that Loz had bequeathed it. That bastard Joe was to blame. The new girl wasn't to know. I thought I ought to introduce myself to her.

'Hello?'

She didn't look up. She seemed to be studying something in her lap. I tried again – 'Hi there' – and had turned to walk away when she came back to me.

'Sorry. In the middle of something. What can I interest you in?'

She had one of those faces that looked angry and happy at the same time. Dark, angled eyebrows met pleasing sea-green eyes. Eyes that caught me off guard.

'All pieces are genuine one-offs, handmade in Ireland from materials I gathered myself on the beaches of County Antrim,' she said. It sounded like a rehearsed spiel. She introduced each item, a mixture of jewellery, knick-knacks and ornaments, everything from pendants to paperweights, fashioned from slate, sandstone, jet, quartz, glass, shells, driftwood and all manner of flotsam and jetsam. Each piece was engraved with a Celtic design. She held up a blue bottle, its glass smoothed and dulled by sea erosion. Her finger traced out the ornate interlocking bands etched cleanly into it. 'This design was reputed to be on the arms of Cuchulainn when he fought for the Red Branch Knights. Of course then, he was known as Setanta,' she said.

118

'Sorry, I don't want to buy anything.'

'It comes with a wee certificate of authenticity,' she offered.

'No really, I just wanted to say hello, welcome you to the market.'

'Oh. Right.'

I sensed her disappointment.

'Sorry, I run the crêperie opposite. The name's Bic.'

'That's nice. Well, I'd love to chat but, as you can see, I'm a bit busy.' She brushed away the wood shavings that clung to her skirt and returned her attention to the half-carved Celtic cross that sat in her lap.

'Don't I get a name?' I asked.

'Roisin.' She said it to her knees. 'And keep your dog away from my stuff, some of it's breakable,' she added.

I looked down. Right on cue, Duncan cocked his leg and marked his territory all over her green velvet drapes.

Roisin reared up, scalpel in hand. 'Jesus, get him off.'

'Duncan, bad dog. Look, I'm really sorry. I've got cloths, I'll clean it up.'

'You idiot. That drape is ruined.'

'Relax, it just needs a soak. I've got a sink. Come on, give it here,' I said.

'Ach just leave me alone. You've done enough damage already.'

She ran round the stall, knocking over a rack of bangles. I went to pick them up and got a DM in the groin for my trouble.

'Don't touch anything. Do you hear me,' she said.

Fine, if that's the way she wanted it, I thought. *I want to be sick*, is what I actually thought. I straightened and sought sanctuary back at my stall. I crouched down behind the counter and unbuttoned my fly to rearrange the family crockery. I checked for bleeding.

'Do you want me to rub something on that?'

It was Sam.

After her no-show that morning, I was relieved to see her. She had been so upset yesterday, I feared she would never come back to the market again. I buttoned up.

'I don't understand. Dunc only ever pees outside my downstairs neighbours' flat. And that's only because I can't stand them.'

'Maybe he's a good judge of character.' Sam watched as Roisin changed her drapes.

'Come to think of it, he did once pee on Loz's record collection,' I said.

'Bic, given the opportunity, I would've peed on Loz's record collection.'

'So you're saying it was worth pissing on?'

Sam laughed, but it was only half a laugh. I remembered her tears twenty-four hours earlier. 'Are you OK?' I asked. 'I was worried about you. Why weren't you answering your phone?'

'I threw it in the river.'

'You did what?'

'I was upset, Bic. I tried to phone Dad yesterday, to get him to pick me up. But I couldn't get a signal, so I just hurled it.'

'Shit, that'll cost you.'

'It's all right, Dad's gonna tell the cab office he had his phone nicked, get me a new one.'

'And you're OK now, I mean, you're not about to throw another wobbler?'

Sam laughed a more convincing laugh. 'OK, so I was upset, but it was nothing that a few friends and a few grams of cocaine couldn't cure.' She sniffed sharply.

'Saaaam?'

'Don't be a daft bugger. You know I don't do that scene, especially after recent events.'

'You mean Loz's performance of *The Pirates of Penzance*, the snuff version?'

'Bic, don't joke, the guy killed himself.'

'Sorry.'

'No, my only vice is vodka and Red Bull,' she said.

'Well, those seem to have done you some damage.' I had noticed something on her neck. I moved her hair back, exposing a blackberry stain of a love bite.

'I fell.' She said it with a smile.

'Who did you fall on, Bela Lugosi?'

'Dunno. I can't remember his name.'

Yep, Sam was back on form.

Like the breeze, business picked up around lunch and died off in the afternoon. Perhaps the brass band had deterred people. Sam made no mention of the girl with the jet black hair. I didn't tell her that I knew her name, and that she was as icy as a Finn's freezer. Sam didn't seem interested.

Roisin had been paying us even less attention. She sat with her DMs on the table and her knees tucked into her chest. She teetered on her stool reading a book, *Amongst Women*, Irish tricolour on the cover. Don't ask me what it was about. She barely moved, only to lick a painted finger and turn a page. Occasionally she'd follow this by moving the same finger to her hair and twisting a long black lock into a tight ringlet. She would pop the ringlet in her mouth and chew on its end. Then she'd gently flick one of her pendulous earrings into swing. It was a very female set of movements and one that I found most alien. I was beguiled by it. Barbara never moved like this. Perhaps she once did, before she became a wife and a mother. I really should phone her and end it, I thought.

Roisin's eyebrows angled more steeply the more she read, like a couple of accents. Why did such a good-looking girl have to be all angry? I was just getting irritated by the Clannad compilation that was emoting from her battered little tape deck when I saw two schoolgirls approaching her. They were skivers from the local comp. I could tell they were from the local comp because they were wearing the uniform: crop tops, navel rings, and patent Nikes.

Roisin set her book pages down, to keep her place. She chatted with the girls and let them try on necklaces in a mirror. She didn't make a sale, the girls clearly failing to be regaled by tales of Cuchulainn. Roisin's expression never wavered throughout. I was beginning to think she only had one expression, like those ageing American ladies who marry plastic surgeons and have so many free facelifts they can't blink; they just become chamois-leather zombies with fixed smiles.

Only, Roisin never smiled.

Sam said, 'We're pissed and she's nuts.'

'What?'

'We need pistachio nuts.'

'Sorry, miles away.'

'I'll run over the road and get some.'

'Here. Take some money out of the float,' I said.

As Sam went off, the schoolgirls came back. Roisin didn't stop reading this time. She peered over her book, saw who it was and left them to it. If they wanted to try something on, they could ask her. They knew the form. The girls fingered some items disinterestedly and were just walking away when I ran across and grabbed them both, one arm each, behind their backs.

'What in God's name are you doing now? These are my customers.' Roisin threw down her book, losing her place.

The girls did their best to wriggle free. To onlookers it must have seemed like I was operating two very uncooperative ventriloquist's dummies. Roisin's DMs hurried towards me. My testicles had a flashback and retreated into my stomach.

'Let them go,' she said.

I let one of them go. I slipped my free hand into the jacket pocket of the other girl and pulled out a fistful of rings. Celtic rings. I had watched her pinch them while Roisin was reading her book.

'Do you want me to call the police?' I asked.

'No. Just give them the rings and let her go. She won't be back here in a hurry,' said Roisin.

The girls had run some distance before they stopped, turned and shouted *wanker!* at me.

I think Roisin was grateful, not that her face betrayed it. She only said, 'I suppose I have to buy you a drink or something.'

'Well, there's an offer I can't refuse. You're really selling it to me.'

'Look, whatever you're called –'

'Bic.'

'Bic?'

'It's my pen name.'

She wasn't amused.

'I haven't forgotten about the dog,' she said.

'No, but you forgot my name. Charming.'

'Bic, where's good for a drink? I don't know the area yet.'

'We can head up the South Bank. Give me fifteen minutes to close up.'

'I'll give you five. I've had it for today,' she said.

'Fine. Can I bring the dog?'

'Don't push your luck.'

Nine

Jewish Jeff pulled up in his black cab. He had driven down to the market to pick up his daughter, Sam.

I liked Jewish Jeff. I called him Jewish Jeff to avoid confusing him with Geoff, my wholesaler. Jewish Jeff could not have been more different from his namesake. He was a motormouth, a thousand words a minute, all fake gold and Old Spice. He wore trousers so tight you could read the dates on the coins in his pockets. You could certainly tell what religion he was. It was a wonder he was ever able to sit down behind the wheel of his cab. Or that he was able to get up again when he did.

Sam said she'd lock up for me, to make up for her tardiness that morning. She offered to take the dog for the night, while I 'took the bitch for the night'. She hadn't forgiven Roisin for occupying her stall.

Jeff insisted on running Roisin and me out to the South

Bank. He said he'd go back for his daughter. Jeff was great like that. I kept his number stored in my mobile as he'd promised to pick me up, no matter where I was calling from, at whatever time of day or night. (My mobile was a necessary evil. When we were younger, Jambo and I would communicate with two cups tied together by string. It was primitive, but at least it worked in a tunnel. I'm a bit of a Luddite when it comes to technology.)

Jeff had even been known to kick people out of his cab to come and get me. And he never let me pay. *Don't offend me like this, why do you offend me son,* he would say, waving my cash away. I think he was grateful that I'd helped his daughter out.

Jeff stuck as close as he could to the river. He sensed that Roisin was new to London and wanted to keep the route as scenic as possible, following the Millennium Mile, past Tower Bridge and on towards Oxo Tower. He avoided Bermondsey.

Roisin was silent. She stared resolutely out the window at all the hustle and bustle of the city, like she was watching the last crucial scenes in a three-hour thriller. Gripped.

I felt nervous. I hadn't felt this nervous since I was forced to act out *Free Willy* in a game of charades. I felt how I would feel if this were a date, sort of prickly. But this wasn't a date. Crazy what your body does to you, isn't it. Just sharing a cab with a strange and attractive woman was enough to bring me out in hives and weeping sores. I felt stupid. She was just being polite, doing her duty, taking me for a quick drink because, in her own words, *she owed me.* Nevertheless, I had to wind the window down. I couldn't think what to say.

Jeff filled the vacuum.

'Are you still living with that couple who write the adverts, son?'

'I live above them, not with them.'

'I reckon the only good ad these days is that PG Tips one. Only they had to go and call the chimpanzee Jeffrey. Stupid bloody name, Jeffrey.'

'That's your name,' I pointed out.

Not that he was listening. When Jeff talked, it was one-way traffic.

'Jeffrey. What sort of person calls a kid Jeffrey,' he said. 'My bleedin' dad, that's who. And it's not even the English spelling, it's the German one. Him a Jew and he uses the German spelling, I ask you.'

'Could've been worse, Jeff,' I said.

'Eh, son?'

'He could've called you Adolf.'

Roisin remained oblivious. She watched the signs for the City become signs for Waterloo, Gabriel's Wharf and South Bank. A scented tree boogied wildly from side to side under the rear-view mirror as Jeff broached sharp lefts, rights, short cuts and the occasional No Through Road. His A to Z only seemed to go up to Q. He had done the Knowledge, but remembered only choice parts of it, in the same way I could recall only small chunks of first-form Latin. *Caecelius est in horto*, to be exact. That and *Latin is a dead language, as dead as dead can be, first it killed the Romans, now it's killing me*. The way Jeff was cutting through the rush-hour traffic, I feared he'd be the one killing us all.

'You gotta hate the Japs though,' he said. Jeff was on his specialist subject: tourists.

'Why's that then?'

'Well, they eat dolphins don't they.'

'Dolphins?'

'And whales,' he added.

'The Welsh eat dolphins?'

Jeff grunted. 'I wish the Japs would eat the Welsh. Do us all a favour.'

He didn't mean it, of course. It was all in jest. I didn't want him starting on the Irish, though, not with Roisin and all. She didn't know Jeff. She hadn't yet learnt to take his banter with a pinch of the proverbial.

'You're an eejit, Jeff.'

'I don't deny it, son.'

'In fact, if there was an eejit contest, you'd come second,' I said.

'Why second?'

'Because you're an eejit.'

I got him to drop us off behind the Royal National Theatre.

London's South Bank is a concrete lover's wet dream. Like their favourite building material, they'd go hard at the sight of it. I wish I had bought shares in Blue Circle cement at the time the plans were approved. The main triumvirate of buildings – the National Theatre, the National Film Theatre and the dominant Royal Festival Hall – date back to the Concrete Age, and were built in the Naive style, a form of architecture that came to be known as Grey Lego. The only redeeming feature of the South Bank is the view afforded from it. That's because, when you're sitting sipping espresso on the south side of the Thames, you don't have to look directly across and be confronted by the South Bank.

I walked Roisin under Waterloo Bridge. Salman Rushdie could often be seen under this bridge. He met here regularly with all the other literary greats – Dickens, Trollope, Joyce, Kundera, Grisham, Cooper and Collins. And this day was no exception, for the booksellers were out in force. Their long tables were so laden with books that some even bowed in the middle. You could sense the weight of words. It wasn't hard to get lost in this maze of historical novels, hysterical novels, hardbacks, paperbacks, biographies, journals, guides, diaries, manuals, self-help bibles, and unput-downables. You could buy a year's reading and still have change from a tenner.

I guided Roisin to a table outside the Theatre Café, under one of the many chestnut trees that peg the river-bank to the flagstones. She ordered me a Budvar and for herself, a bottomless pot of tea.

'Do you not want anything stronger?' I asked.

'I don't drink alcohol.'

'Any reason?'

'I have my reasons.' She poured a little tea. Pale yellow. She moved the pot in small circles until the liquid ran amber. I got the feeling she didn't really want to be here.

'So, you're from Ireland,' I said.

'You're perceptive.'

'I'm from Ireland as well.'

'Isn't everyone,' she said. '*Riverdance, The Commitments, Father Ted* . . . sure doesn't everyone want to be Irish at the minute. It's so fashionable.'

'No really, I was born in Bangor, lived there till I was ten, then moved to Scotland. You could say I'm

129

half-Irish and half-Scots. Oh and half-cut, on my father's side.' I raised my beer to toast the joke.

'So you're Scots Irish,' she said.

'Northern Irish, Scots Irish, London Irish. I've even been Welsh Irish in my time. I *am* the Irish diaspora.'

'Whatever,' she said.

I knew what she was doing, of course. I had been dismissed as a plastic paddy many a time. I never understood why the native Irish did that to me. So what if my accent wasn't as true as theirs? What other nationality is so ready to be disparaging to their own people? Nobody ever called Loz a plastic Jamaican. When the Republic of Ireland football team had its good run it was led by an Englishman and was suitably stocked with 'plastic paddies'. Did the Irish swelling the bars round Lansdowne Road pass judgement upon them? Did they heck.

We watched as a riverboat puttered off from Festival Pier, taking a load of suits out on some office jolly. I didn't want confrontation so I decided to change tack.

'So, how long have you been over in London?' I asked.

'Just a week.'

'Have you come to see if the streets are paved with gold?'

'No, I'm only here for the summer. Once I make enough money, I'll head back to Cushendun.'

'Cushendun?'

'Loosely translated as brown river. In Irish.' She was doing that point-scoring thing that the 'genuine' Irish often do. 'The family farm's there,' she added.

'No, I know it. There's a nice little bay. My folks used to take me there on bank holidays, for picnics. You wouldn't get me in the water for love nor money. Freezing, if I remember rightly.'

Roisin either laughed or she'd swallowed her tea the wrong way.

'So, you speak Irish then?' I asked.

'Yes. I used to teach it. Nothing serious like, just a couple of evening classes at Queen's University. I had to stop, though. The extra money was eaten up by the cost of petrol to and from Belfast twice a week.'

'I assume it was just Catholics you taught. I imagine all the Orangemen studied Mandarin.'

Her eyebrows relaxed into arcs, like two dark humps arching elegantly out of Loch Ness. We were getting somewhere.

'I never even did the Scots Gaelic at school,' I said. 'I wasn't allowed. I went to Stranraer Boys, a Protestant grammar school. We were forced to learn German. I remember the teacher, old Mr Greenfield, always breaking his chalk on the blackboard, always handing out detentions. A real Nazi he was. Not that his classes were like concentration camps. More like lack of concentration camps. So we weren't surprised when they brought in a younger tutor, one with more progressive teaching methods. He was a fan of those subliminal language tapes.'

Roisin looked sceptical.

'Seriously,' I said. 'He got us all to lie on the floor and tried to sort of hypnotize us, to put us in a state that he called near sleep.'

'So, when he played the tapes, did you assimilate much of the language?'

'No,' I said. 'I slept.'

131

A waitress kept us sweet for Budvar and bottomless tea. Roisin had begun to open up a little.

'Did you know that in Irish, there's no word for no,' she said.

'God, can you imagine if the word no was removed from the English language? The Unionists would be speechless – *Ulster Says Um, Er?*'

Roisin looked serious again.

'Are you political, Bic?'

I hated that question. Especially when asked by a Northern Irish tongue. It sounded so loaded, like an armalite.

'Not any more,' I said. 'The Monster Raving Loonies threw me out.'

'Seriously though.'

She was persistent, all right. I turned the tables. 'Why, are you political?'

'It's hard not to be when you've seen your parents blown up by the UVF.'

'Shit.'

We sat in silence for a bit. A group of kids on skateboards were doing their best to break femurs and tibias by leaping onto the handrail that descended the steps of the Festival Hall.

'I'm sorry,' I said.

'Don't be. You didn't kill them.'

Roisin rubbed an unopened sugar packet between her thumb and finger, grinding the granules to dust. She looked like she was trying to sort her words into the right order.

'The Troubles have touched most people in Northern Ireland,' she said. 'Everyone knows someone who knows someone who's lost someone. Jeeze, it's like the title of a bad song.'

'I thought things had improved over there, since the ceasefire.'

'Yeah, sure isn't Northern Ireland all happy-clappy now. Complete strangers smile at you. Protestants and Catholics ask each other where they get their hair done. As opposed to asking where they get their knees done. Even the joyriders crash their cars more elegantly.'

'No need for sarcasm,' I said. 'I'm out of touch. I haven't been over there for years.'

'Clearly,' she said.

I left it at that.

'What age were you when your parents died?' I asked.

'They didn't die. They were murdered. I was five. But my brothers brought me up well. Not bad for the Three Stooges.'

'Eh?'

'Ach it's nothing. They're good boys all of them. They watch out for me.'

'So are they back home on the farm?' I asked.

'My eldest brother, Rory, he and I run the farm. The other two, well – I'm staying with Eamon up in Kilburn. And Cathal, the youngest, he's in the Maze.'

'In prison?'

'Yes, but we're going to get him out. He shouldn't be there. He was a student at Queen's. Had the misfortune of sharing digs with Dessie Donnelly, the guy responsible for shooting two female RUC officers in Lisburn, back in '92. My brother's car was spotted driving away from the scene. Cathal was sent down as an accomplice

133

despite the fact that he was at a U2 concert in Belfast at the time of the shooting.'

'Could nobody give him an alibi?'

'No. Bono couldn't actually swear he'd seen Cathal in the audience. He wasn't a reliable witness.'

More sarcasm.

'No, I mean, surely your brother was with friends,' I said.

'He'd gone to the gig on his own. It was a weekend and all of his mates had gone back to Cushendun for the big hurling game with Cushendall. But Cathal wouldn't miss the gig. Do you know he queued up outside Golden Discs at midnight, on a Sunday night no less, to be the first person in line to buy *The Joshua Tree*.'

And I thought Barbara had baggage.

Roisin sandwiched her tea bag between the inside wall of the pot and the back of her spoon. She squeezed the life out of it.

'So, no need to ask which foot you kick with,' I offered.

'Oh God. Oh that. Yes, I'm sorry Bic, I hope I haven't done any lasting damage. I meant to kick your dog but you were sort of, there.'

It wasn't quite what I had meant but she brightened, so again I left it.

Roisin explained that she had to get back to her brother. He'd be wondering where she was at this hour. Eamon was a worrier.

I offered to walk her across Hungerford Bridge to Charing Cross station. She could take the Jubilee Line to Willesden Green and bus it to Kilburn. I might as well have told her to take the Washing Line to Hughie Green,

134

judging by the look of total incomprehension that she gave me.

The bridge shook under our feet as the trains overtook us.

'Thanks again for catching those girls, Bic.'

'Oh, you know, it was nothing.'

'It was something. I can't afford to have my stuff nicked.'

'It's nice stuff. In fact, that bottle you showed me, the Cuchulainn one, I want it. How much?'

'It's yours,' she said.

'Cheers. I meant to ask, how come you're selling Celtic stuff in London?'

'The ceasefire's not holding back home, Bic. There are so many splinter groups springing up you'd think guns were made of wood. And despite what you may have seen on your English news, the tourists are staying away. They're over here, though. Why go to the north of Ireland when you can buy all your Irish souvenirs from the safe distance of London?'

'Well, I suppose it's better than buying plastic bobbies' helmets,' I said.

'Oh cheers. I should hope so.'

'No, I don't mean your stuff's tacky or anything. In fact, Sam, the girl I work with, she's very impressed with your work. Says it's quality. Sam makes jewellery. I reckon you two girls would get on.'

'Maybe. But I'm only here for the summer. I've no time to be making friends.'

I stopped. She stopped.

'So we can't be friends?' I asked.

'Uch, don't be stupid. You know what I mean.' She

135

pushed me forward, to get me walking. 'But I'll be going home when I make enough money.'

'How much is enough?'

'Enough to fund a campaign for Cathal's release. And if we don't get him out by next summer, I'll fly over to Boston and sell stuff there. The Americans will buy anything with a shamrock on it.'

'Aye. I read that there are more Irish dancers in New York than there are in the whole of Ireland. Hard to believe,' I said.

'Not for me. I loved my Irish dancing as a wee girl. I guess the Irish in New York are just trying to keep their culture alive,' she said.

'Well, I don't understand all that *Riverdance* stuff. All those women thrashing about, looking like they're dead from the waist up.'

'Isn't that how most men like their women?' asked Roisin.

We had walked into the polished concourse of Charing Cross station.

Roisin said goodbye. She slid her travelcard into the slot in the gate. Some red words flashed up – *seek assistance* – and the gate refused to open. Her one-week card had expired. I helped her navigate the ticket machine, a tortuous process, even for Londoners. I lifted a pink single from the tray, but I couldn't give it to her. Tomorrow was Monday. There would be no market. I wouldn't see her. I wanted to see her.

'Have you been to Hyde Park yet?' I asked.

'No.' She sounded unsure.

'I could meet you there tomorrow.'

'What for?'

So that we can hold hands, perhaps kiss, and then embark on a new and beautiful life together, was what I wanted to say.

'A picnic,' I said.

'Do people still have picnics?'

'What, in London? Oh yes, all the time. We're picnic crazy over here.'

'I don't believe you,' she said.

'Come on. I'll bring some baps and a bottle. Two o'clock at Speakers' Corner. Jubilee Line to Bond Street, Central Line to Marble Arch, then ask a policeman.'

I was begging. I was about to fall on my knees and tug her skirt, when she said, 'OK. Two o'clock. But Bic . . .'

'Yes?'

'Make sure it's a bottle of lemonade.'

Ten

Roisin stopped at a Chinese takeaway on Kilburn High Road. Emerald City it was called. Its sign sported two back-lit shamrocks. An Irish Chinese, she thought. Kilburn also had an Irish butcher's, an Irish grocer's, an Irish 24-hour garage, a host of Irish pubs and any number of Irish newsagents selling Irish newspapers – the *Kerryman*, the *Laois Nationalist*, the *Limerick Leader*. Her brother had been right when he called Kilburn the thirty-third county.

Roisin had never tried Chinese food. Cushendun was barely big enough for a burger van, never mind a Chinese. It did have the smallest pub in Europe, though. She liked to tell people that. She played safe and bought a couple bags of chips, a regular for herself and large for her brother. The guy serving – Irish – tossed in a couple of free Cokes.

Eamon was waiting at the window when his wee

sister got to the gate. 'Where in God's name have you been?' he asked. His cheeks were as red as his hair.

'I brought you chips,' said Roisin.

Eamon smacked the parcels out of her hand, spilling the chips on the hall carpet. 'Damn it Roisin, I don't want bloody chips. I had your dinner ready four hours ago.'

Roisin bent down and silently picked up the hot yellow crescents.

'Well? Answer me, then. Where have you been?'

'I went for a drink with one of the stallholders. He caught someone stealing from me this afternoon,' she said.

'Roisin, what have we agreed? You're not to get too friendly with the natives. You're over here to do a job.'

Roisin ignored him and walked through to the kitchen.

'It was just a wee drink, to say thanks. Where do you keep your big plates?'

'Fuck the plates,' said Eamon.

Roisin tried a cupboard, but it was full of Eamon's medicine and pills, stuff he brought home from work. She found the plates in the cupboard under the sink. She grabbed some bread and butter and made a piece.

'Are you listening to me, Roach?'

'Yes, Eamon. I hear you loud and clear.'

'You've got to keep your head down. We have a job to do. In six days Admiral James Sutherland will be at Greenwich Pier launching the Tall Ships. It's our job to find out as much as we can about security arrangements on the day so our boys can get in there, kidnap him and get out. If this is to happen, you and I have to gather as much information as possible – the time the admiral arrives, the time of his speech, the time of his walk-about, his route in and out of Greenwich. There's a lot to be done.'

Roisin didn't need reminding. It was all Eamon had talked about since her arrival in London. She removed some carpet fluff from a chip. She placed the chip on the buttered bread and folded herself a buttie.

'I'm not happy with this, Eamon. I still think we should start a legitimate campaign to get Cathal an appeal.'

Eamon was having none of it. 'That could take years. And even then he has little or no chance of winning an appeal. Jeez, have you not seen *In the Name of the Father*? Remember, it's two female officers that Cathal is accused of murdering. Public sentiment is too strong, Roach. There are people back home baying for Cathal's blood.'

'Promise me no-one will get hurt.'

'No-one will get hurt if we do our jobs properly. And that means we don't go making friends. Least of all a stallholder. I mean, Christ, what have you told him? Did you mention Cathal?'

'No.' Roisin couldn't look him in the face.

'Good,' said Eamon. He walked over to his wee sister and rubbed the outsides of her arms. The gesture was designed to reassure her, but Roisin only felt more vulnerable, like he was rubbing away a protective veneer.

'Look,' he continued. 'I'm sorry for shouting. I don't know, perhaps it's the adrenalin. I won't blame you if you want to back out. Just tell me now and I'll have a word with the boys. But think about it. Those Brit bastards are doing their best to destroy our family. They murdered Mammy and Da. They tried to murder you. And now they've stuck our brother in the Maze with no prospect of release until he's an old man. And you know what Cathal's like. He can't handle it inside. He'll do something stupid. They've robbed us, Roach. The Brits have robbed us.'

Whether it was the light, or the way he angled his head, at that moment Roisin saw her father in Eamon's eyes.

'Yeah,' she said. 'Yes. I want to do this. For Da and Mammy. And for Cathal.'

'It's the only way, sis. Once we have Admiral Sutherland the British government will listen to us. Either they accede to our demands and release Cathal or Her Majesty's Navy will have to start looking for another overdecorated eejit to take the helm.'

'You said no-one will get hurt.'

'And they won't. Not if we do our jobs properly and get our brother back. Then we can all leave this god-forsaken country and begin our new lives in Boston. Just think Roach, it'll be a fresh start.'

Roisin remembered the old friends in Cushendun who used to disappear off to Boston for whole summers to find work. Of course, she could never just go galli-vanting off like that. She had to stay home with Rory and look after the farm. She had to look after Rory, more like. She had to undress him and put him to bed most nights, wash the puke and the whiskey out of his shirts, and the piss out of his trousers. No way could she go gallivanting off. Her friends would come back and fill

141

her head with softball, skyscrapers, and plates of pancakes piled like pallets. They brought back new words and phrases: diner, gasoline, over easy, subway, Redsocks, the john. They ate Hershey bars and used ice-making machines. They called their bottoms fannies. It all sounded like great craic. It all sounded a million miles away.

Eamon rinsed the kettle, filled it and set it to boil. He helped himself to some cold chips. 'So this stallholder, does he have a name?' he asked.

'Bic, you call him. He's nice enough.'

'Bic?' Eamon's tongue stuck to the roof of his mouth. It had become suddenly dry.

'I know. Odd, isn't it. He's from County Down originally. Eamon, are you OK?'

'You're not to speak to him again, Roach.'

'Well that's going to be hard, I'm supposed to be mee—'

'I mean it. You're not to go near this Bic character again.'

Eleven

Destroy the heart you said,
very soon you will be quite dead,
she wanted freedom not a shackled man,
but I need her more than I need air

I hadn't pogoed in ages. The last time I pogoed it was
the sort you did with a stick. Pogoing was punk and
slightly before my time. But that morning, with House
of Love playing full blast, I pogoed round my flat like a
mad 'un. I was a frog in boiling water. I pogoed with the
energy and confidence of someone who is not being
watched. I pogoed while eating triangles of toast and
spilling coffee.

yes I need her more than I need air

A stone hit the window.

I turned the music down. Bloody kids. At least Crouch End wasn't as bad as Clapham, where Jambo lived. They started them really young down there. Jambo once claimed he had a Stickle-Brick thrown through his window.

I opened my window. 'Piss off!' I shouted.

'And good morning to you too.'

I looked down to see Barbara. Shit. I suddenly remembered I'd forgotten to phone her and end our relationship. Somehow it had slipped my mind.

'Let me up,' she shouted.

She had her youngest in tow, Ben. At least, I assumed it was Ben. I knew all her children by name, but I had never seen them. I guessed that this was Ben. Either that or Barbara was now in the habit of picking up four-year-olds. And I thought I was her toyboy.

Why was she with Ben? I threw my keys down.

'Shit,' said Barbara, when I let her in. 'Those nearly hit me.' She handed me the keys.

'Shit!' repeated Ben.

'Oi! Watch your fucking language.' She grabbed Ben by the arm and slapped the back of his leg. He burst into tears. Barbara burst into tears. She picked him up and cradled him on her shoulder.

'I've left him,' she said.

Some people really don't suit tears and Barbara was one of them. She looked awful. Her mascara would have run if she had bothered to put it on. I had never seen Barbara without her make-up. I was in shock. Not because of the way she looked, but because I couldn't believe what she was telling me.

144

'You've left your husband?'

'No, I've left Bruce Willis. Who do you think?'

'Fuck,' I said.

'Fuck!' said Ben.

His mother ignored him.

'You haven't told him it's because of me, have you?' I asked.

'No, Bic. I told him I was off to become a nun. Of course I told him.'

'But your husband's very large.' I was genuinely scared. 'He's a fireman. He can lift heavy objects, like people, and throw them great distances.'

Barbara was unsympathetic. 'He's a pussycat once you get to know him,' she said.

'Yeah, and I'm a ball of wool.'

I offered her the sofa. She sat down, letting Ben loose. He occupied himself using my CDs as frisbees. A Red Hand of Ulster had surfaced on the back of his leg.

I went to the kitchen to fix Barbara a coffee. She had her fag down to the filter by the time I brought it up to her.

'So what are you going to do?' I asked.

'Well, my other three are at school today. I'll phone them when they get home. Steve can look after them till I get on my feet. I thought Ben and I could stay here in the meantime.'

'Listen, are you sure you've done the right thing, Barbara? Think of the kids. I know what it's like to have a parent run off. My dad's been running away all my life.'

Barbara chuckled. 'So are we running off together, then?' she asked.

145

'You know what I mean. Maybe you should go back to Steve. Tell him you're confused.'

'Oh cheers for the support, Bic. I've left my husband for you. Do you not want me now or something?'

'Look. I've been meaning to—'

There was a dull crack. The window imploded. Something heavy hit the floor. Ben picked it up.

'Brick!' he said.

'Good boy. Now come away from the window and give the brick to Mummy.' Barbara prised the half-brick out of his tiny hands.

I slid over to the window and looked down.

'It's your husband,' I said. 'Bollocks.'

'Bollocks,' said Barbara.

'Bollocks!' said Ben.

'I've an idea, Barbara. Why don't you go down, kiss, make up and live happily ever after.'

'I'm staying right here.' She threw herself back onto the sofa and folded her arms. 'I don't respond to violence,' she said.

'Yes, but I do. Usually by bleeding. And this is a new carpet. The last one was smoke-damaged. I don't want this one blood-damaged.'

Steve was shouting. I looked down to see him shouldering the front door.

'Jesus, not only did you name me as the other man, you told him where I lived. Are you wise in the head?'

'I didn't tell him anything. He recognized your name from the fire report,' she said.

'What fire report?'

'The chip fire downstairs. Steve's watch put it out. He remembered you because you only gave one name in

146

your statement. Just Bic. He said it sounded like prick, and filed it. There aren't many just Bics in London. When I told him I was leaving him for a guy called Bic, he must have put two and two together.'

'He can add?'

I heard thumping on the stairs. It wasn't getting any quieter.

'Shit, he's kicked the door in,' I said.

'He's trained to do that,' said Barbara.

'Well, that's OK then. As long as I've had my door kicked in by a professional.'

Barbara grabbed Ben and held him close. She lit up. She cocked her mouth and funnelled a blue plume of smoke out the side of it, channelling it away from her son.

'Does my hair look all right?' she asked.

'Your husband is about to come in here and kick seven shades of shit out of me and all you can do is fix your hair.'

'Daddy!' said Ben.

Steve burst into the room. He didn't go for me straight away. He took a moment to survey the scene before shouting, 'Christ, this place is a dump. Who did your decorating, pal . . . Alan Titchmarsh?'

'Actually, Alan Titchmarsh does the gardening programme,' I corrected.

'Exactly,' he said.

'Steve, leave Bic alone. This isn't about him.'

'Ah, so this is the famous Prick. The bloke who's been shagging my missus.'

'I love him, Steve,' said Barbara.

This was news to me.

147

'Look at him, Babs. He's a streak of piss,' said Steve.
I nodded in agreement.

'I'm moving in with him,' said Babs.

'I don't know how you could live with the wallpaper, never mind living with him,' said Steve.

'Well, this has been lovely. Thank you both for coming round. Shall I show you the door?' If I couldn't go down fighting I was at least going to go down in a blaze of sarcasm.

'No, Prick. Allow me.' Steve grabbed my arm and twisted it behind my back. He marched me over to the broken window and pitched me forward, half-in, half-out of it. Four storeys up.

'There it is,' he said.

'There's what?'

'There's the door. Or perhaps you need a closer look,' said Steve.

I felt a large hand ram between my legs and grab on, scrum-like, to my crotch. He hoisted me further forward so everything above my knees was outside the window. The blood filled my head. It felt like a watermelon.

'Stop this,' I said. 'You can have her. You can have your wife back.'

'Bic!' Barbara's voice.

'Go on, mate. She's yours. I don't want her. Honestly. I was going to phone her, tell her I'm not interested any more.'

'What? My wife not good enough for you is she?' asked Steve.

'No, I mean—'

My body was pulled back through the window. I

would have breathed a sigh of relief had a fireman's fist not smacked me in the jaw. I fell to the floor.

'What's wrong with my wife, Prick?'

'Nothing, I—'

'You little shit.' Barbara stepped forward and drove her heel into my hand.

'Never, ever, insult the woman I love,' said Steve.

'Oh Steve,' said Barbara. I didn't look up, but I could tell by her voice that she was suddenly smitten. When we had first gone out together she had spoken my name in the same coy falsetto.

'Stay away from my wife, Prick.'

'Oh I will.'

'Prick!' said little Ben and the three of them walked out the door.

It took a while to clear all the debris. I stuck on my Marigolds and a more sobering soundtrack – Nick Drake. I sealed the broken window with a scorched bath panel retrieved from the skip outside the flats. I shovelled up what glass I could, those bits visible to the naked eye. I resigned myself to finding the remaining chips in the coming weeks, every time I walked round barefoot. I couldn't bring myself to wash Barbara's lipstick off the coffee cup, so I threw it in the bin. The half-brick I set on the mantelpiece as a reminder never to screw another man's wife (Resolution Number Two). Maybe I'd get a little walnut plinth made for it, you know, to really set it off.

My jaw smarted. I went to the bathroom to throw some water on it. The bathroom was filthy. While all the other rooms had benefited from my redecorating since the fire, the bathroom had suffered. I wasn't paying it enough attention. The sink alone looked like a science project. I filled it from the cold tap and caught sight of myself in the mirror. My chin was a blue plum.

How would I explain this to Roisin? I was due to meet her in an hour. I couldn't say *the dog did it*. Dunc was with Sam. Nor could I shrug and say *hey, you should see the state of the other guys*. Women aren't impressed by that macho stuff. But then, paradoxically, I couldn't tell her I'd been beaten up. They're not impressed by that either. What about *I fell*? No. I had used that too many times as a teenager and Aunt Sylvia always saw through it. She could always tell when I was lying. At least, she thought she could.

I decided to phone Roisin and cancel our date. But I didn't have her number. Shit. Maybe she wouldn't notice. I held a wet flannel to my chin to reduce the swelling. Of course she'd notice.

There was only one thing for it. This sort of situation demanded honesty. I would have to come clean. I would own up. I would tell Roisin that I hurt myself while trying to open a packet of bacon.

Twelve

The trees in Hyde Park let out a continuous healthy rustle, like they were made of crêpe paper. The park wasn't too busy. It was only Monday, after all.

A gaggle of office girls hitched their skirts and spread themselves on the grass to catch some rays in their lunch hour. An old fella who should have known better was dancing on rollerblades. He was wearing one of those hats with built-in headphones. I tried to guess the song from his swishing and sashaying – 'Disco Inferno'? I walked past him, towards Speakers' Corner. I touched my jaw. It sat out like a drawer handle. Children took one look at me and fled.

Dunc snapped at my heels. Jewish Jeff had dropped him off. The poor, tortured dog could smell the barbecued chicken in my Tesco Metro bag. It was accompanied by the other essential ingredients for a city picnic: a bottle of Paul Masson Red (screw top, no need for a cumbersome corkscrew); a tall snake of twenty-four shrink-wrapped plastic cups (they only sold them in packs of twenty-four but hey, no washing up); cherry tomatoes (no need for a knife); cheese slices (ditto); and a few sachets of salt and pepper stolen from McDonald's. (I had popped in to use their toilet. Isn't that what McDonald's is for?)

I had brought cherryade for Roisin. Dunc had his frisbee. Everybody's happy, I thought, and walked with renewed purpose, twirling a French stick about my head like I was leading the Pride of Whitehill Blood 'n' Thunder Knock-Yer-Pan-In Flute Band.

I chose a spot on the grass with a good view of the Marble Arch tube exit. The grass was still a little dewy, so I sat on the frisbee, further torturing the dog. It was so unlike me to be early.

'Got twenty pee?' A thick, Dublin brogue.

I looked up and was forced to shield my eyes from the sun. A blur of a man slowly came into resolution. He smelt like a shop doorway.

'Excuse me?' I asked.

'Got twenty pee?'

'Yes thanks.'

He wouldn't go away. I didn't need this. I needed to share barbecued chicken with a beautiful woman.

'Could you spare the price of a cup of coffee?' he asked.

'Well that depends, doesn't it. I mean, do you want a regular coffee or a cappuccino? Perhaps you're a double decaf skinny vanilla latte man?'

I seriously doubted it.

'Got twenty pee?' he repeated.

I reached into my trouser pocket, a difficult thing to

do when you're sitting down, and when your hand is still smarting from the heel of a slighted woman.

'If I give you twenty pee, do you promise you'll use it to get a cup of coffee?'

'As God is my judge, sir.' He necked the last of his Special Brew.

I accidentally pulled a pound coin out of my pocket, an unfortunate habit of mine when asked to contribute change. His Irish eyes were smiling. I gave it to him anyway.

'Here. Coffee for you and four of your friends.'

'Ach you're a saint and so you are,' he proclaimed.

'Don't worry about it.'

'No, sir. May you get a playground in heaven. You're a saint I tell you.'

'No really, it's nothing. I only wish I could give you more,' I said.

'Got twenty pee for me bus home?'

The cheek of him. And why did everything suddenly cost twenty pence – cups of coffee, buses home, bites to eat? Had the Chancellor suddenly slapped some radical new uniform pricing policy on us, and told only the drunk and the homeless? *Excuse me, I'd like to purchase that BMW 5 Series Coupé out there on your forecourt. An excellent choice sir, that'll be twenty pee.*

I had already given him a pound.

'I've already given you a pound,' I said.

'You're a saint sir, but I still need twenty pee for me bus home.'

'But if you buy a coffee for twenty pee, then you have twenty pee for the bus home and sixty pee to, I don't know, buy three speedboats or something.'

'Please sir. May God smile on your gracious soul.'

'No. You've had your lot.'

'Well feck you ya dirty fecker. Ya dirty lyin' bastard ye. Feck off ya wee gobshite.'

You could still hear him shouting from the other side of the park. I couldn't catch all of it, but I think he left the lunchtime throng in no doubt that I was Satan himself.

Twenty past two. No sign of Roisin.

The office girls, who had by now adopted Dunc, picked themselves up and adjusted their hemlines. They headed back to their offices to photocopy their breasts, or whatever it is you do in offices.

A crowd had started to gather at the park gates. It looked like some sort of demo. The few policemen in attendance seemed unconcerned.

So where was Roisin? She was new to London. I shouldn't have assumed she could find her way to Hyde Park. Surely she could, though. The park is so big and so well mapped, it should be easy to find. It's not as if it's a G-spot.

Maybe she just decided against it. She had only just met me, after all. I had probably been a bit forward, made her feel like this was too much of a date. She said she didn't have time for friends, so why make time for dates? I was confused. Perhaps she had hurt herself trying to open a packet of bacon.

I tore a cold and stringy strip of barbecued chicken and gave it to the dog. I gave Roisin another hour, but she didn't show.

In that time the crowd at the gates had almost trebled.

154

A bearded guy carrying a megaphone had organized the rabble into a slow, ordered march. The marchers waved Irish tricolours and carried placards with swiftly aero-soled slogans. 'Ban Sectarian Marches' and 'Re-route or Riot' gave me the gist of their grievance. This was the run-up to the Twelfth of July, or 'The Twelfth' if you're a particularly proud Belfast Protestant. It was marching season back home. This lot were marching to ban marches. File that in irony corner.

Beardy joined the leading group, who paraded a large bedsheet on which was painted 'Brent Irish Centre'. He sang into his megaphone, leading the marchers in a chorus of 'Orange Order, Out of Order'.

They all wore green ribbons.

The police looked a bit livelier now. Nannies rustled up their kids and left the park by other gates. A Japanese couple took photographs.

As the marchers approached, I stood up and scanned the park for Roisin. A young man in a woolly football hat – half Liverpool FC, half Celtic – approached me. He thrust something into my hand. It was a Sinn Fein newsletter.

A policeman tried to grab the newsletters off him. That was all it took. The marchers steamed in from all directions, punching and kicking the officer to the ground.

From nowhere, scores of fluorescent, flak-jacketed police baled in.

Dunc was barking so I re-attached his lead and wound it round my wrist. I tried to make for the south exit, but it was too late. Mounted police galloped in, forcing me into the melee. Into the clop and froth of blinkered horses. Huge flaring nostrils on legs. Hooves that could crack heads.

It was as if I'd been sucked into a vacuum. All sound disappeared. Then my picture went dead.

'Fuckin' move over, hey.'

A woman or a man, I couldn't be sure. Pushing me sideways.

I heard a yap.

'Is that your fuckin' dog, hey?'

The woman with the man's voice pulled Dunc out from under her feet. His lead was still wound tightly round my wrist. My hand was completely dead. I recovered my senses enough to work out that I was in the back of a police van. I counted six of us, excluding the dog.

Jesus, why was I in a meat wagon?

'Oh he's with us now, is he. Well fuckin' sit up and give us some room, hey.' She sounded like she was from Derry, hey.

'That's a fuckin' chin you've got on ye,' she said. She touched my jaw. I recoiled.

'Yeah and it's *my* chin. Hands off,' I said.

'Did one of them Brit bastards do that to ye?'

'Well, not exact—'

'Never worry, hey. This'll make the national news. You're a soldier, so you are.' She patted my knee.

'Look, I'm no soldier. I was in the park with my dog, minding my own business.'

'That's right, son. You tell the police that and they

156

can't touch ye, so they can't. Looks like a nasty bruise though. You could claim for that, hey.'

'No. I don't want to claim for anything. I just want to get out of this van.'

She continued, undeterred. 'My Brenda got two grand out of Islington council for tripping on a fuckin' paving stone and cutting her face. She didn't really trip on it, but hey, they don't fuckin' know that. Her boyfriend did it. He beats her. He's a thief and a drunk. Such a shame really, coz he's got such a beautiful singing voice.'

I thought that if I ignored her then perhaps she'd go away. I stuck my head up to the grille and appealed to the better nature of our uniformed driver.

'That's fine mate, you can drop me off here,' I said.

The copper said nothing.

'Where are you taking us?' I asked.

'To Euro Disney, you thick paddy bastard.'

Well, that got a response.

'Am I under arrest?'

'Listen sunshine, if I had my way I'd shoot the lot of you. You're all murdering IRA scum.'

'Does that include my dog?' I asked.

No response.

It must have been the horses. I must have passed out. That would be it. The police had mistaken me for one of the demonstrators and bundled me into their van.

I have been terrified of horses ever since my accident. The accident that resulted in the distortion to the base of my skull, the medical term for which is 'a big lump'. If I ever did forget to be terrified by these great, hulking, unpredictable beasts, I needed only to rub the back of my head to remind me. Even the sound of someone clacking two coconut shells together inspires in me a fantasy legion of oversized equine creatures playing hoof-ball with my head. It can send me giddy. I don't like the fact that I can't control the fear and I rarely mention it.

My father used to admonish me, saying my phobia was a small thing that I should get a grip on and sort out. He sought psychiatric help when I began to suffer from turbulent horse-filled dreams, recurring 'night mares'. I enjoyed several visits from a Dr Reginald Arbuthnot, the foremost authority on matters phobic in County Down. This boisterous individual, unruffled by the prevailing winds of twentieth-century psychology, put my phobia down to 'unresolved sexual conflicts'. My father was suitably alarmed: *you mean he wants to fuck horses?*

But by the third or fourth session I had read extensively from a copy of *The Home Doctor* that had been gathering dust in Dad's library. Well, I'd read the section on phobias, so I had an answer for the doctor.

'Behaviourists, on the other hand,' I precociously retorted, 'would say that all fear is learned.'

'Dear oh dear,' said the venerable Arbuthnot. 'Your child is transferring the anger of his childhood onto the untamed sexuality of the horse.'

It never occurred to him to ask me if I'd fallen off one of the fuckers.

Edgware police station was busy. They had managed to round up most of the demonstrators. I was made to stand in line beside Derry woman while a duty sergeant took down our particulars.

'What's your name, love?'

'May, hey,' she said.

'May Hay.' He wrote it down.

'No, May McFetteridge.'

The sergeant crossed out what he had written and started again.

'And where do you live, May?'

'I live at home,' she said. 'Doesn't everybody?'

'And where is home?'

'Home is where the heart is.' Derry woman elbowed me and cackled unhealthily. I held my breath for fear of infection.

The sergeant didn't share the joke.

'You're not doing yourself any favours.'

'Neither are you, hey. Not with that moustache.'

'Right.' He nodded at two officers fresh out of officer school. 'Throw her in a cell,' he ordered.

The two men dragged the kicking and cursing Derry woman to her cell, grappling with her like two puppies pulling apart a rag doll.

The sergeant moved to me. I was in no mood for this. I hadn't asked to be abducted by his goons and brought here. Did having a picnic now constitute a criminal offence in London?

'Name?' he asked.

'Bic. I mean, Anthony Bickmore.' I thought it better to give my full name in case I ended up sleeping with his wife. Less chance of detection.

'Your dog?'

'Duncan. D.U.N.C—'

'No I don't need his name, thanks. I was just asking if it was your dog.' The sergeant blew a sigh. He seemed to be having a bad day.

Not as bad as mine, pal.

'Address?' he continued.

'It's engraved on his collar.'

'*Your* address. Just co-operate, son, and we'll get out out of here a lot quicker.'

'Ninety-two Crouch Hill, N8.'

'Are you a member of the Brent Irish Centre?'

'No, but I'm in the Desperate Dan Cow Pie Club if that's any use to you.'

I sensed he was about to call the Chuckle Brothers back, to escort me to a cell.

'Are you a member of Sinn Fein?' he asked.

'What is this?' I replied.

The sergeant pulled a rolled-up Sinn Fein newsletter out of my coat pocket. He flicked through the pages, pretending to read it.

'No, I'm not a member of Sinn Fein, Brent Irish Centre, the IRA or anything else for that matter.'

'Who mentioned the IRA?' he asked. Cryptically. He dropped the newsletter and jotted something down on his pad. He squared up to me once more.

'Are you a sympathizer?'

'Well, my friends say I'm a good listener.'

He could only shake his head. 'That's a nasty knock on the chin, son. Do you want to press charges against the police?'

'No, I want to press charges against the Fire Brigade.' I was serious. I had a case. He didn't see it that way.

'You're lucky, sonny. If the cells weren't already full to bursting, I'd have no hesitation in banging you up.'

'I didn't think I was your type.'

'Quit while you're ahead, son. Take this.' He ripped

a yellow slip of paper from his pad and handed it to me. 'Anthony Bickmore, I am cautioning you. These details will be held on police record for a period of six months, after which time, provided you do not re-offend, they will be erased. Do you follow?'

'No, I'm a born leader.'

'The police nurse will see to your chin. Sadly she can't do anything about your attitude. Down the corridor, second left. Take this card.'

I walked down the corridor, checking behind me to make sure that Tweedledum and Tweedledumber weren't following. I didn't want to accidentally fall down some stairs on the way to the nurse.

'You've been in the wars,' she said as I entered.

'Hey this is nothing, you should see the other guys.'

'I'm not impressed. Take a seat on the bed.'

She cleaned my chin and secured the small cut with steri-strips. She noticed the bruising on my hand, where Barbara had stamped on it.

'Can you bend those fingers?'

I bent them.

'Well, they're not broken. Pity,' she said.

'What do you mean, pity?'

'If they were broken you'd be able to put in a bigger claim. A broken finger's worth about a grand. More if you play the piano.'

The gall of her. I had to ask –

'You're not from Derry, by any chance?'

Thirteen

'What happened to your chin?' Sam was laughing.

'I did it shaving.'

'What were you shaving, a bear?'

'Sam, can we just get on with this?'

I wasn't in the mood. There was stuff to be done, things to be sorted. There was a rota to be drawn up and a menu to be finalized. And we had to change our name. Joe Carlin deemed Life's Crêpe somewhat inappropriate for the visit of Her Majesty's cousin.

'What about something posh?' ventured Sam. 'Something French, but still on a seafaring theme. Something like La Crêpe de Mer?'

'No,' I said.

'And why not, grumpy face?'

'Sounds too much like the crap in the sea.'

'OK, what about something rustic and wholesome? Hearty Fare?'

'And a hey nonny no.'

'Right, I give up. I'm not playing this game any longer. Be in a bad mood if you want, but don't take it out on me— Bic? Where are you going? Bic, come back. I can't serve this lot by myself. Bic!'

Roisin was open for business. I made sure I was her first customer.

'So where were you yesterday?' I asked.

'I didn't fancy it.'

She started up a small lathe and held a nugget of something purple and crystalline to it. The crystal burred and barked as she shaped it.

'You didn't fancy it? Fair enough then. Silly old me for buying a load of food, sitting for three hours in a park, fainting, and getting arrested for civil disobedience. You didn't fancy it. Like what's that supposed to mean?'

Roisin blew on the crystal. She hadn't heard me. The lathe had drowned me out. I reached down and wrenched out the extension lead, pulling the plug.

'Do you mind. I've got work to do,' she said.

'I want an answer, Roisin. If you didn't fancy it, why did you agree to meet me in the first place?'

'Look, I bought you a couple of beers. I changed my mind about the park. I don't owe you anything, all right.'

'You owe me an explanation,' I said.

'Something came up, that's all. You'll survive. You're a big boy now.'

What was her problem? It was no use my getting angry, her eyebrows alone could shout me down from forty paces. And she was right, she didn't owe me

163

anything. I was a stranger to her. For all she knew, I kept the dismembered limbs of previous girlfriends under my floorboards. I made a mental note never to let her into my bathroom, the smell alone would fuel her macabre thoughts. I had to slow down.

'Sorry. I had a bit of a day of it yesterday. Look, why don't I take you out on the town, take you for dinner, I dunno, take you brass rubbing in Westminster Cathedral, whatever?'

'I can't,' she said.

'Why not?'

'I just can't.'

'See, what does that mean, I just can't?'

'Does everything require a reason?' she asked.

'Yes.'

'Right then.' She set the crystal on the table and removed her protective gloves. The gloves obviously worked. Her hands were soft and unmarked, her nails polished and unbroken.

'It wouldn't work out,' she said.

'It?'

'You and me. So let's stop it before it starts. I'm a good Catholic sort of a girl, if you know what I mean.'

'No actually, I don't.' Yes actually, I did.

'Look, we had a nice evening, but I don't even know you,' she said.

I knew it. She wanted to know what was under my floorboards.

'You could try getting to know me, Roisin.'

'No, I can't. I'll be back in Cushendun in a matter of weeks. It's just better that I don't. I can't say I'm not flattered though.'

'Uch, save it. Don't patronize me.'

'There's no need to get arsey. Accept it, Bic. You and I, it can't work.'

I took myself down to the old boathouse. The Thames lapped against its jetty like a slick. It was all very peaceful.

The boathouse comprised a simple white box with some metal steps whizzing round it – a fire escape. The surrounding ground was littered with green and brown beer bottles. A faint breeze rolled them from side to side. They kissed each other in clinks, the sound of marbles in a bag. A foetal figure was sleeping off his drink in the boathouse doorway. This was no tramp, however, for he wore a tuxedo. He was probably the last refugee from some boating function held the night before. One of his eyebrows was missing.

I walked out to the end of the jetty and sat against the buoy. I stared at an upturned shopping trolley jutting up from the water's edge. Dark green weed hung lopsided from one of its wheels, like an ill-fitting wig. The weed trailed downriver in the water's continuum.

After six years in London I admitted defeat. I was a wasp in a jam jar. The city was slowly stifling me. I had to get out before I got dragged under.

I wasn't sure I could do it alone, though. I needed someone. Barbara, well she was a non-starter. Roisin, on the other hand, was like a breath of fresh Antrim air, after six years of smog and sulphur. When I thought of her, I thought of that Smiths song – 'I want the one I can't have'. Christ, things must have been bad, I was regressing into the self-absorbed teenager I used to be. I had to snap out of it, move on, before I started walking around with daffodils hanging out of my arse.

I was getting tired of my own company. I used to love it. Sitting here by the Thames reminded me of Stranraer when I used to bunk off school and go sit at the ferry port, watching the loch. Some mornings the water would be so still, as viscous as glass. I'd sit under cover of the disused bandstand by the dock. One of my school-masters, the Head of Chemistry (he reeked of vinegar), would walk past the bandstand each morning and I'd have to duck down behind one of its stanchions. I remember the acid-warm smell of urine where people had pissed. My blazer smelt of the bandstand and of the menthol cigarettes that I stole from Aunt Sylvia. I had been trying to teach myself how to smoke. Earlier experiments sucking lit cinnamon sticks were even less successful. I loved the thrill of it, though. I loved the fear of getting caught. My nerves would lace me up like boots. But it was a nice feeling, like going over bumps in the road.

I couldn't believe Roisin, pulling the religion card on me. Who did she think I was, some Lambeg-drum-lugging, sash-wearing, field-frequenting son of Ulster? I hadn't asked to be Protestant. I was born with the caul over my head.

OK, so on one occasion I had stood with Jambo and his Hearts crew at an Edinburgh derby, and I joined in when they sang a song that expressed some slight anti-Catholic sentiment, urging people to engage in sexual relations with His Holiness the Pope. But I was sixteen and drunk and, anyway, Roisin couldn't have known that. Not unless she'd been standing in the Hibs end.

Roisin's mother and father had been murdered by Protestant paramilitaries and I felt genuinely sorry for her, but why tar me with the same sectarian brush? And why couldn't she just get on with her life?

She had been right, though, when she said that in Northern Ireland everyone knows someone who knows someone who's lost someone. My Aunt Sylvia had lost the man she was going to marry. In the same instant, Jambo had lost his father even before he was conceived.

11th July, 1968

'Sylvia, come here.'

'Leave me alone Ken.'

'Sylvia, listen to me, I'm your brother. That Davey Jameson's a bad egg, he's mixed up in all sorts.'

'Ken, let me go!'

'Wait'll I tell Mum and Dad about this.'

'You tell them, Kenneth Bickmore, and I'll tell them about those magazines I found under your bed.'

'You wee hoor. You wouldn't dare.'

'Try me.'

Sylvia took her place back among the crowd at the bonfire, her long hair bobbing as she ran. Her younger brother was at that age when, for the first time, she wished she didn't have one. She locked her arm into that of the thickset young man by her side. All the girls in Bangor fancied Davey Jameson. He was the first of the lads in the town to possess his own car, a reconditioned Bentley. Sylvia stood pinned to his chest like a badge. The huge mass of flame licked colour into their hot faces.

'Fancy a wee sip?' asked Davey.

'I'm not really allowed, but –' Sylvia accepted the brown beer bottle from Davey's hand. She tipped its weight onto her thin lips.

'Tcheeeewt!'

A jet of liquid shot out of her mouth and hissed on the bonfire.

'You all right, Syllie?' Davey threw an arm round his girl as she spluttered into a corner of her cardigan.

'What is in that, Davey?' She held out the brown bottle as though it were a soiled nappy.

'Poteen. Some of the boys use it to pep up the beer. Just on special occasions, you understand.'

'It tastes like petrol,' said Sylvia.

'Now, when have you ever tasted petrol?' laughed Davey. It was a big laugh and one that drew looks from round the fire. Sylvia loved the way people looked at Davey. Because when they looked at him, they were looking at her too. She loved being the centre of attention.

Davey was right to laugh. Of course she had never tasted petrol. But she had smelt it often enough that summer, in the back of his Bentley.

She made him take the bottle. She turned her nose up in wrinkles, like a child who has tasted their first Brussels sprout. Davey pulled her close. She let his warm, beery tongue slide into her mouth.

Ken threw another tyre on the bonfire and stared through the intense wobbling heat at his sister. If the rumours were true, Davey Jameson had killed and there was going to be trouble. The appearance of Ciaran

Donnelly, leading his three remaining brothers out of the shelters, confirmed Ken's worst fears.

These were the last days when Protestants and Catholics could share a bonfire on the Eleventh Night. Yet there were raised eyebrows and nudged elbows as the Donnellys idled up to the fire, tossing their fag butts like fireflies into the black July night. People talked behind hands, what with young Sean Donnelly barely in his grave and all. The low muttering was only punctuated by the snap, crackle and pop of burning wood – pallets, telegraph poles, fencing, furniture, For Sale signs, dead Christmas trees.

The Donnelly brothers joined the queue at the beer table. It was well stacked with bottles donated by, of all people, the 1st Bangor Presbyterian Mothers. Davey was one of the few not to notice them. Sylvia and he were entertaining his young nephew.

'Watch this, kid,' said Davey, setting his beer on the scorched grass, evidence of bonfires past. He rolled up his sleeves and cupped his hands over his mouth and nose. The child looked at Davey with the same awe that everyone did. Ever so slowly, Davey used his hands to bend his nose to one side. Suddenly it cracked, like he'd broken it. The child screamed and ran back to his mother.

Sylvia looked at Davey disapprovingly. He played the innocent.

'What, Sylvia? I didn't really break it. I used my thumbnail on my tooth,' he protested. He repeated his sleight of hand.

'Davey, you're awful to that kid,' said Sylvia.

Her cardigan fell away from her shoulder, exposing a porcelain neck. Her silver locket glinted the fire into Davey's eyes.

'I've been thinking, Syllie,' he said.

'That's dangerous.'

'Seriously. I thought that you and I should, that is, we— aw heck!'

A sliver of burning, sappy wood had rocketed into his groin. He doubled up. He took the remainder of his poteenbeer and sloshed it onto the front of his trousers like cheap cologne.

'Heck!'

Sylvia suppressed a laugh with her hand.

'You and I . . . ?' she asked.

'Eh?'

'You and I should what?'

'Huh? Oh aye. Maybe we could get—' He wiped his wet hands over his thighs. Satisfied they were sufficiently dry, he put them round Sylvia's narrow waist. 'I was thinking we could get married,' he said.

'Married?'

Though there wasn't much of Sylvia, it was all Davey could do to keep her upright.

'Yes, married. And we could have kids of our own to tease and we could do up my gran's old house out at Groomsport and I could even sell the Bentley and get a smaller car so we'd have furniture because we'd need something to sit on wouldn't we and you'd love the kitchen it has a wee pantry off it and there's even a spare room for you to make your dresses in and . . .'

'Yes.'

'. . . there's a chance of more work coming in at the shipyard and me da says— yes? You will?'

'I will,' she said.

He lifted her off her feet so her head was level with his. Their tongues danced again in each other's mouths. He set her down and pulled her tight. Sylvia felt a hardness pressing against her belly. She could feel the wet of the poteenbeer as it seeped like a transfusion from the front of his trousers, through the thin cotton of her dress and into her knickers. She pressed hard against him and felt her bottom tighten.

She led Davey away from the fire and the singing, towards the old air-raid shelters. He walked behind with his arms round her. The front of her thighs slid up and down in his palms as she walked forward.

A warm gust bounced through the shelter, throwing her hair across his face. He lifted her up onto the sill of an open square cut into the shelter wall. Her skirt gathered round his wrists as he raised it. Sylvia felt herself being pulled forward, onto him. It went straight in, first time, not hurting like those aborted attempts in the back of his Bentley. The glorious cold of the sill reached into her anus as she bumped herself further forward, taking him deeper. She threw her arms round his neck, pulling him in and easing him out, in and out, until, with one almighty blow, their heads cracked together, and their locked mouths clotted up with Davey's blood.

'That's for Sean, you murdering Proddie bastard.'

Sylvia's back hit the shelter floor. She was sucked down under Davey's limp body. He lay on top of her, still in spasm, with a claw hammer in his head. She

*found herself unable to scream under his weight. She
silently picked tats of his brain out of her hair. As
the bonfire raged, dead Davey came inside her.*

'What time is it?' someone asked.

'Huh?'

The guy in the tuxedo had joined me on the jetty.
Only it wasn't a tuxedo at all, it was a morning suit.

'I think I've missed my wedding,' he said. 'I knew I
shouldn't have had the stag do the night before. My wife
will kill me. Well, technically she's not my wife yet, but
she won't let a small matter like that stop her.'

I never wear a watch, so I checked the time on my
mobile.

'It's exactly one,' I said.

A loud explosion corroborated my story. Every day at
one o'clock, a cannon fired from the *Cutty Sark*.

'Shit,' he squealed, like his voice had just broken.

'What, is it too late?' I asked.

'No.' He shook his head. Small bits of broken glass
showered out of his hair. 'Shit, I've been bottled. Have
I been cut?'

I checked his head.

'No.'

'Well that's something. Cheers, pal. Now I gotta get
me to the church on time and all that.'

'Before you run off, tell me, why did you wear a
morning suit on your stag night?'

'Well, I thought it appropriate to wear a morning suit
on my last night of freedom. Think of it as mourning
with a "U".'

'A point well made,' I said.

He scratched at a stain on his lapel. 'Also, I knew I'd get drunk and something like this would happen. It saves me going home and getting changed. Got a mint?' he asked.

'Sorry.' I shrugged.

'Never worry.'

He jogged off, hawking and spitting.

One o'clock. Sam would be fuming. I made my way back to the stall.

I had just got to within sniffing distance of buttered batter when I saw Roisin. She was kissing a man. She climbed into his car.

The lying cow, I thought. She might have said there was someone else. All that 'good Catholic girl' stuff, how it wouldn't work between us, what was that all about? Women. They're like oncoming traffic. You can't trust them.

Sam saw me.

'I've got it, Bic. What about Taste of the Thames?'

'Whatever.'

Fourteen

Roisin turned a rough piece of rose quartz against her lathe. It was polishing up well. Dusty purple gave way to smooth pink, the legacy of manganese within the rock. She blew the redundant dust off the stone. This was gem quality, she thought. And it had rutiles, which meant it did something very special when you held it to the light. It was rare to find rose quartz in such a small crystalline form. She knew from her books that it was usually found in large chunks, as a product of granite pegmatites. The Antrim coast wasn't known for its granite. This piece must have found its way across the Irish Sea bed, from Scotland. It was a rare find, but find it she did amid the shingle and stones, amid the rusty Harp tins, hollow crab carcasses and marooned jellyfish that washed up on her Cushendun shore. It had taken a keen eye to spot it and a keener one to fashion it into a sea horse. She held the hard pink arc up to the sun, allowing the light through. Beautiful stars appeared within the stone.

She had already made an anchor, a filigree of green copper wire, into which the celestial sea horse would be set. Joe Carlin had mentioned that he wanted one of the stallholders to make a presentation to Admiral Sutherland as part of the pomp and ceremony surrounding Saturday's regatta. Roisin was making the sea horse as a gesture on behalf of Greenwich market. Joe Carlin would be impressed by her industry and let her present it. Not only would he then make her privy to the admiral's itinerary – the times, the places, the whole shebang – but, more crucially, she would be given a legitimate opportunity to get close to the main man. Close enough to lick the salt off his ruddy face. Close enough to choreograph a kidnapping.

The lathe barked and burred. Roisin knew that rose quartz had the power to transform intuition into intellectual thought, so that plans could be implemented. It was also said to encourage the ability to love.

Her thoughts turned to Bic. She had been cruel to him, but that was the way it had to be. Cathal was rotting in some anonymous Belfast cell and she had to get him out. Bic would survive. He was a good-looking, resourceful sort of guy, a bit pushy, a bit cocky, but perhaps he was used to getting what he wanted. It would do him good to get a knock-back or two.

No, the only men in Roisin's life were her brothers – Rory, Eamon and Cathal. The Three Stooges. Where would she be without them? She owed them everything. She was not about to let them down.

Her concentration was broken by the sound of a

cannon and the insistent call of a car horn. Eamon had pulled up in his van. What was he doing out of work this early, she wondered. Eamon wound his window down.

'Lock up, Roach, there's some people I want you to meet.'

'I can't just lock up like that.'

'Yes you can. This is important,' he said.

'Who are we meeting?'

'You'll find out soon enough. Now close up and come on.'

Roisin grabbed the corners of her drapes and hastily bundled her wares into the resulting makeshift hammock, taking care not to break anything. She threw a tarpaulin over the metal frames that bookended her stall. There was no need to secure it, she thought. She wouldn't be gone long. Eamon was probably taking her to meet 'the boys', the unseen and the unnamed who needed her information; the guys who'd get their hands dirty on the day. Eamon had assured her that if any of these men were IRA, they were no longer active under the ceasefire. No weapons would be used. This would be a good, clean kidnapping. Queensberry Rules – nothing below the gun belt.

Eamon sat in the van while Roisin sorted herself out. A young man dressed in a morning suit came up to him, out of breath. He propped an elbow on the driver's window.

'Excuse me mate, any chance of a lift to the Woolwich registry?'

'Sorry fella, I'm heading north of the river,' said Eamon.

'Got a mint?'

'No. Sorry.'

The young man lightly slapped the van roof. He turned and ran.

Eamon got out of the van and opened the passenger door for his sister. She kissed him and climbed in.

'What the fuck's he staring at?' asked Eamon. He had spotted a guy looking directly at them.

'Shit. That's him. That's Bic,' said Roisin. She hid her eyes.

Eamon looked again, more intently this time. He knew this guy. This was the guy with the tongue. The guy who came into the pharmacy wanting clove oil. He put the face to the already familiar name. So this was Bic.

He turned the ignition.

'Remember what I said, Roach. You're not to go near that fella.'

'Oh, don't worry. After this morning I don't think *he'll* be coming anywhere near *me*,' she said.

An image of Bic moved slowly across her passenger window as they drove past. It was a slideshow she chose to ignore.

Roisin spent much of the journey trying to cajole names out of her brother, the names of the people he was taking her to meet. But Eamon was staying schtum. He had probably been instructed to, she thought, or perhaps he didn't know their names and that was the way it had to be. The less they knew, the better off they'd be, or so she figured. She didn't care what their names were, as long as they got Cathal back. They could be Zig and Zag, as long as they got her brother back.

They drove into Kilburn. Christ, she thought, the boys are at Eamon's. She felt a sudden and unpleasant euphoria as a strange chemical released itself giddily into her bloodstream. Adrenalin. The reality of what they were about to do had hit her. It had punched her in the guts.

Eamon led her into the house. She could hear the television. She didn't remember leaving the television on that morning. Eamon slammed the front door behind them. Roisin heard the television being switched off. She heard a cough, followed by a familiar voice:

'Roach, is that you sis?'

'Cathal?'

He appeared at the living-room door.

Before she had time to ask the hows, whys and wherefores, Roisin felt herself being picked up in a fireman's lift. Cathal hoisted her over his shoulder. He twirled her round and round and round, her hair fanning out like a splayed paintbrush.

'Cathal, put me down. Cathal my head nearly hit the door there.'

He set her on her feet, but they might as well have been jelly roller skates for she had little control over them. Disorientated, she pitched forward into Cathal's arms. Was he real?

'Bet you didn't expect to see me, eh Roach?'

'God no, Cathal. I can't believe it. You got out.'

'I know, I know, it's great isn't it,' he said.

Roisin's face began to fall. 'Sorry. I think I'm going to cry. This is just the best thing ever. I can't believe they let you out.'

Cathal looked at Eamon, who in turn looked at his car keys, using one of them to exhume some dirt from under his thumbnail.

'They didn't let me out, Roach,' said Cathal. He mouthed something to his older brother. Eamon lip-read it as: *you didn't tell her?*

Roisin was confused.

'They didn't let me out, Roach. I escaped.'

'When?'

'Last night.'

'Jesus, Mary and Joseph, Cathal. They'll be looking for you. You can't stay here.'

'Calm down, Roach. Nobody knows you're sheltering us.'

'Us?'

A long-haired, slack-jawed, gaunt-looking guy, the wrong side of five and a half feet, walked into the living room carrying a knife. He also carried a block of cheese and Eamon's biscuit tin. Without saying a word he plonked himself on the single-seater and switched the television back on. He dispensed with the knife and instead bit straight into the hunk of Cheddar. A Rich Tea followed in the same hole. He chomped and chewed, breaking them down into a cheese 'n' biscuit cement.

'And who is this?' asked Roisin.

'Geowmot,' said the little guy. His cheeks ballooned as he chewed, like he was storing food for winter.

'Dermot escaped with the rest of us,' explained Cathal.

'The rest of you. Shit Cathal, should I check all the cupboards?'

'No need, Roach. Only Derm and I made it across the water. There were six of us escaped. The other three were stopped on the border, on their way to Dundalk.'

'The other three?'

'That's right.'

'Cathal, either your maths is worse than mine or you're forgetting someone. You said six of you escaped.'

'Yes, that'll be Declan,' said Cathal.

'Geclam, ha!' said Dermot. He laughed loudly, showering the carpet in biscuit crumbs.

'There are plates, you know,' said Eamon. He went to his kitchen to get the dustpan and brush.

'You'll have to forgive Dermot,' said Cathal. 'When we escaped he was into the sixth day of his hunger strike.'

'I'm fuckin' starvin',' shouted Dermot. 'Here Eamon, got any Tayto Cheese 'n' Onion?'

'Derm, I knew you were on a hunger strike, I didn't realize you were on a dirty protest as well,' said Eamon. He brushed up the crumbs.

Derm held up the last three Rich Tea, announced that a drink was too wet without one and stuffed the lot into his mouth.

Roisin did her best to ignore him. 'So anyway Cathal, what happened to this Declan bloke?'

'Declan didn't make it. You see, we escaped by hiding in the prison laundry bins. It was so clichéd, it had to work. And it did work, for all of us except Declan. He was never the best at taking instructions. He hid in a wheelie bin.'

'He got minced,' laughed Derm.

Roisin wasn't amused. 'That makes me ill, Cathal. That could've been you.'

'Jesus, Roach, I'm not a complete eejit. I know the difference between a laundry bin and a wheelie bin.'

Roisin sat down. She tried to take it all in, but it was too much, too fast. The implications of this were manifold and her brain had become a bag of snakes.

Eamon offered to put the kettle on.

'I'll have one of those beers in your fridge,' said Dermot.

Roisin felt a nerve going in her eyelid. 'Cathal, you can't stay here, the police will be knocking that door down any second.'

'Well, isn't it just as well our brother Eamon works under an assumed name. Isn't that right, Ian Dunne?'

Eamon came in carrying a four-pack. 'Aye, that's my name, don't wear it out.'

'Eamon, you never told me that,' said Roisin.

'He never told you I escaped,' said Cathal.

'I still think the police will find you here. Sure won't they go to the farm and quiz Rory. He's bound to let slip that I'm over here staying with Eamon.'

'Rory's already been in touch,' said Eamon. 'He told the RUC you were off hitching round Europe.'

'Great,' she said. 'So when they find me here I'll have become an accomplice to the escape. I suppose it's better than being an accomplice to a kidnapping. Thank God we don't have to perform that little operation any more.'

'What do you mean?' asked Cathal.

'Well, you're out. We don't exactly need to keep the pressure on for your release.'

'Yes, but there are a lot of our guys still in the Maze. I saw them with my own eyes. Jesus, I've beaten most of them at table tennis. We've got to get them out before they get too good at it.'

'But I was doing this for you,' said Roisin.

'I'm touched sis, I really am, but think of the guys still stuck in that hellhole. They're guys like me, with wives, girlfriends and sisters who haven't seen them in years. We're in a position to do something here. We can get them out, Roach.'

Cathal had always been a persuasive bugger. Roisin would have done anything for her brothers, but for Cathal she did anything and everything. He was her favourite, possibly because he was closest to her in age. He knew this and had always played on it. He used to get her to steal coatfuls of sweets for him from the Spar in Cushendun. He'd even let her keep one or two for herself. Cathal was dead generous like that.

But now she wasn't so sure. He wasn't talking about liberating a few packets of Pacers and Parma Violets. He was talking about a kidnap.

'Look Roach, the plan's exactly the same. All we need is a bit of information. Leave the nitty-gritty to Derm, Eamon and myself. Come on. What have you got so far?'

'Well, I had hoped to see a Mr Carlin, the market owner, this afternoon. I'll be able to get some of the specifics off him, where the admiral will be and when, that sort of thing. Aside from that, well, not much as yet. The place has been crawling with security. They're running checks on the dock every six hours. I was speaking to a bandsman who told me the checks were pretty thorough. One policeman even stuck a hand up his French horn. They're a sea-scout band. I've done a sketch of their uniform. You can probably buy it standard issue. I thought it might be something you could wear on the day, you know, to get close without arousing too much suspicion.'

There was a loud cough and half a biscuit hit Roisin's shoe.

'Without arousing suspicion, she says. Do we look like fuckin' sea scouts?' howled Derm.

'Shut the fuck up, she's trying to help,' said Eamon.

'Imagine the fuckin' headline – Admiral Sutherland Kidnapped by Sea Scouts. Catch yerself on, wee girl.'

'Enough, Derm,' said Cathal. 'Carry on, Roach.'

'Well, the band are due on stage at ten a.m. So I guess Sutherland's entourage will be at the ship and seated by then. I heard the band rehearse the same bloody tunes over and over last Saturday and I reckon that they only have enough material to play for twenty minutes at most. Unless they've got a wee Glenn Miller medley tucked away for the big day. So that means the admiral should be on the podium and speaking, no later than ten thirty. I might be able to wangle my way onto the stage to make a presentation. His walkabout follows immediately after that, then there's a reception at one of the local pubs, the Seagull's Arms. But as I say, I'll have to speak to Mr Carlin before I can get the exact times.'

'You're doing a cracking job. Eamon has you well trained,' said Cathal.

Derm turned up the television volume while the siblings chatted. They had nothing to dunk in their tea.

'How is Rory anyway?' asked Cathal.

'Roach would know better than I would,' abdicated Eamon.

'To tell you the truth, I'm worried about his drinking.

183

He's getting a name for himself in the village. He was caught feeling up Fiona McAllister.'

'Fiona? Francis McAllister's youngest? Sure she isn't fifteen.'

'I know,' said Roisin. 'Well Frannie shouldn't let her work the bar in the Lurig Inn then. That was Rory's local till Frannie threw him out on his ear.'

'Still, Rory shouldn't be touching the wee girls.'

'Fiona? A wee girl? Jeez, Cathal, you have been inside too long. You should see the size of her, she's an arse on her like a barn door.' Roisin made herself big.

'Roar was lucky that Frannie didn't rip his arms off,' said Eamon. He stabbed at his tea with his top lip and retracted it as quickly. Too hot.

Cathal was laughing.

'It's not funny,' said Roisin. 'The farm's going to seed. Rory's sold half our livestock to settle his bar tab. I'm glad Mammy and Da aren't alive to see it. They left that farm to all of us. I can only do so much.'

'Sure, won't we all be off to the States soon enough,' said Eamon.

Roisin knew that this would mean selling the farm. That was something she swore she would never do. To sell the farm would be to erase all memory of her parents. She only needed to take a walk into one of the fields or down to the midden and she was five years old again, in a duffel and wellies, helping her da to lug a big zinc bucket of feed out to the cattle. He would tell her not to let go of the handle. But he knew she would, and when she did, he'd let the bucket pull his arm to the ground, rooting him to the spot, pretending it weighed a thousand million tonnes. Then she'd grab a hold again and they'd be able to lift it, light as a feather. Her da made her feel strong.

She only needed to sit on her parents' bed and she was all small and frightened of thunder. She used to worm in between them like a bolster.

'Maybe I should just pack my bags now and go back to the farm,' she said. 'I don't have the heart for this. And I don't want to see you back in prison, Cathal.'

'Roisin, you don't understand, if we don't do this I might as well be in prison. Look at me. I can't go back to the farm. I can't get a job, or sign on. These guys in H Block, they're names, they're the top men. They'll make sure I get into the States to join you.'

'You shouldn't be making promises to those sort of people.'

'Roach, they're going to fix me up with a green card, dollars, everything. They're well connected.'

'And what if you don't deliver? Your knees won't be well connected to your legs,' said Roisin.

'All the more reason why we have to do this.'

Roisin could feel the heat that precedes tears. But she was determined not to cry. She could tell by the look in Cathal's eyes that he was scared. She knew then that if they didn't go ahead with the kidnapping, he was a dead man. She didn't have a choice.

And then what? She could kiss goodbye to the farm and live the rest of her life in the States as an illegal alien, eternally indebted to some nameless, faceless paramilitaries. And would the kidnapping be the end of it, or would there be other wee jobs to do? Was this the life that she had to look forward to?

'It's all about freedom,' urged Cathal. 'I've already had

my freedom taken away by the Brits. Mammy and Da had their freedom taken away. But we're not the only ones. There are thousands like us back home. We have to do something about it. If we can hold some bloke in a house for a few days, as a bargaining tool, then we'll be doing something. Nobody needs to get hurt, Roach. Not me, not the admiral. We'll look after him, feed and water him.'

'Well I hope he doesn't like cheese 'n' biccies,' yapped Derm. 'Cos I've caned the lot.'

Cathal sat on the arm of the sofa, beside his sister. 'Seriously Roach, if you get us the information we need, it means that everything can go smoothly. We won't be keeping the admiral here. You needn't have any contact with him. But I'll make sure he's looked after. I don't have any grudge against him personally. I'll make sure he's comfortable.'

'Jesus H.,' said Derm. 'The way you're talking, you and this admiral are going to end up as fuckin' pen pals.'

Roisin was resigned to it. 'I'll see what I can do,' she said. It occurred to her that there was one other source of information as yet unpumped. 'The guy that runs the stall opposite me, I think he said he was doing some of the catering on Saturday.'

Eamon was onto her like a shot. 'Is that the guy I told you to stay clear of?'

'What's this?' asked Cathal.

'Our little sister has been getting a bit too friendly with the natives.'

'Give it a rest, Eamon. He's just a guy I had a drink with.'

186

'What do you know about him?' Cathal was all ears.

'Not much. He sells pancakes. A girl helps him out. He's from County Down originally.'

'Interesting,' said Cathal.

'What's interesting? What are you thinking?' asked Roisin.

'Well, maybe it wouldn't be such a bad idea for you to get to know him.'

Roisin stood up. She grabbed the remote control off Dermot and switched the television off. She kept the control just out of his reach while she shouted at her brothers. 'I don't believe you two. First Eamon tells me to stay away from Bic, then you tell me to get to know him.'

Eamon apologized to Cathal. 'I didn't think he'd be useful,' he said.

Roisin wasn't done. 'So yesterday I stood him up and this morning I as good as served him with an exclusion order.'

'You could try lifting it,' said Cathal.

'Are you wise? He'll think I'm a complete nut, some sort of bunny-boiler.'

'Tell him you weren't feeling well. Tell him you were having your period or something.'

'Thanks Eamon, he'll be putty in my hands after that.'

'Look,' said Cathal, 'ask to meet him somewhere neutral. Does he drink?'

'Does the Pope shit in the woods?'

'Good. Take him out and get him hammered. Find out about this catering lark, see if he needs any extra hands on the day,' said Cathal.

'Hold on a second,' said Roisin. 'I'm doing nothing on the day. You lot can throw the onion sack over this admiral bloke, but I'm not getting involved.'

Eamon and Cathal said it in unison.

'You *are* involved.'

Fifteen

The Tropical Ravine is a peculiar place. It is essentially a collection of weird and wonderful plants from all corners of the globe, all hothoused in a long, low building in Greenwich Park.

You would think that a tropical ravine in a British park would be easy to spot, but you'd be wrong. Bushes and trees mask the entire building and even its orange brick is disguised in yellow-green lichen. Only an apologetic glimmer of girders and glass juts up to betray its hide. It sits in the park, camouflaged and rarely discovered, like something Aztec. It is also a deceptively small building, Tardis-like, for a gulch the size of a meteor swallows up its interior, plunging it well beneath the ground level outside. It is one huge botanical bunker, yet, from the outside, only the condensation that bleaches the building's windows hints at any life within.

And what myriad lives it holds. The lives of the South American Indians, who courted death when falling asleep under the leafy angel's trumpet; or the Mexicans, who smoked its poisonous foliage and large white fluted flowers as an asthma remedy. The life of John the Baptist, who stood in the wilderness eating locusts, the fruit of the Ravine's locust tree.

The Ravine also accounted for many deaths, for the small museum at its rear is reputed to hold a dormant reminder of Ireland's worst tragedy: the Famine. In 1845, when the famine started, withered leaves from infected potato plants were removed from Ireland and taken to Kew Gardens for analysis. There they identified the *phytophthora infestans* fungus, some fifteen years after the blight. Fifteen years too late, some might say. The dried leaves were taken to Greenwich to be stored in the Ravine's Mycological Herbarium.

Botanists now believe that extracting fungal DNA from the leaves might resolve one of the great unsolved questions: how did the blight get into Ireland? But the question remains unanswered and the leaves remain under lock and key.

I often visited the Ravine and its museum as an antidote to the hullabaloo of the market. It was like having a jungle on my doorstep.

The humidity poached my lungs as I first entered. I scythed an arm out in front of me, moving gingerly through the dinosaur flora that lined the throat of an interminable tunnel. Some of the leaves were the size of surfboards. This leafy tunnel ran round the entire perimeter of the interior and acted as a mezzanine to the ravine beneath.

I was struck by the sheer profusion of greens; greens foreign even to Ireland. Within the space of a dozen steps I found myself charting an entire atlas. From the papyrus on the banks of the Nile, to the rose of China and onwards to Hawaii, where the shoe flower is made into garlands to welcome visitors. A few steps further and I landed in Europe to enjoy the Swiss cheese plant and the lemon-scented Dutchman's pipe suspended by fine stems that seemed too frail to support its blooms. If I desired, I could return home with an impressive booty of king's crowns, and a cargo of dates, grapefruit, guava, and star anise, from my journey through the Ravine's hangers and reachers, climbers and creepers.

I found the end of the tunnel and hit light. I eased up beside an elegant, dark-haired figure. Roisin had draped herself over some railings that fenced off a large pond. She was immersed in the life that sputtered round its lilies. She watched the dash of carp in the furry brown water. She giggled at the dizzy water boatmen as they harassed the turtles. The yellow-cheeked creatures extended their pinstriped necks in arrogant riposte.

Roisin had, that morning, pinned a note on my stall instructing me to meet her here. The note was written on a sheet of paper from the very pad in which she was now sketching, the same weight and grain. I stood at her shoulder and watched her draw. She was using scant, minimal lines to sketch the tall water plants that bobbed and dallied in front of her.

'I like your elephant's ears,' I said.

'Bic?' She caught her pencil before it fell into the water. 'Sorry, you gave me a shock creeping up like that. What do you mean, I've got elephant's ears?'

'Those plants you're drawing, they're called elephant's ears. And that ugly fella above them is an oilcloth flower.'

Father's investment in my mythical botany degree was paying unexpected dividends.

'Nice names,' she said. 'There are some great plants in here, unusual structures. I wanted to make a few sketches. I might base some pieces on them.' She snapped her sketchpad shut and fanned herself with it. 'Sheesh, it's hot in here, like the calm before the monsoon.'

'Roisin, what do you want?'

'Oh charming.'

'Well come on, what do you expect?'

'Yes. I'm sorry about yesterday. I didn't mean to be rude.'

'So it just comes naturally.'

'Bic. Look, can we forget yesterday? I actually wanted to apologize for Monday, our picnic in the park.'

'Ach don't mention it. Dunc and I had a great time. We had a riot.'

I could tell the joke was lost on her.

'I owe you an explanation,' she said.

I wanted to make this difficult for her. I wanted to force her to come clean about her boyfriend, to level with me. I wanted her to feel more guilty than she already did. I wanted her to beg. Then I wanted her to roll over and let me rub her tummy.

'Save your breath. I know about your boyfriend. You could have just told me, you know.'

Something happened to Roisin's face. It formed a new

expression, one of total and utter incomprehension. Imagine handing a chimpanzee some sheet music.

'Whoa, rewind a little there. What boyfriend?' she asked.

'Seriously, it doesn't bother me. I only wanted us to be friends.'

'What boyfriend?' she repeated.

'I saw you kiss him. It's OK.'

Confusion.

'Yesterday?' I said.

Puzzlement.

'About lunchtime?'

She needed more.

'He picked you up from your stall? In a van?'

Her memory rebooted itself.

'Oh, that'll be Eamon. My brother.'

Her brother. I wanted the ground to open up and swallow me whole. Then I realized I was standing in a ravine, so it already had.

'You thought Eamon was my boyfriend. Ha! Wait till I tell him.'

'Yes, very good. You have a good laugh there. So I made a mistake, but it still doesn't explain why you stood me up.'

Roisin looked serious again.

'Well, you weren't totally wide of the mark. It did have a lot to do with Eamon.' She smoothed the back of her skirt and sat herself down on an ornamental toadstool by the pond. 'My brothers have always been quite protective of me. They've had to look after me since I was five. They washed me, dressed me, lifted and laid me.'

'I hope they didn't lay you.'

'You know what I mean, Bic. They had to do everything for me. So maybe there's a part of them that still sees me as their wee sister, that still thinks I need looking after.'

'So, Eamon didn't think I'd look after you?'

'I can look after myself, thanks.'

I didn't doubt it. My balls were still smarting from her left boot.

'Look,' she continued, 'he's just watching out for me. It's nothing personal. I'm new to London, he doesn't want me to go waltzing off with any old freak now, does he.'

'But I'm not just any old freak. I'm a very special, funny, lovable freak.'

'Let me be the judge of that,' she said.

'So what would Eamon say if he saw you in here, alone, with me? I mean it's dangerous in this jungle. Fall in that pond and the carp will strip you to the bone in thirty seconds. And what if we get lost? We may have to eat each other.'

'Don't take the piss. Eamon means no harm. He just feels responsible. Anyway it was his idea that we meet up today. Now come with me –'

She stood up and took my hand, but couldn't decide which direction to pull me in. I didn't care.

'You're right about getting lost,' she said. 'I haven't a clue how to get out of here. You'd better lead.'

'What makes you think I can find my way out? I normally drop bread on my way in, but this morning I was all out of Hovis.'

'Just get us out of here before it closes, Bic, otherwise we won't be going out on the town tonight.'

'We're going out?'

'Yep. And Eamon approves, in case you're worried I'll stand you up.'

'I can't. Not tonight,' I said.

'How come?'

'I'm waxing my bikini line.'

Roisin ushered me to the door, stabbing at my arse with a 4B pencil.

Four hours later I found myself sitting in an O'Neill's off Covent Garden, nursing a Guinness and checking the time on my mobile. 'Waiting for Roisin' had become my new hobby. If I'd still been in the Cubs, I wouldn't have been a kick in the arse off earning my 'Waiting for Roisin' badge. But I'd been expelled from the Cubs some time ago for making a primitive pipe bomb by igniting a tin of Bird's Custard powder. I never did get my badge for terrorism.

I have never understood the English and their fascination with Oirish chain pubs. Most are about as Irish as lederhosen. The O'Neill's in which I sat was no exception. Everything was just so *forced*. Instead of cheese 'n' onion crisps they sold Letterkenny Cheddar and Scallion Kettle Chips. It's the sort of thing that makes you wish the potato famine had never ended. The decor was equally libellous. From the assorted busts, hairpins, ostentatious hats, old shop signs and tin advertising posters, you'd have sworn that every pub on O'Connell Street once doubled as a milliner's. I had to take my hat off to them for getting it so wrong.

This was not the sort of pub in which novels would be written. Banned as many Irish writers were under the Censorship Act of 1927, it is a legacy unique to Ireland that they congregated in pubs, pleading with journalists to see their work through to print. The genuine Irish pub respected the need for privacy. The snug was the place where plots were put down as privately as pint pots. Not much privacy in this O'Neill's, however, where the object of the game was to see and be seen. The place was starting to fill up with young professionals. They had intermittently picked off four of the five stools from my table. I hooked my leg round the last one. It was mine.

'Is someone sitting there?' asked John Hart, IT Manager at somewhere called InvoTel. I knew it was John Hart, IT Manager at InvoTel, because his name badge was pinned to his breast pocket. The badge also carried a photograph, in the unlikely event that some-one might want to steal it and pass himself off as John Hart, IT Manager at InvoTel.

'Yes,' I said.

Johnny boy grabbed the stool.

'Yes, someone is sitting there,' I elaborated.

'Sorry mate, couldn't hear you above the music.'

He returned the stool and with it, my leg.

The music was loud. An Irish band was playing. An Irish band from Watford.

This I had established from their one, well-oiled fan. I think he was called Derm, but he'd had a few, so it came out as Germ. This seemed more apt judging by the cut of him. Long chip-fat hair. Thick, white nails ingrained with crescents of black dirt, like pints of Guinness in negative. He told me he hadn't had a drink in three years and, right enough, he seemed to have lost the knack. He kept missing his mouth. He sat at the next table, Black Bush dripping off his chin and onto a mixing desk. He twiddled the small bank of multicoloured knobs and dials with a confident, authoritative, *ooh I wonder what this one does* expression. He appeared to be the band's fan, soundman, roadie and, for all I knew, their manager. U2 could sleep well.

Germ pressed a flyer into my hand on which was a badly reproduced black and white photograph of the band – Lughnasa – looking windswept and interesting on the Giant's Causeway. I was about to suggest they should have called themselves Cliché, when Germ pointed out the significance of the band's name.

'Lughnasa, you know, it's an Irish festival, as in *Dancing at Lughnasa*,' he spat.

I sat and watched the band, one of only two people in the packed bar doing so. I saw no dancing at Lughnasa. But somebody did throw a beer mat at them.

I was just reaching across the table for another beer mat when I felt a tug at my leg, the one wrapped round the stool.

'Is someone sitting here?'

'Yes.'

'Who, your dog? I suppose he's up at the bar getting a round in.'

I looked up.

'Roisin,' I said. She looked different. 'You're wearing lipstick,' I added.

'And you have hair. God we're observant, aren't we.'

197

She set her bag on the stool and removed a small purse. 'What's your poison?'

'Guinness. Ta.'

I watched Roisin force her way to the bar. Actually, very little force was required, men just seemed to peel off her as she wriggled through. I knew what they were up to. An attractive girl like that. I knew their game.

Lughnasa rounded off their set with a sincere and heartfelt rendering of 'Teenage Kicks' played on uillean pipes augmented by bodhrán. There wasn't a dry eye in the house. I, for one, practically pissed myself it was that hysterical. The band exited stage to a level of applause that almost prevented me from hearing a fresh Guinness lightly suckering the tabletop as it was set down beside me.

'I didn't know whether you wanted normal Guinness or Extra Cold Guinness, so I got you normal,' said Roisin.

'Normal's fine. What is it with this Extra Cold nonsense anyway? I mean, it's already supposed to be cold, isn't it. Any colder and they'll be serving it on a stick. A stick with an Irish joke on it.'

'These'll cheer you up.' Roisin produced a bag of crisps.

'Are they normal salty or extra salty?' I asked.

'Galway Gammon flavour. Funny or what,' she said.

I cried into my normal Guinness.

Roisin emptied a bottle of Ballygowan mineral water into a tall glass so stacked with ice cubes it hardly warranted buying the water in the first place. She could've just waited for them to melt. I absently read the back of her bottle, the way I read the backs of Domestos bottles when I've forgotten to restock my toilet with copies of *National Geographic*; the way tube passengers read and reread adverts for Leeds Castle and thrush cream to avoid catching each other's eyes. The water, it claimed, had been filtered through layers of Irish basalt and andesite, naturally purifying it and imparting precious minerals in a process that took thousands of years from cloud to bottle. It also said: 'Best before Nov 99'.

Roisin drank the water, no doubt relieved that they'd bottled it in the nick of time. If they'd left it unbottled any longer it might have 'turned'. She folded a crisp on her tongue and asked, 'What's your story, Bic? How did you end up running your own business selling crêpes?'

'Well, I started off selling iced fingers at traffic lights and worked my way up,' I said.

'You don't take anything seriously, do you?'

'It's a defence mechanism. In fact, I'm quite high up in the Ministry of Defence Mechanisms.'

Roisin sucked an ice cube out of her mineral water and crunched it with such ferocity I thought she'd dislocated her jaw.

'I wish I could be like you,' she chomped. 'I wish I couldn't give a damn.'

'Couldn't give a damn about what?'

'Oh, I don't know. Everything. Nothing.'

She looked out the window. The pub had spilled its patrons out over the pavement and onto the road. People propped their pints in the window boxes and did their drunken best to obstruct traffic. Roisin wasn't looking at them. There was a distance in her eyes, a thousand-yard stare. It was ground that I desperately wanted to make up.

'You know, when I first saw you I thought you looked angry,' I said.

Roisin looked angry. She forced her face into mine. 'And what made you think that?' she shouted. She broke it with a laugh.

'See, now you're taking the piss. It's not so hard, is it.'

But I could tell it was. Roisin only ever seemed comfortable when she had something to rail against, something to feel aggrieved about. As soon as she looked like she might be starting to enjoy herself, letting go a little, it was as if something inside pulled her down again, kept her in check. Not happy unless she was unhappy, that was Roisin.

You hear about Catholic guilt. Was that why she was so uncomfortable around me? Then again, I had barely known her five minutes and she had told me how her parents were murdered. That's not the sort of thing you discuss with someone you don't feel comfortable with. Maybe she had wanted to talk more about it the first time she mentioned it. I had steered our conversation round the bomb. It was either that or drive right over it. I mean, what do you say?

'Do you still blame the Brits, you know, for your parents . . . for the bomb?' I blurted. Jeez, ask a silly question why don't I.

'No, I blame Wile E. Coyote,' she said. She let me wait just long enough to wish I hadn't opened my mouth before she added, 'See, that's the sort of sarcastic thing you'd come out with, isn't it.'

I didn't argue.

200

'Of course I still blame the Brits, the loyalists, the murdering scum, whatever you like to call them. They planted the bomb. OK, so they thought they were going to get a busload of Gaelic footballers, not a family on a day trip. But they'd still be murderers either way.'

A few heads turned and Roisin sensed that her voice had become raised. She sipped from her glass, allowing it to cover her nose and mouth as though it were a mute.

'It must have been awful. I'm sorry,' I said.

She perked up. 'Ach don't be. I appreciate what you're trying to do, with the psychoanalysis, but I'm fine. I've just got stuff on my mind, things to sort out. What with Cathal in prison and all.' She suddenly bristled, like she'd caught herself falling asleep at the wheel. 'Speaking of sorting stuff, how are your preparations going for the Tall Ships race? Not long now.'

'Tell me about it. Thank God I've got Sam, she's been working her socks off.' I made a mental note to buy Sam some new socks. Really nice ones. 'I wish I shared her enthusiasm,' I continued. 'If it was just a Tall Ships race, then fine, all of Greenwich having a grand day out like they do at the marathon . . . great. But we all know there's a hidden agenda. The Government have already hijacked the race to publicize the Dome, and the local council is no better. They're using the event to lobby for more lottery money to buy, I don't know, bigger fireworks and more outrageous party hats for Millennium Eve. Then there's that Admiral Sutherland, PR-ing his way to a knighthood. Did you see him on the news doing his "Britannia rules the waves" spiel? And this from the guy who, they reckon, was really behind the sinking of the *Belgrano*. Apparently Thatcher had a crush on him, she did whatever he told her to do. He's an oily seabird if ever there was one.'

'Really?' said Roisin.

I caught myself on. 'Sorry, two pints and you can't shut me up. I'm getting on my high horse again. Still, it's the only horse you're likely to catch me on.'

'No, keep going, it's nice listening to you.' She looked like she meant it. 'So, this admiral, will you get to meet him?' she asked.

'I'll be the second hand that he shakes after he gives his address.'

'The second hand?'

'Aye, after Joe Carlin. He made sure he got himself first in line, it makes him feel important. These walk-abouts aren't spontaneous, you know. The whole charade has to be orchestrated well in advance. The police have to know exactly who the admiral's going to meet and greet. Sutherland's practically royalty, they don't want him shaking hands with just any old scum – lepers, international assassins, Women's Institute. It would be bad PR.'

'And you're not bad PR?' asked Roisin, turning the question mark on its side, to form a wry smile.

'No. I represent the honest, hard-working Londoner, the lifeblood of a Greenwich community enjoying massive regeneration under a new Labour government as we approach a new millennium. At least, that's the spin they'll put on it. I'd rather not have anything to do with it, but Joe insists we make some sort of presen-tation on behalf of the market. Correction, he insists on getting his face on the box. I mean, if you had a face like Joe's, would you really want to beam it to the nation?

He had the audacity to ask me to bake a special cake for the admiral. Like *I* bake cakes. He wasn't happy when I suggested the compromise of a custard pie. I even offered to deliver it to the admiral personally.'

'Maybe I could make him something, a little trinket. Save you the bother,' said Roisin.

'Don't worry your head.'

'No, really. I'd like to help out. You've got enough on your plate. As it happens, I've been working on a piece that might be appropriate. I could finish it on the stall tomorrow.'

'Well I hope you work quickly, Joe wants us all to shut up shop at one,' I said.

'One? He can't, that's half a day's takings gone. I can't afford to lose that sort of money, not with the market so busy.'

I made another mental note to buy the drinks for the remainder of the evening.

'We have no choice, he's under instruction from the Met. They're doing one last security sweep on the stalls tomorrow afternoon. I'll just be glad when it's all over and the market gets back to normal. Christ, the Beeb have even been doing the weather live from the dock all week. The forecast for the next two days is bleak – politicians moving in from the west, bringing in a lot of hot air with occasional scattered photo opportunities.'

Roisin laughed through her nose. 'As I said, if you need a hand.'

'You'll wish you hadn't said that when you're lugging a twenty-kilo barrel of batter across the dock at six in the morning.'

203

I got us fresh drinks and introduced Roisin to the big-city sport of people-watching. This involved teaching her how to bitch, a skill that she had never learned, surrounded, as she had been in her formative years, by men. And nuns. If you were looking for something to bitch about, Covent Garden had the edge on convent school. Post-theatre thesps, postcard punks, city boys, silly girls, lousy street entertainers, Angus Steakhouse diners, a cast of thousands had descended on the square. All prime bitching material.

But Roisin couldn't bring herself to be catty about any of them. She had too much good in her, that was her problem. It was best that she didn't stay in London longer than one summer, long enough for that goodness to be corrupted. Any more time in London and she'd wind up becoming as wound-up and vitriolic as the rest of us.

I nudged Roisin in the direction of a demure young woman sitting at an outside table. 'See yer woman, with the Pioneer pin and the tomato juice?'

'Aye.'

'It's Bloody Mary,' I said.

'You know her?' asked Roisin.

'No, her drink's a Bloody Mary. She's got a wee quarter-bottle of vodka stashed in her bag. Every time her boyfriend goes up to the bar, she secretly tops up her tomato juice with vodka.'

'But doesn't a Pioneer pin signify abstinence?' said Roisin.

'Exactly,' I said.

'Leave her alone. It's not fair to bitch.'

'Come on, what about the guy who took our empties?'

'Bic, there was nothing wrong with him. He was a good-looking fella. Nice muscles.'

'Come off it. He was as camp as a pink chiffon tent.'

She harrumphed. I could tell she didn't know what camp meant. Not in the context I meant it. And how would she know? She was from the sticks after all, where men were men. Hurley players aren't known to mince round the field of play and I doubted she'd met an Antrim farmer who was light in his wellies.

'I don't like this bitching thing,' she said. 'You're just picking one small flaw in something that's not, on the whole, bad. Then you're getting a cheap laugh from it.'

'By George she's got it,' I exclaimed, in my best Henry Higgins.

'OK,' said my Eliza Doolittle, 'but that's too easy. Let's see you do it the other way round. I'll give you something that's obviously bad or flawed, and instead of bitching about it, you have to compliment it, find some good in it. I don't think you're capable. In fact, next drink says so.'

'You're on.'

'And it can be anything?' she asked.

'Anything,' I confirmed.

Roisin surveyed the bar with I-spy eyes.

'Got it,' she said, a little too confidently.

'Fire away then,' I said.

'The Troubles. Tell me what's good about the Troubles.'

Was she serious?

'*The* Troubles? The ones with the capital T?' I asked.

'Them's the ones,' she said. 'But hey, I didn't have you down as a Horslips fan.' I could tell she was enjoying this. She had thrown me.

'Could you not have picked a lighter subject, say, Third World debt or female circumcision?' I asked.

'No, the Troubles are fine.'

I thought about it a long time. My Guinness went extra cold. Finally, I plucked something from the ether.

'Well, if it wasn't for the Troubles, Northern Irish novelists would have nothing to write about.'

She weighed it up.

'They'd only be left with Daniel O'Donnell, soda farls and a whole load of hard-drinking, world-beating sportsmen,' I added. 'Hardly the most fertile subject matter.'

I was exaggerating when I said *a whole load*. Everyone knew that Northern Ireland only boasted four hard-drinking, world-beating sportsmen: George Best, Alex Higgins, Barry Maguigan and David Feherty. Except Maguigan, who was teetotal, and Feherty, who was hardly a world-beater (though he did win the Bob Hope Classic once, beating Bing Crosby and a cartoon bluebird by two shots).

'I thought Daniel O'Donnell *was* the Troubles,' said Roisin.

'See. You *can* bitch.' My Fair Lady, indeed.

Roisin shrugged, conceding the game. She lifted her purse and nodded at my disappearing pint.

'I'll have the same again, on one condition,' I said. 'Let's get out of this place. I don't want to hang around for another bunch of bodhrán-bashing sweater-wearers

206

to take the stage and assault us with their fiddledy-diddledy toora-loora music.' (I find the drunker I get, the more hyphens I use. Or over-use.)

'Oh shit.' Roisin inhaled the words sharply.

'What's wrong?'

'You mean I've missed Lughnasa? I've missed my brother's band?'

'That was Eamon's band? Jeez, I wondered why you dragged me here. Which one was he?'

'He's one of the fiddlers. The smaller one,' she said.

'Does he always play second fiddle?'

'Ha ha.' Roisin wasn't laughing. 'He'll kill me. Are they off stage long?'

'No, they were finishing as you came in.'

'Watch my bag. I'm popping out.'

'I have the same problem. Button missing on my boxers.'

'Just watch the bag, Bic. I'm going out the back lane.'

'Can you not use the ladies like everyone else?'

'You're not funny. I want to catch Eamon, he'll be loading the van.'

She was gone before I could protest.

I dabbed at the crisp packet, sucked the salt off my finger and mentally typed page one of the new existentialist play that I'd been researching, entitled *Waiting for Roisin*. I didn't get very far. Typing isn't easy when you're sucking your finger.

'Enjoy the gig?'

'I'm sorry Eamon, I thought you were on at nine,' said Roisin.

Her brothers were helping two other men to lift a large orange amplifier into the empty van. Derm stood further up the alley, urinating.

'You missed a cracker,' said Cathal. 'Eamon set his fiddle on fire and played it with his teeth.'

Eamon glared at his younger brother and coiled a long blue microphone lead a little more tightly round his forearm.

'Derm said he spoke to your new friend in there, the Bangor man,' continued Cathal. 'This Bic fella's made his peace with you, then.'

'I think he likes me, though Lord knows why. I've been stringing him along something rotten,' said Roisin. 'You should come in and meet him, have a jar.'

'Can't Roach, got to drive Alan and Kevin back out to Watford,' said Eamon.

Cathal guided his sister further up the alley, some distance away from Alan and Kevin. Out of earshot. The Watford Gap.

'Well, what have you got?' he asked.

'Bits and pieces really. We're to close up at one o'clock tomorrow, big security operation. On Saturday, Bic opens up at six a.m. He'll be joined by Sam, the wee girl he has working for him. He said something about barrels and batter. Twenty kilos. Em, what else? He's making a presentation to Sutherland, but he doesn't want to. Bic called him an oily seagull, whatever that means. I reckon I could take his place, I've as good as offered. Oh, and he wants a copy of Lughnasa's demo, signed by the band.'

'Good work, Roach.' Cathal planted a careful kiss on his sister's forehead. He rubbed it off as deliberately.

'I'd better go back in,' she said, 'before Bic gets himself arrested.'

Cathal waited for Roisin to disappear into the bar before he called Eamon across. Dermot shook himself dry and joined them. Cathal put a hand on his brother's shoulder.

'Eamon, is that Semtex still buried in your garden?'

Slowly, a warm pool of urine collected at their feet.

Sixteen

I gave her a choice.

We could head into Soho and grab a jar in any bar that didn't have the words *fir* and *mna* painted on the doors to its bogs. We could get a table in Chinatown and roll our own duck 'n' plum cigars. We could go for a Ruby (Roisin did not understand why the English chose to name their curry after a Belfast chanteuse). We could hire dog costumes in Covent Garden and go heckle at *Cats*. We could stand outside a rubber club and sell puncture-repair kits. We could buy rucksacks, adopt Norwegian accents and stand on the left-hand side of an escalator. We could pay eight pounds to see a film, four quid for popcorn, two-fifty for Coke. Then we could visit a cyber café, log on and remortgage my flat to cover the cost.

In short, I gave her every possible option except the one she chose.

'Let's take a ride on an open-top bus,' she said.

I had never seen her so excited as when she mounted the small half-spiral staircase to the top deck. Understandable, when I thought about it. The only open-top buses you got in Northern Ireland were black and charred, their roofs blown to kingdom come.

Roisin chose a Blue Plaque tour. She wanted to see the homes of the distinguished and the venerable who once resided in London, each building marked out by a small blue circle, a name, a vocation, and a bracketed set of dates. She wanted to peek through a window and see the desk at which *Oliver Twist* had been written. It was the first proper book she had read. She wanted to catch a glimpse of the stairs that Newton once went up and invariably came down. She was curious to see if Gandhi had lived above a launderette, what with all those loincloths. She wanted to see the homes of the great composers: Chopin, Mozart, Elgar. It was quite a Liszt.

I was only interested in visiting royal homes, elegant brick buildings with plaques that read 'the King George', 'the Prince Albert', or 'the Queen Vic'. I needed alcohol. There's nothing like an open-top bus to sober you up. Especially if you hit a low bridge.

I pretended to enjoy myself as we scuttled the city streets. Or rather, I pretended to pretend to enjoy myself. I was actually having a ball, but I couldn't let Roisin know that. I wanted her to think that I was doing her a favour, sacrificing the pub to do something she wanted to do. And if she thought I was making a real effort to look happy about it, all the better. Win, win.

We stopped at 23 Brook Street, outside the home of

George Frederick Handel. There was something very peculiar about his plaque. Right next door to it was another plaque, for another musician: Jimi Hendrix. We stared at both plaques and chose to ignore the dates. Though their stays in London were separated by 250 years, it was much more fun imagining the two men living there at the same time, as next-door neighbours. You could see Jimi banging on the wall: *Hey, Handy, keep the harpsichord down man, I'm trying to screw my guitar.* And would Handel have helped his neighbour to revolutionize guitar technology by inventing the Hallelujah Chorus pedal? We will never know.

The bus deposited us in Trafalgar Square, full of pigeons. Not us, the square. We hadn't eaten a thing.

'Do you want to grab a bite somewhere?' I asked Roisin.

'I'm all right, thanks.'

I was down, but not out. I thought I'd go one better. 'Would you like to visit the home of Anthony Bickmore, Barroom Philosopher, 1971 to the present?'

'I can't, Bic. I'd better head. Charing Cross is just over there, isn't it.'

She knew the way.

'I'll walk you,' I said.

'No need. Really.'

I had forgotten how nippy these summer evenings could get. I rubbed my arms. My goosebumps read like Braille, reminding me that I was still in short sleeves. Strange, I hadn't felt this cold on the exposed deck of a bus, with Roisin by my side.

She took my arm.

'I've had a great time. I'll see you tomorrow,' she said.

She pulled me closer. I closed my eyes. I slowly bent and guided my lips onto hers. But she turned her head at the last second, forcing me to abort the landing and settle for a hug.

The pigeons looked at me. They nodded their heads. They gossiped. How come you never see pigeons sleeping, I thought. I wanted to go to sleep right there, on Roisin's shoulder. But as my eyelids grew heavy she broke away and caught a green man across the road to the station.

My goosebumps had gone.

I walked towards Leicester Square with the intention of catching the last Piccadilly Line tube. But I never made it. I wasn't ready to go home. Nights like this were rare. Nights like this had to be savoured.

I entered the Bay of Bengal and uttered those immortal words:

'Table for one?'

Roisin was surprised to find nobody home. They were probably on their way back from Watford, wherever that was. She knew nothing about Watford, only that Elton John once managed their rugby team.

Her Watford theory was blown out of the water the second she opened the door to the garden. There, between the well-stocked borders, stood Derm. She was torn between asking him where her brothers were, and asking him why he was standing bare-chested and knee deep in a muddy hole with a spade in his hands. She didn't have him down as the green-fingered type. Green-livered, yes.

213

'Have you forgotten where you buried your bone?' she asked.

'It's a pond. It's for the fish.'

He was drunk. Roisin had seen it all before with Rory. She recognized the subtle signs that betray the drunk. His speech slows. His words become deliberate. His eyeballs appear to move in slightly different orbits. He begins to excavate a fishpond at one in the morning. Subtle, almost imperceptible giveaways.

She knew from all her experience that it is best not to interrogate the drunk. There is no reasoning with him. The drunk will justify anything: a fall, a broken shop window, a crashed car, an affair. The drunk believes he is above the law. He believes he is always right. He believes the laws of physics do not apply to him. His capacity to woo women is as undiminished as his ability to hurt men, or so he reckons. He could have been a contender, not a bartender. More significantly, the drunk believes he is not drunk.

She would be wasting her time interrogating the drunk.

Rather than ask Derm why he was turning the garden into Seaworld, she told him he was filthy and offered to switch the immersion heater on. There were many things that Derm had been denied in the Maze. Alcohol was one of them. Roisin believed that a good bath was another.

'There's a clean towel in the airing cupboard,' she said, as he walked mud through the hall. 'Where are Cathal and Eamon?' she asked, before he got away.

'Out on a reccie.'

Of course, thought Roisin. It was best they scouted the

214

market at night. No security. And what would be the point of taking Derm with them? He wouldn't remember anything he saw.

'The bathroom's upstairs,' she said. 'First on your right.' Roisin knew that Derm had been in the house a few days but she wasn't entirely convinced that he'd yet found the bathroom. He smelt like a damp coat.

Derm entered the strange room that contained a bath, a toilet and a sink. He carried a washbag. It had the word Oddbins on it and held a bottle of Bushmills relaxing all-over body lotion.

Roisin left him to it. She fixed herself a tea. Tiny liver spots of grease cannoned off each other on the drink's meniscus. She rued that Eamon didn't clean his cups properly. She remembered how her mammy would rub salt round her cups as a cheap abrasive cleaner. How soon her brother had forgotten. Such lapses were unforgivable. She believed they all had a duty to keep their parents' habits alive, to practise what they had practised. Otherwise their mother and father were truly dead.

Some of their little quirks she had inherited as a matter of biology. She often chewed the ends of her hair as her mammy had done. She had her da's laugh, though she didn't use it as often as he did. But these were unconscious bonds. They were forged naturally. The McKay genes dictated them. It was her parents' many other little idiosyncrasies that needed working on if they were to be kept alive. Roisin believed their memory was as fragile as the Irish language. Unspoken and unpractised, it would die.

Roisin went to her bedroom. She stripped down to bra

and knickers. She sipped tea and opened her book. She caught herself reading the same paragraph for the third time, so she snapped the book shut. Not a word had gone in.

Derm had the bathroom radio on full blast and was drumming along in time to some gangsta rapper, slapping the skin off his bath water. His percussion rat-a-tatted through the wall like cartoon gunfire.

Roisin reached for her personal stereo. She flicked through her cassettes, all Irish bands: Cranberries, Chimera, Ash. Roisin only listened to Irish bands. In the end she plumped for a tape with no label. She would surprise herself. She donned the headphones and pressed 'play'. She stretched out on the bed and closed her eyes.

'Loveless' by My Bloody Valentine.

Roisin didn't hear the bath coughing wetly, like catarrh, as it emptied itself. She didn't register the loud clatter, the bathroom cabinet vomiting its contents onto the sink as Derm searched for a plaster. Nor did his awful rendition of 'I wish I was back home in Derry' make her wish she was back home in Derry. Or Cushendun, for that matter. It would have, had she heard him. In fact, she only remembered that Derm was even in the house when she felt his hand over her mouth and his dick inside her knickers.

He looked mad. He was screaming something at her but she couldn't hear him. She thrashed her head from side to side, not from the pain of his persistent attempts to enter her, she was trying to free her headphones. Her arms were no more than ghost limbs, unco-operative under his weight. She couldn't speak, her mouth covered. She couldn't hear his filthy words, her ears encased. She had lost all feeling, her body numbed. And even though his mouth gabbled and spat and gnawed at her face, she couldn't smell his breath (all hot, and sour as turps). It was as if the deprivation of three senses had resulted in the loss of a fourth.

All she could do was look at him. And when she did, only one thought came into her head – that 'Loveless' was an appropriate soundtrack to get raped to.

She could feel his half-hard penis jabbing unsuccessfully at her belly, at her thighs, at her bottom. He tried to encourage her hand onto it, to rub him. But she couldn't form a grip. There was even less blood in her arms than there was in his dwindling erection.

Then, without warning, Derm turned his head to the door. He ripped himself away from her and tiptoed out of the room.

Roisin lay a while and let the apocalyptic guitar course through her. She wanted to take her headphones off, but was frightened to do so. The whole thing might not have happened. She might have merely dozed off while listening to her tape and experienced a horrible, lucid dream. She wanted to take the headphones off and hear Derm next door, splashing about in his bath. Then she could be certain she had dreamt it.

But what if he wasn't in the bath? She groped for her teacup. It retained heat. She felt immediately exhilarated. Derm had been on top of her for some time, or so it had seemed. If such an ordeal had really happened, her tea would be cold.

She pressed 'stop' and immediately regretted it. Through her headphones she heard the terrible sound

217

of Cathal calling her name. Terrible, because it explained one thing and confirmed another. It explained why Derm had got up from her bed so quickly. Which in turn confirmed that Derm had been on her bed.

She wrapped herself in a dressing gown and made her way across the dark landing. Cathal shouted again. The downstairs light acted as a beacon. It chased her name up the stairs, to fetch her. She groped for the banister but her hand found something warm and hairy and Irish – Derm's forearm.

He said nothing. He pointed at her. He moved the same finger to his lips and made to zip them closed. He then dropped the finger below his chin and sliced it slowly across his throat. And even though she wasn't deaf, Roisin understood the sign language.

She joined her brothers in the living room. They both had a sweat on and seemed buoyed by some new enthusiasm. They talked and talked. They talked for Ireland. Roisin said nothing. Their words hit her like persistent rain. She hadn't the energy to take refuge from them. She accepted everything they said.

They told her their plan. Tomorrow was the eve of the regatta, the day before their big day. Eamon unclipped the hood of a green plastic box, the one he often brought home from the pharmacy. Roisin must go home with Bic tomorrow night, he told her. He filled the chamber of a syringe from a small brown bottle. He held it to the light and gauged the measure. She might even have to stay the night at Bic's place, he said.

Cathal told her not to get too frisky. Derm laughed.
Roisin felt sick.
Eamon syringed a light, syrupy liquid into an empty

218

reservoir normally used to hold contact lenses. He set the reservoir on top of the television. He placed a fresh sealed syringe beside it. The minute Bic falls asleep Roisin must inject him, he said. She needn't worry. It's just a little something that'll knock him out for twelve hours or so. Enough time for her to grab his mobile phone and the keys to his stall. Enough time for them to carry out a kidnapping.

Eamon told Roisin to text Sam from Bic's phone. That way, Sam wouldn't question that Bic had sent her the message. In it, he would claim to be ill – food poisoning – and inform her that he wanted Roisin to take his place at the regatta. Bic's message would also say that Roisin and Sam would be joined by two hired caterers, Kevin and James. They would be played by Cathal and Derm. This would give them every opportunity to get to the admiral. Eamon would be the driver, he said. He had the van and, because he worked in Greenwich, a parking permit. On production of the permit, the police would allow him into the area on the day.

Eamon asked Roisin if she had any questions.

She had plenty questions. They came thick and fast and in no particular order. Why did she agree to this? Which part of Bic's anatomy was she to inject? Why was there a hole in the garden? Why were her brothers sweating when she was so cold? Why had they left her alone with a rapist? Why her?

So many questions and she couldn't ask any of them.

She went to bed.

Cathal and Eamon followed suit.

Derm closed the door behind them. He walked to the television and switched it on. He noticed the contact lens reservoir sitting on top of it. He lifted it and shook its contents. It frothed slightly. He opened Eamon's little green box of tricks. He selected three bottles – Diprivan, Narcan and Ketalar – because they sounded like baddies in *Star Trek*, the sort of blokes who'd finish off Captain Kirk. He syringed a little of each into the reservoir. He returned the bottles to their green box and set the reservoir back on top of the television.

Everything was just as it was.

Seventeen

On 20th March 1923, the partners of the London wine merchants Berry Bros & Rudd invited a well-known Scottish artist – James McBey – to lunch. One of the topics discussed was a possible name for the new Scotch whisky that the company had distilled. The rosy-nosed McBey held his glass to his good eye. The whisky was the colour of urine. For him it conjured stories of dehydrated sailors losing their bearings off some faraway cape and finding themselves in the unenviable position of having to drink their own piss. McBey rolled the whisky round his mouth, numbing his gums. He swallowed hotly, declaring it be named Cutty Sark, after the tea clipper that had just returned to English waters. The artist then took his napkin and sketched a design for the label, complete with hand-drawn lettering. It was a design faithfully reproduced on the hundreds of yellow sails, banners, hoardings,

T-shirts, hats, balloons and badges, that announced the heavily sponsored Cutty Sark Tall Ships Regatta 1999 to the denizens of Greenwich, myself among them.

The Tall Ships Regatta. For many these words usher an exciting kaleidoscope of images: giant square-riggers with towering masts and billowing sails leaning sturdily to the wind; sleek schooners slicing the seas. The race brings its own language, sails and rigs with names as curt as birds: ketch, barque, brig, sloop and yawl. It admits vessels even more voluptuous than their monikers suggest: *Morning Star of Revelation*, *Ocean Spirit of Moray*, *Regina Germania*, *Jolie Brise*.

To me it meant only one thing: money. And business was brisk.

Over two thousand crew had descended on my patch, my little section of the Thames, to make final preparations on the eve of the race. I noted flags from Holland, Germany, Finland, Croatia, Norway, Mexico, Greece, Italy, Poland, Sweden, USA and Russia. An Austrian crew had even managed to enter a boat, seemingly undeterred by the fact their country is land-locked. Theirs was a country that also boasted a navy and a whaling commission. You had to admire their pluck.

I watched as the crews soaped decks, climbed rigging, furled sails, and executed all connotations of the humble knot. It was hungry work, judging by the cash going through my till. But it filled me with a new paranoia. I began to worry that I had seriously misjudged the scale of the event. Tomorrow would be three times as busy, when the crowds congregated to see off the ships.

Sam had sorted the menu. Jambo was still off work on full pay and free to muck in. And I resolved to take up

Roisin on her offer of help. I would have enough hands, I just wasn't sure I had ordered enough food to feed the hordes.

This situation wasn't helped by my being robbed. I had arrived at the stall to find that, overnight, someone had kicked out one of its wooden panels and half-inched a barrel of batter. Why would anyone want to steal a barrel of batter? To cut it down and pass it off on the International Pastry Market? It was a theft made more unusual because they hadn't stolen my float. I had stupidly left it in the till in my haste to meet up with Roisin at O'Neill's the previous evening.

The place was crawling with police. Every boat had to be given the once-over. I don't know what they expected to find on the old vessels – drugs, guns or holds full of shackled slaves lashed to mighty wooden oars. They used sniffer dogs, so drugs were probably high up their list. Dunc had even mounted one of the cocker spaniels in a foolhardy attempt to impregnate him. I resolved to sit him down some day and teach him about the dogs and the bees.

I was sweating like a Grand National winner. Sam too. Her skin shone like a greased hotplate as we diced, chopped, sliced, buttered and drizzled. A cool breeze was not forthcoming. This was stifling work, but I didn't mind. I was thriving on it. I turned the radio up. I was on a high. I hadn't come down since I left Roisin at Trafalgar Square.

A Danish crewman placed his order. He wanted a crêpe with raisins. I didn't do a crêpe with raisins. In normal circumstances I'd have slapped him with my spatula. Going off-menu is not a practice I like to

223

encourage. But today was different. I poured the batter on the hotplate, spun it into a disc and, by the time it had solidified, I had returned from the newsagents with a packet of raisins. Actually it was a packet of mixed nuts and raisins, but I picked the nuts out, such was my dedication.

I had to be nice to the Danish guy. We could soon be neighbours. It is a little-known fact that the island of Ireland is moving north-eastwards at the rate of one inch per year. In fifty millennia Ireland will be where Denmark is today. We will eventually have our revenge on the Danes for all that pillage in the ninth and tenth centuries. The Irish have long memories.

Roisin sat across the way. She seemed unusually demure. Her hair was tied back in a slick and pointed ponytail, a black sable brush. Her face was unpainted. She rarely wore much make-up, but this morning she wore none. If you can gauge a dog's health by the wetness of its nose, then Roisin's eyebrows were as sure an indicator of her mood. Normally dark and angled and volatile as calligraphy, they had settled flatly on her blank brow, like two minus signs. They didn't make a positive.

I asked Sam to give me five minutes. I didn't let her answer. I threw off my apron and went over to Roisin.

'Hello stranger,' I said. Well, she hadn't spoken to me all morning.

Roisin had something in her hands, wrapped in a velvet cloth. She rubbed the material vigorously like she was polishing what was inside.

'Oh, morning. Bic.'

She added my name like an afterthought.

224

'Enjoy last night?' I asked.

She stopped rubbing. It wasn't the most difficult question I'd ever asked, but it took her some time to fathom an answer. And when it arrived, it was a question, not an answer.

'Can we talk about it later?'

Those weren't the words I wanted to hear. I wanted her to say yes, she'd had a great time, that I was a great big laugh, that she'd never met a man who understood her so well and could she please do it all over again, say, every night for the rest of her life. *Can we talk about it later* was not good. It sounded like she had something portentous to say. Something ominous. Something that required the right time and place. Something that demanded more than five snatched minutes in a crowded market.

'Sure,' I said. I wasn't going to argue. Roisin was hot and cold all right, like a temperamental shower. Just when you're all nice and warm, she switches on a tap and leaves you frozen and exposed, hyperventilating.

She set her velvet cloth on her knees and peeled open its corners to reveal a plump pink sea horse.

'Nice,' I offered. I had taken to speaking in single-word sentences.

'It's for tomorrow. To present to Admiral Sutherland.' She fished a small, greenish anchor up from under the table. She clipped the pink sea horse neatly into it. She handed it to me.

I turned the anchor over in my hand. Its metal, though it looked rough and aged, felt coolly smooth. The sea did that to anchors. That Roisin had made this was not without irony. The anchor is a powerful symbol of stasis, stability and settlement. The very things I needed. The very things I had hoped Roisin could offer me.

I returned the anchor. She could present it.

'Thanks,' I said, doing nothing for my word average.

She unclipped the sea horse and resumed her polishing. I was about to ask her where we could meet, later on, to get whatever it was off her chest, when Joe Carlin appeared. One o'clock was upon us and Joe was walking through the market and talking through a megaphone, asking all key holders to co-operate with the constabulary and shut up shop. He wasn't five feet away from me when his voice thundered through the megaphone: 'Bic, did you ever see a doctor about that bowel problem?'

Far out on the horizon, people got the joke.

I smacked the loudhailer off his lips.

'Very funny Joe. Now if you don't mind, I've got to pack up.'

'No you don't,' he said. 'You've got to go over to that boat and chat to Sir David Frost.'

And so it came to pass. I found myself on the deck of an impressive three-masted brigantine. I was one of a tripartite of interviewees for Sir David's new series of ten-minute topical interviews on Radio Two, entitled *Frost Bites*. To my left stood Culture Secretary Chris Smith. To my right, Heidar Gudmundsson, an Icelandic captain and winner of the 1998 race.

As Sir David shook my hand he sussed my accent. He wasn't going to let another irony escape me. That morning I had been an Irishman cooking food for the English, among others. This afternoon, so Frost informed me, I stood on the deck of *Dunbrody*, a faithful replica of an Irish famine vessel. He thought he was funny.

A soundman positioned a boom above our heads. A skinny bottle blonde made last-minute adjustments to Sir David's make-up. I couldn't believe he wore make-up. On radio.

I had never been comfortable being interviewed on national radio. I had never actually been interviewed on national radio. I wondered why I was even there. I supposed that the three of us represented the three core aspects of the event. Heidar represented the race itself. I represented the community benefiting from its patronage. And the Culture Secretary represented a fawning, idiotic government with more lottery cash in its pockets than it knew what to do with.

Not that I could get a word in edgeways. Which suited me fine.

Heidar talked Frost through the race route. From Greenwich to Ålesund in Norway, an apparently beautiful art nouveau setting spread across several islands at the entrance to the 'world-famous' Geirangerfjord. The town, he told listeners, was devastated by fire on a winter's night in 1904, razing eight hundred houses to the ground. During a remarkably short period of time the new Ålesund rose from the ashes in a continental, turn-of-the-century style, a myriad of turrets and spires. From Ålesund, Heidar would set sail for Bergen, the fjord capital, and a city that had enjoyed an entire millennium welcoming sailors. The Tall Ships would take their final berth in Esbjerg. Heidar said he was very excited at the prospect of reaching Esbjerg, 'the fifth largest town in Denmark'. Copenhagen aside, I struggled to name numbers two to four.

Chris Smith wasn't short of a sound bite either. It was a massive coup, he said, securing the Tall Ships Race for Greenwich. It demonstrated his government's commitment to ensuring that Britain led the rest of the world into the next millennium. 'Tomorrow, when Admiral Sutherland fires the starting cannon,' he said, 'it will be the start of something much bigger. Six months of national celebration and festivities, of cultural, educational and artistic projects coming to fruition, culminating in one hell of a party when Big Ben strikes twelve and the Millennium Dome opens its doors.'

I reminded him that until a certain pair of black redstarts finished rearing their young, the Dome would have no doors to open. He laughed with all the sincerity of a politician.

Frost asked me what the regatta meant to the people of Greenwich. I told him I didn't know, he would have to ask them.

'Surely such an event must be a boon for the local economy. Especially for a small-time trader like yourself,' he retorted. The bitch.

I decided to toe the party line: 'Yes, Dave, tomorrow will be a great day. I'll make a killing. And may I take this opportunity to wish Heidar good luck in the race. It should go off with a bang.'

Frost wrapped up the interview quicker than a last-minute birthday present. His producer – all Hawaiian shirt and eczema – was immediately besieged by Chris Smith's cronies. They donned cans and demanded playback. They had secured the right to selectively tinker with the Culture Secretary's words before broadcast. I guessed they'd jostle a few of my words around while they were at it.

I returned to land. Sam had all but closed the stall. Everything had been appropriately cleaned, bagged and refrigerated. She was enjoying the luxury of a fag in the sun.

'Did you get his autograph?' she asked.

'No,' I said. 'Sure he's only an Icelandic sailor. Nobody's heard of him.'

She shook her head and blew smoke at me, ear to ear.

'Where's Dunc?' I asked.

'Dunno. But he shouldn't be too hard to spot. Last I saw, he was walking round with a yellow Cutty Sark helium balloon tied to his collar.' Sam laughed impishly. 'My little joke,' she added.

As I often did, I turned, fanned my hands round my mouth and shouted, 'Duuuuuuuuuuuuunc!'

I counted my elephants. *One elephant. Two elephant.* On *three elephant* I saw a stirring in the crowd. On *five elephant* I saw people looking towards the ground and laughing affectionately. *Seven elephant.* A yellow balloon coming towards me, bobbing like a sinker. I'd got a bite. *Nine elephant.* I caught a familiar flash of red hair and knew it was Duncan. *Ten elephant.* I saw his happy eyes. *Eleven elephant.* I saw a car reversing – a big black Lexus. *Twelve elephant.* The most horrible sound, like the squeak of soles on a basketball court. But it came from the mouth of my dog. It was the sound of sudden desperation, of unadulterated pain. *Thirteen elephant.* A balloon popped. The car stopped. Duncan flapped. One of his legs stayed trapped under a wheel. He looked at me like I had let him down, like he was so disappointed in me.

I ran to the car and slapped the windscreen. I screamed at the driver to reverse. He fiddled with his gears. His clutch barked. The car rocked back. Duncan scuttled out from under it, legs splayed, chin not an inch from the ground. He ran like a lizard, his head skimming this way and that. He zigzagged towards Roisin and buried himself under one of her drapes. It was as if he had decided on a nice place to die.

A man opened the rear door of the Lexus and stuck a leg out. It was Chris Smith. I slammed the door against him. He fell to the ground. It took three minders, his press officer, and a BBC film crew to pull me off him. The police were last to the scene. The bastards had me on my belly.

'My dog. Let me see my dog.'

'Calm down, sunshine,' cooed the officer, doing his best to deglove the skin from my forearm.

'Let him go.' It was either the realization of what his driver had done, or it was the public scrutiny of a BBC camera in his face. Whatever the reason, the Culture Secretary had decided to speak up for me.

The police escorted me over to Roisin. She didn't say anything. Her tears said it all.

I stared at the pathetic lump that had cocooned itself in the drape. The purple material bloomed black with blood. It had become a shroud.

'I'm sorry,' said Roisin.

I peeled back the sticky velvet.

As quick as a cobra, Dunc uncoiled his neck and bit the skin off my fingers.

I felt no pain. He was alive. He didn't know who I was, but he was alive. There was barely a breath in him, but he was breathing.

He fought for air, clacking and wheezing, his tongue as white as an egg. He rolled onto his side. He pissed himself.

'Sam, call Jeff . . . call your father. I need to get Dunc to a vet.'

I wanted my dad. He would know what to do. For the first time in thirteen years, I needed my dad.

'You're not phoning anyone, love.' A police officer stopped Sam's arm as she brought her phone to her ear. If I'd had a gun he'd have been whistling out the back of his head. It was as well that I hadn't, for he added, 'It'll be quicker in the squad car.'

I swaddled Duncan in the drape and carried him to the car. Its siren was already wailing. Roisin climbed in beside us.

The traffic was bad. London's arteries were blocked. The adrenalin of a flashing light and a police siren did little to unclog them.

We had barely got a mile from the market when Duncan perked up. He looked at me like he wanted to ask me something, but he seemed to have forgotten what it was. Then, with an almost apologetic cough, his insides came out his mouth and his head fell on my knee.

He was gone.

Eighteen

I dreamt of a red dog chasing ostriches round a green, green field.

I passed Dunc over to Roisin. He felt lighter in death, hollow somehow. I didn't say goodbye, I just kissed his neck like a big, burbling galoot.

I stayed in the squad car while Roisin took his body to the vet. I couldn't bring myself to do it.

The police officer wound down his window.

'Sorry about the mess,' I said.

He said nothing. He offered me some gum.

After some time, long enough for a stick of Wrigley's to lose its flavour, Roisin came out of the surgery. She carried only a dog collar and a receipt.

'Crouch End,' she told the policeman. She held my hand.

We drove in blood-soaked silence.

I didn't apologize for the state of the flat. Somehow I felt less proprietorial about the place, like I no longer lived there. The moment I walked in the door I felt out of context.

I showed Roisin into the kitchen. She accidentally kicked a plastic dog bowl, scooting it into the middle of the floor. A couple half-chewed, bone-shaped biscuits remained cemented to its sides. I threw it out onto the fire escape.

'I'll make us a coffee, you get out of those clothes,' she said.

Roisin released the force of the tap into the kettle, dousing herself in the process. I found it funny, but I couldn't summon a laugh. Neither could I perform the simple alchemy of turning thoughts into words. My vocal cords felt like the kettle's lime-hardened element.

Roisin sensed my predicament. She just looked at me.

'I know,' she said.

I snatched a bin-liner from under the sink and went to my bedroom. I stripped, throwing everything – socks, trousers, trainers – into the bag. I caught sight of my naked form in the mirror. The tops of both my legs were covered in a large tea stain of dog blood, where it had come through my trousers. I sat down on the edge of the bed and brought my knees together. A big brown heart formed itself on my lap.

I had a sink wash and threw on the only clean clothes I could find. It's hard to cut a dash in red cords and a grey V-neck, but I cared little. The V-neck still had my name sewn in the back of it, Sylvia's stitchwork, a reminder of school. The sleeves barely covered my elbows. Yet there was something so reassuringly familiar about having my school jumper next to my skin. It was like I was twelve again and my future hadn't happened. It was like I'd never come to London and my dog hadn't died. My life felt unmapped, uncharted, so full of possibilities. Like I'd been given a second chance, another shot at it.

I began to draw consolation from the bin bag of soiled clothes that sat by my bed. It was as if this black bag contained all the refuse of my past. I fastened it with a tight knot and set it out on the landing. Tomorrow was Saturday – Bin Day. On Saturday my life would begin again, with all the fresh hope and raw urgency of its *Grandstand* theme tune.

I climbed under the bedcovers.

'You're all out of coffee. There was a free sachet of hot chocolate stuck to my magazine, so I made you that instead.' Roisin waited for me to respond.

I pretended to sleep.

I heard her sniff, like she was crying again. I heard her set the mug on the bedside table. I felt a momentary draught on my back and my weight pitched down towards the centre of the bed as she climbed in beside me. She was fully clothed, the leather of her boots meeting the soles of my bare feet. She wiped her nose on my shoulder.

I dreamt of a red dog chasing ostriches round a green, green field.

'Shit.'

Roisin lifted her head and experienced the sudden vertigo of someone who has just woken up. She found

234

herself in Bic's room. The skylight above her head was a perfect black square with a single white fleck, like someone had missed a bit. It was the moon. She consulted her watch. Someone had spun it forward five hours.

'Shit.'

A skin had puckered itself over the not-so-hot chocolate. Bic was dead to the world. She prised herself out from under the covers, making sure he stayed that way.

Roisin found the kitchen light and emptied the mug into the sink. She opened Bic's fridge and stole a few glugs from a carton of orange juice. She wouldn't have been so brave had she checked its sell-by date. Her bag sat on the kitchen table. She made to open it, but stopped, leaving her hands hovering over it, a parody of Tommy Cooper. What did she think she was doing? Why was she even carrying a contact lens bath around in her bag, when her sight was twenty-twenty?

Then she saw it all so clearly. She unzipped the bag and retrieved the reservoir. She had a job to do. If she did it properly, it would all be over in a matter of hours. She *had* to do it. For her brothers. How else could they get to the States and build lives for themselves? There was no other way.

She tipped out her bag, spilling the contents. The syringe hit the linoleum. Before she could pick it up, the doorbell rang.

Roisin waited a beat, tuning her ears into the bedroom next door. No movement. Good. Bic was out for the count.

She went to the door to let Sam in.

'Oh. Hello. I'm Leslie and this is Charley.'

'Hiiiiiiiiii,' enthused Charley.

'Hello,' said Roisin. Why had she expected to see Sam?

'We live downstairs. Is Bic in?' asked Leslie.

'I'm afraid Bic's having a wee snooze.'

'Oh yeaaaaaah. We get ya.' Charley looked Roisin up and down and saw that her clothes were all crumpled, like she'd just thrown them on. 'We're sorry, we didn't mean to interrupt you two lovebirds.' She threaded her arm through her husband's and jostled him away from the door.

'No really, he's sleeping. He's had a bit of a day of it.' Roisin had taken an instant dislike to these two, with their insipid giggles and their insinuations. When Roisin took an instant dislike to someone she was rarely proved wrong. Bic was the one exception.

'Well if he wakes in the next hour, tell him Charley's got a pot of her chilli bubbling away downstairs. You're both welcome,' said Leslie.

'Thanks.'

Roisin motioned to shut the door, but Charley stuck a foot into the flat.

'I love your accent. Are you from Dublin?' she asked.

'I am,' lied Roisin. She couldn't be bothered to argue.

'Have you ever been to Belfast?' asked Leslie.

Roisin shook her head.

'Oh you just *have* to go,' said Leslie. 'It's so goddam raw. They had snipers on the roofs. We practically got strip-searched going into Boots. Course that was before peace broke out. Shame, really. Charley and I spent a mad weekend there, on a shoot.'

Roisin was unaware that the Northern Ireland Tourist

236

Board offered weekend breaks to trigger-happy tourists.

'Yeah, we were shooting an ad for Pimm's.' Charley talked Roisin through the script. 'It was a pearler. Open on the Ormeau Road. There's a stand-off between local Catholic residents and the marching Orangemen. Bricks and insults are being exchanged until, from one of the bars, a young man comes out clutching a jug of Pimm's. The brick-throwing stops as the warring factions eye the ruby liquid and bits of cucumber. The young man, realizing that Pimm's is made for sharing, offers his jug to both sides. The ad ends on a wide shot of hundreds of people from right across the divide clinking glasses. *Come together with Pimm's*, the voice-over says. We used Primal Scream for the soundtrack. You might remember it on TV. It won an award.'

'Can't say I do,' said Roisin.

'That's right. You're a Dublin girl. They only aired it in the North,' said Leslie.

'Well that explains it,' said Roisin. 'We only get RTE. Which reminds me, I hope my folks are taping the Angelus for me while I visit London. I watch it religiously.'

It had the desired effect. Leslie and Charley looked at her like she was some sort of alien, a little green woman. They returned to their chilli before she beamed them up to her mothership.

Roisin moved quickly. She grabbed the syringe and the reservoir and made her way to the bedroom. Just keep your head down, get on with it, she thought. But it wasn't as easy as that. She knew that once she did this, once she inserted that needle, she could never see Bic again.

Bic had thrown off his duvet. He lay prostrate on the bed, his legs as sprawled as the Isle of Man flag. He looked like he was running after something.

Roisin felt like a twit. She had never administered an injection before and she wasn't entirely sure that she knew what to do. She managed to fit the needle without puncturing herself, a feat made all the more remarkable because her hands were shaking. She examined the clear liquid in the reservoir. It seemed an awfully big dose, but she supposed her brother knew what he was doing. She unscrewed the cap and felt compelled to smell it, in the way children feel compelled to drink bleach. Her nose registered its disapproval in the form of a sneeze.

Bic stirred. He brought his arm across his eyes like he knew what was about to happen, but didn't want to witness it.

Roisin filled the syringe. She flicked the chamber with her finger because that was what they did in the movies. She ejaculated a little of the liquid into the plant pot by the bed, to eliminate air bubbles.

She hovered the needle over Bic's body, not knowing where to stick it. Trying to find a good vein would be like trying to find a truffle in a peat bog. His head, wrists and feet were the only bits of skin readily exposed. She knew the feet were too sensitive, he might wake up. She had heard of people slashing their wrists, but not injecting them. And she couldn't even contemplate injecting his head. It seemed so brutal, even if it was just to make him sleep a little longer.

There was really only one accessible point of entry. Bic unconsciously adjusted his position, jutting his bottom further towards her. He remained blissfully ignorant as she emptied the syringe.

Roisin grabbed his mobile and his keys. She went to the landing and unpicked the knot in the bin-liner. She lifted out one of Bic's discarded socks and balled the syringe and the reservoir into it. She threw them in the bag and secured it again. She stopped at his bedroom door. He was all curled up like a dog. Not for the first time, he drew tears from her eyes.

But she had made a decision and there was no going back.

Roisin dumped the bin-liner in the skip outside the flat. It brimmed with burnt furniture and wet carpets. She waited until she was on the top deck of the Finsbury-bound W7 before she text-messaged Sam.

Back in Bic's bedroom, a pepper plant began to experience the slow chemistry of death.

Nineteen

'For fuck's sake Derm, sit down,' said Cathal.

Eamon's telly could pick up the new Channel 5. They were trying to catch the last few minutes of the Republic's friendly with Andorra. Still nil-nil. It didn't help that Derm was pacing round the room like a cur in a kennel.

'I can't help it,' said Derm.

'Are you nervous about the match or about tomorrow?' asked Eamon.

'Fuck off. Nervous, he says. I'm fuckin' excited. This is like Christmas Eve times ten. I haven't been this pumped since I did that bookies in Portadown.'

Cathal and Eamon said nothing. They fixed their eyes resolutely on the game, even though play had stopped for an injury to Ian Harte.

They didn't like to talk about the Portadown thing. It had been a botched job by all accounts. Derm and a few of his drinking buddies from the Wolfe Tone Bar and Pool Rooms in Andytown had been under orders to go into a Protestant bookmakers – John Eastwood's – and shoot on sight. It was a simple tit-for-tat, my-dad's-bigger-than-your-dad retaliation for the UVF shooting of three Sinn Fein party members who'd been canvassing the local elections at the time. Unfortunately the lines of entrenchment in Northern Ireland were not always so well defined. Portadown wasn't the strict Vatican of Loyalism that they imagined. In the space of sixteen seconds, Derm managed to kill four Prods and two Catholics, spawning a new phrase in the jargon of the Troubles: 'a spray job'. In the blackest of ironies, one of the two dead Catholics happened to be a prominent businessman from South Armagh who'd been bankrolling IRA activity in the area for years. Kieron Fintan of Kieron Fintan Carpets was shot twice in the neck. To ask what a Catholic was doing in a Proddy bookies would have been as futile as a Donegal trawlerman asking how a dolphin ended up in his tuna net. Such was the indiscriminate nature of Northern Ireland's patented brand of terrorism.

This incident hardly ingratiated Derm with the top boys back in West Belfast. But they were prepared to forgive him. It had been badly planned and he wasn't solely to blame. What they were not prepared to forgive, however, was the death of a six-year-old girl in the same incident. The girl had been running into the bookies with a 99 melting over one hand and her daddy's change cupped in the other, as Derm was running out. She got in his way, which didn't please him. He put a bullet in her stomach. At her funeral, mourners consoled each other that at least the poor wee girl never made it inside the bookie's door, where her father lay in bits.

The order was given to kill Derm, cleanly, quietly and without trace. The IRA wanted to make him disappear. Derm was counter-productive. He did nothing to advance the cause. He was a fucking embarrassment. Then it occurred to them that this would send out precisely no message at all. Far better to distance themselves totally from the incident. They got Derm to make a phone call to the *Belfast Telegraph*. He used an IRA code word, but claimed responsibility for the shooting on behalf of the 'New IRA', an invented splinter group. They bought it.

Derm couldn't believe his luck. He had thought his number was up. The boys even drove him home that night. They went the mountain road, towards Aldergrove airport. Derm was sure he lived nowhere near the airport. He'd have heard planes every ten minutes for the last eight years if he lived near the fucking airport. It came as little surprise, then, when the boys dropped him off in a field outside Glengormley with four bullets, knees and elbows, for company.

Cathal examined the scars on Derm's arms as he brought them across the TV screen again, impeding his view. Derm had near perfect circles of skin grafted onto them, restricting the joints. This new skin had been taken from his bottom. Some said this was the reason that Derm didn't know his arse from his elbow.

'I need a fuckin' drink,' said Derm. He rubbed a hand all over his mouth. 'Eamon, what drink have you got?'

'There's a pint and a half of semi-skimmed in the fridge.'

'Alcohol. I need alcohol.'

'No can do, Derm. Even if you hadn't already drunk me out of house and home, we agreed, no drinking the night before a job. We've an early start. We've got to be focused. We don't want another cock-up do we?'

Eamon didn't like Derm. He hadn't expected to be working with him. It made him nervous. Derm hadn't done a job since Portadown. He'd spent the intervening years in the Maze. But he'd made some friends in there, the big men, the Names. They wanted Derm in on this one. Cathal assured Eamon they couldn't argue. Cathal had been inside, he knew what these boys were capable of. Their reach extended far beyond the prison walls. It extended beyond the border, beyond Ireland herself. What these guys said, you did. Derm was part of the operation whether they liked it or not. Like the name of the wee girl he murdered, it was set in stone.

'Where the fuck is Andorra anyway?' asked Derm. He fell onto the sofa.

'It's just north of Fermanagh,' said Cathal.

'Why is it that all countries whose names begin with the letter A also have to end their names with an A?' asked Eamon. 'Think about it . . . Andorra, Austria, Angola, Australia, Armenia, America, Argentina, Antigua.'

'Algeria,' said Cathal.

'Armagh,' said Derm.

'I said countries, not counties, you daft prick,' said Eamon.

Their laughter was cut short by a goal, Luenazalez, a minute from time.

'What sort of a fucking name is Luenazalez?' shouted Derm, lambasting the replay.

'Not as bad as the Moldovans we beat last month,' said Cathal. 'Bumpypic. Nervustwic. Wikidwic.'

'Femininic,' said Eamon.

'Sukmicocubic,' added Derm.

They heard the momentary amplification of the street as the front door swished open and closed. Roisin entered the room just as the final whistle was blown.

'Oh fuck right off,' shouted Cathal.

'And good evening to you too,' said Roisin.

'Not you. We just lost one-nil. To the fucking Andorrans. Bring back Big Jack.'

Roisin threw Bic's stall keys into Cathal's lap. 'It's done,' she said.

Eamon followed his sister into the kitchen.

'So, is Bic sleeping well?' he asked.

'Sleeping? He's hibernating.'

'Did you get his phone?'

'Yes. It's in my bag,' she said.

'And you sent the message to this Sam girl?'

'Yes, Eamon.'

'You remembered to say that Kevin and James would be helping out?'

'No, Eamon. I used the names Cathal and Dermot. In fact, I gave her your surnames as well. And this address. And I told her they'd just escaped from prison. The police are due any minute. Do you want me to stick the kettle on?'

'OK, OK. I'm just checking. You know what I'm like, Roach.'

He gave her a hug. Eamon's hugs felt strange in comparison to Cathal's. They were formal things, like you were his partner at a tea dance. They were the hug equivalent of air kisses. And he rarely bestowed them. Cathal's hugs were a different beast altogether. Your feet left the ground and your ribs bruised. Roisin preferred Cathal's hugs, but right then any hug would do.

'Eamon, we've got to talk. It's about Derm,' she said.

'I know. I'm as nervous about working with him as you are. But if each of us sticks to our task, there won't be a problem. Sure we'll be shot of him in a week or two. He reckons he's heading down under when the dust settles. He's got family in Perth.'

'No, it's not that. Last night, Derm, he tried to—'

'Are you sure you've no drink, Eamon? Isn't that a bottle of Windolene above the sink?' Derm nudged himself past Roisin, rubbing his body all over hers. 'Jesus this kitchen's narrow.' He looked her square in the eye as he said it.

'Listen Roisin,' said Eamon, 'we're all going a bit stir crazy in here. You wouldn't pop out and get us a few tinnies? Cooking lager will do. We can't afford to get hangovers, can we Derm?'

He took Roisin's hand and pressed a tenner into it.

'OK, but give us a minute, I need to get out of these clothes.'

Derm had already spotted the blood on Roisin's skirt. 'Jesus, Mary and Joseph. Have you not heard of tampons?' he asked.

'Oh piss off.'

'What happened, Roach?' asked Eamon.

'Nothing. Bic's dog got hit by a car. I had to carry it. Poor sod didn't make it. Bic was in a right state. We're

245

probably doing him a favour knocking him out for a while.'

'A long, long while,' said Derm. He stretched his O's, giving *long* a curious onomatopoeia. He knew something they didn't.

'That's right, sis. It helps to think positively. We're doing a good thing here. We're only after a bit of justice. Try and remember that tomorrow,' said Eamon.

'I will,' said Roisin. 'Now give us five minutes and I'll go out for your beers.'

'Get yourself something nice with the change,' said Derm.

Roisin gave him the finger out of view of her brother.

Roisin's bedroom was tidy. She introduced chaos. She jammed her bed against the door. She pulled out all her drawers and threw them onto the duvet. She stood on a chair and reached her rucksack down from the top of the wardrobe. Dust found its way into her throat. She ripped clothes off their hangers like she'd been caught on a shop's security video. She stuffed them into the rucksack. Socks, bras, knickers, jeans and T shirts followed until the drawers sat in a redundant stack. She was conscious of time. She grabbed only one coat, the one with the most pockets. She filled every one of them: toothbrush, money, cards, Bic's mobile. She unpicked the photo of her parents from the wall. The knobs of Blu-Tack snagged on her inside breast pocket as she tried frantically to slide the picture in. *Slow down, Roisin,* she thought, but it was a thought that didn't translate into action.

She opened the bedroom window. Eamon's neighbour was a builder. Roisin threw her rucksack onto the pile of sand in his driveway. She pulled her bed back from the door. She composed her face in the bathroom mirror before she descended the stairs.

Mick McCarthy was apologizing to Cathal, Eamon and Derm for his team's lacklustre performance.

'Anything else while I'm out?' asked Roisin.

'Aye Roach, you could get us a video. The card's in the hall, by the phone,' said Eamon. 'Something to relax us. Something funny.'

'Yeah. Get *Far and Away*. I piss myself every time Tom Cruise opens his mouth,' said Cathal.

Then Roisin left Eamon's house for the last time.

She retrieved her rucksack from the neighbour's sand pile, cursing the dogs that had used it as their toilet. She ran as fast as she could down Kilburn High Road. She fought through the Friday throng that had gathered under the dome of the National Ballroom. She passed the Goose and Granite, with its marble floors and its staff in aprons, closing up. She didn't stop to be reminded of its origins as the Earl Derby, where Irish workers used to gather on Sunday mornings to be offered 'the start'. Her only concern was to put as much distance between herself and that house as her lungs and legs would allow.

She sought asylum in the door of a church. She tried three pockets before she found Bic's mobile. She switched it on. The screen illuminated her face from the chin up. She scrolled through Bic's pre-set list of names. She found 'Jeff' sandwiched between 'Jambo' and 'Joe'. She called him.

He answered on the first ring.

'Bic? What can I do for you, son?'

'Hello, Jeff? This is Roisin, Bic's friend. You took us out last week . . . I'm fine, thanks . . . no . . . no . . . no, he was the perfect gentleman . . . yes, I will. Listen Jeff, quick question – how much to drive us to Edinburgh?'

Twenty

'Wakey, wakey.'

Roisin's voice. She was sitting on the end of my bed, bouncing on my feet.

'It's half past midnight. Time to get up,' she said.

She didn't seem real.

'Roisin, I know there's a lot to do, it's a big day and all that, but Christ . . . half past midnight? The first tube doesn't run until six,' I said.

'Come on. Get up, Bic. Here, I've brought you a drink.' She offered me a small glass of orange juice.

'Did you get that from my fridge?' I asked.

'Aye, what of it?'

'I meant to throw it out weeks ago. It's out of date.'

Roisin looked uncomfortable. She cleared her throat. She set the glass down, untouched, beside my pepper plant.

'Shit, what happened to my plant?'

249

Its leaves were crispy.

'Sorry, my fault,' said Roisin. 'This afternoon I must have fallen asleep beside you. I had my lenses in. I never sleep with my lenses in. When I woke up, they felt like a couple of tiddlywinks wedged under my eyelids. I had to take them out and stick them in clean fluid. I was too lazy to go to the bathroom. I'm afraid I emptied the old stuff from my lens bath into your plant pot.'

'I didn't know you wore lenses,' I said.

'There's a lot you don't know about me, Bic.'

'Shit, if that stuff kills plants, what is it doing to your eyes?'

Roisin puffed her cheeks and exhaled, like it was all a bit mad. 'Come on, we need to get a move on. I took the liberty of packing your bag.' She drew my attention to the fat Adidas holdall sitting by my stereo. 'Unfortunately the only clothes I could find were the ones in your laundry basket. I threw them all at the wall and the ones that didn't stick, I packed.'

'Hold on. Why do I need a bag of clothes?' I asked.

Roisin remained out of focus, like vaseline-lensed romance, as my eyes tried to ungum themselves.

'We're going to Scotland,' she said.

Had she taken leave of her senses? Perhaps she was still asleep and this was just some weird somnambulistic enterprise she was literally 'dreaming' up.

'Why are we going to Scotland?' I asked.

'Well, I thought you could do with a break. What with Dunc and all, the last thing you should be doing in the morning is working your arse off at this regatta. You don't need the hassle.'

Of course. Dunc was dead. She wasn't dreaming. I so wished she was. I so wished we both were.

'But what about Sam? She won't be able to cope,' I said.

'It's all sorted. I called Sam and told her that we're getting out of London for a while. She understands. I've sorted out some hired help for the catering. Oh, and I took the liberty of offering her a two-hundred-pound bonus. I knew you wouldn't mind.'

Why was she doing this? Why was she being so lovely? Why now?

'It's totally impractical. I can't do it, Roisin.'

'Yes you can. And I think you've known me long enough to call me Roach.'

'Roach? I can't call you Roach.'

'Why not?'

'Roaches live behind fridges. You stamp on roaches.'

'They come out after dark and you can't get rid of the things. It's dark, I'm still here and I won't take no for an answer. Come on, splash some water on your face and we'll head.'

'How do you propose we get there? Like I said, the tubes are closed. And all the night trains in and out of Euston have been stopped. They're carrying out track repairs.'

'Calm down, Bic. Our carriage awaits.'

At that moment I could have sworn I saw Jewish Jeff walk into my bedroom with a carton in his hand.

'Bic son, this orange juice tastes like nail varnish.'

I found myself in the back of a black cab, shooting north out of London, like a ball bearing being fired into a pinball Britain.

'Where do you want me to drop you off?' asked Jeff. 'Edinburgh's a big place.'

Roisin lifted her head off my chest. 'I hadn't really thought.'

'Well start thinking, we'll be at the border in four hours.'

'Where shall we go, Bic? You know Edinburgh. That's why I chose it.'

I shrugged. I didn't care where we went. My chest was getting cold without her head on it.

'I've never been to Edinburgh,' said Roisin. 'I only know the castle. Drop us near the castle. We can get a hotel with a view of it.'

'Your wish is my command,' said Jeff.

'How long will it take?' asked Roisin.

'In a normal vehicle, seven or eight hours. In my cab, we're talking five and a half. I'm allowed to do whatever speed I like on these roads. It says so on my licence. Seriously. It says *tear along dotted line*.'

The last window disappeared on the west wing of the Kensal Rise Nursing Home as the light inside was extinguished. The building vanished with it, into the night sky. A nurse had called in on Collette Breen to check that she'd taken her pills, before switching her light off.

Collette lay in almost total darkness. She loosened her bedclothes a little. They were too full of starch for her liking. How were you expected to breathe under sheets as taut as these? Were they trying to mummify her?

Collette couldn't understand this pills business. She was 106 years of age. What use were pills? She was

252

about to enter her third century on God's earth. She didn't need pills to get her there. She had achieved 106 years by eating modestly and working hard. Three jobs on the go most of her life. Six children reared. Sure she never had time to get ill. Collette never had the time or money to indulge in any vice that might have halted the onset of her years. Well, she did allow herself a Woodbine and a glass of the black stuff on a Sunday evening. But where was the harm in that? There's iron in stout. It thins the blood.

She liked to sleep with the curtains open. She liked to look into the gardens. You are nearer to God in a garden than anywhere else on earth, she believed. The gardens were still. The cherry trees stood petrified. Their black trunks formed crooked stripes against the blue night, like wet gloss running down a door.

Three centuries, she thought. Collette could just about remember the eighteen hundreds – the Act of Union, the Famine, emancipation – Ireland had been busy. She had been born at the tail end of it all. Ten of them grew up in a mud cabin on the West Coast. Ten became eight when she lost two sisters to pneumonia. The twins were only three weeks old. Them only three weeks and her getting to 106. It didn't seem fair.

Collette wondered why the papers were making such a fuss of her. They said she was the oldest person in Britain. The year 2000 was fast approaching and every-one wanted her story. She was unaware that she had a story. Her life was all bits and bobs.

Her family had moved to Wexford. The Wexford house was a rambling house. They cut turf to make ends meet. This was done in May, in the space between setting the root crops and saving the harvest. In the evenings, the kitchen would be crowded. The men would play cards while the women sat by the fire tracing relationships. Who married who, that sort of thing. They went back generations. When the cards finished, the story-telling would start. When the subject was a ghost or a fairy story, Collette would hang in until exhaustion got the better of her, afraid to go to her room.

A river bordered their land. She used to stand in it, knee-deep, with her brothers and sisters. If they kept still and got their timing right, they could whip a salmon right out of it. Their mammy would cut the salmon in half, boil the front bit and fry up the other half. She liked the front bit herself. The eyes, when boiled, would pop out like marbles. She would chase them round her plate with a fork before giving up and using her fingers.

She remembered the 1916 Easter Rising, as she was hoping to marry her boyfriend that year. Noel he was called, he made her as happy as Christmas. He dropped dead on Dublin's Sackville Street. Appendicitis. She took the first boat to England. No-one thought of staying in Ireland back then. She would get letters from the girls in London and Birmingham, all having a whale of a time. She wanted some of the fun.

She kept various domestic jobs on the go, sometimes a cook, sometimes a housekeeper. Beggars couldn't be choosers, and Collette could turn her hand to anything. She married above herself – Charlie Breen. He owned a bed and breakfast in Sussex Gardens, in London's West End. Together they ran it, while raising a family. Charlie died in 1960. The kids had flown the nest by then and

Collette needed to fill the hole. She took her last job as a dresser at the Theatre Royal, Drury Lane.

Wasn't it all just bits and bobs.

Collette turned to the two photographs that presided over the pillbox on her bedside table. Even though the room was pitch black, she felt she could see the images in their frames. Herself and Charlie under Piccadilly's Cupid. Herself backstage, zipping Judy Garland into a dress.

Her head was heavy with reminiscence. Though it was dark, she closed her eyes to blank out thought more than anything. She needed to get some sleep. In the morning they were taking her down to the river to watch the boats. She would be the guest of Greenwich Council.

Collette found it all a bit ridiculous. She had never been invited to anything in her life and now they wanted to present her with a specially commissioned millennium clock, to commemorate her years. Sure what did she want with a clock, she thought. She was 106 years old. She was older than trees.

She slept like a log.

Stafford Services. If Jeff had been charging them for the journey, his meter would have clocked 149.8 miles and almost as many pounds. He paid for petrol while Bic slept in the cab.

Roisin had got out to stretch her legs. The M6 sounded at her back like a printing press working through the night. It was chilly. She could smell gas. Her teeth were coated in fur.

She thought about Eamon and Cathal. They would have to carry out the kidnapping without her. She was letting them down. But what choice did she have? She had to get away from Derm. He was dangerous. She just prayed he did nothing to harm her brothers. She would phone them in the morning and tell them what he had tried to do. But she wanted to get a safe distance first.

She looked in on Bic through the taxi window. If she couldn't bring herself to inject him to keep him away from the market, then she had to remove him some other way. This was the other way. It would do him good. She felt sure he needed to get out of London as much as she did. Scotland was the obvious choice. Bic knew Edinburgh. He could show her round, take their minds off things. Once they got themselves north of the border things wouldn't seem so bad.

'There you go, love.' Jeff spoke through the receipts in his teeth. His arms were full of cans, bottles, crisps and sandwiches. He let Roisin have first pick.

She grabbed a Diet Coke. It tasted of the tin, but at least it was cold. It acted like mouthwash.

Jeff pulled onto the motorway.

'I once had a naked woman get in the back of my cab,' he said. 'Not a stitch on her. I asked her how she was going to pay. You know what she did, she opened her legs wide apart. So I took one look and said, love, have you not got anything smaller?'

He drummed on his steering wheel.

Roisin didn't catch the end of his joke. She rested her Coke on Bic's knee. She knew she was falling for him.

Siobhan Cullen woke up in a strange room in a strange city. There was no movement from the other bunks in the dormitory. She wondered how her classmates were

256

able to sleep. Siobhan was the only one of the girls never to have visited London. How could they sleep? She considered London too big and exciting a place to be slept in. Even the tube map looked like coloured streamers flung from a party popper.

The sounds that filtered into the dormitory from Great Portland Street were different to the sounds Belfast made. Back home in Belfast, Siobhan would wake to the wok-wok of helicopters patrolling the skies. One time, a bomb went off and shook her whole house.

She heard a plane fly over.

Siobhan had only just taken her first flight – from Aldergrove to London Stansted – with her school. They had been awarded first prize in a national competition. All the primary schools in Britain had been asked to write a play imagining life in the twenty-first century. Her school, the Sacred Heart of St Mary, had won. Tomorrow they would visit a place called Greenwich, where all the clocks in the world were made. In Greenwich, a very important man would present the school with their prize: five computers installed with Windows 2000. This man was an admiral and he was the Queen's cousin, or so her teachers claimed. Siobhan had been told to mind her Ps and Qs in such company.

The school had already been invited to return to London in 2000 and perform their play in the Millennium Dome.

Siobhan was excited. She was having the time of her life. She had already seen Big Ben, Buckingham Palace, and Nelson's Column. She had visited Madame Tussaud's where she had her photograph taken with the Spice Girls. When she got home, she would tell her wee brother they were the real Spice Girls. He was only four so he wouldn't know they were made of wax. She went to Planet Hollywood, but had to stand outside because the burgers cost eight pounds. That was nearly all her money.

Siobhan could see the Post Office Tower from her bunk. Her mum had told her that the Post Office Tower had a restaurant at the top that spun round and round. She wanted to go there. She fell asleep wondering how she would keep her peas on her plate.

The first light of morning jumped into the cab. The sky was intensely pink, like someone had picked away the scabrous night to reveal a new crimson skin underneath. The hills were purple with heather and polka-dotted with sheep. If only Monet had been a Scotsman, I thought.

'Are we over the border?' I asked. My joints needed oiling.

'Just gone through Gretna Green,' said Jeff. 'Now are you two sure you don't want to turn back and get hitched? I'll be a witness.'

I looked at Roisin.

'One step at a time,' she said.

She kissed my cheek.

From that moment I knew I would never go back to London.

Liam McAlindon dipped his comb in Brylcreem and ran it through his thinning hair. He couldn't have found a straighter parting if he'd used a T-square. He tipped a bottle of aftershave onto both hands. He slapped

258

his cheeks twice and winced when they burned. He fastened the top button of his shirt and secured his collar with a tie. It had been a while since he'd worn this tie. He proudly centred the words Cumann Luthcleas Gael directly below the knot. Liam McAlindon had once been treasurer to the London Exiles Gaelic football team.

Liam had his papers delivered every morning. Battersea Council now offered this service to the over fifty-fives. Liam was fifty-three, but took them up on the scheme regardless. He lifted copies of the Irish Times and the Racing Post from his doormat. He boiled an egg and checked the form.

The horses had been his ruin when he first came to London. It was 1966 when Liam had started working on the Victoria Line. He had just left the Merchant Navy following the seamen's strike that year. Construction was the only job going, so Liam lived in the tunnels, helping to build the new tube line.

The tube system was getting bigger and bigger. There were so many tunnels, Liam feared London would cave in on top of him. Baker Street had been the first tube station ever built. That always made him laugh. Sure who would use it, where would they go?

They were all Irish on the Victoria Line. It was powerful craic. The money was good too, but no-one put a penny away. Liam would do one week on days, one week on nights. The week he was on days wasn't too bad. But the week he was on nights, well, he was in the bookies all day, and even the couple of bob he'd saved the week before would be gone.

But this morning Liam picked his winners with a new

and extravagant abandon. Ballgawley Boy, 6/1 in the two-thirty. Emperor Ming, 7/4 favourite in the two forty-five. And in the three o'clock? Euthanasia. It was 40/1, but what of it. This morning Liam was rich.

Liam was first through the door of his bookies. He placed three fifty-pound notes on the counter to accompany his bet. They didn't know whether to accept it or phone the police. This was a man who usually bet in shrapnel. Still, business was business and they ran it through.

Liam popped the pink slips into the pocket of his GAA blazer. He felt just grand. He walked to Chelsea Bridge. He wanted to stand somewhere special to hail his first London cab. He was off to Greenwich, after all, to be presented with a cheque for seven million pounds.

Liam's numbers had come up.

We drove into an inferno of red sandstone. Edinburgh Castle filled the windscreen like a tacky postcard, a parody of itself. The sun picked the city out like a light sketch.

Roisin was asleep in my lap. Jeff was in full flow.

'The thing was, it kept blocking the toilet. I couldn't flush the stuff. So I wrote to the manufacturer and complained about the density of their toilet paper. And they sent me a reply, a 124-page dossier explaining the physics of bog roll. I mean, what was I supposed to do with a 124-page dossier . . . wipe my arse on it?'

He dropped us outside Waverley Station.

'If you give us a second, I'll go to the cashpoint,' I said.

'Don't insult me, son. I don't want your money.

You've been good to my daughter. I'm just returning the favour.'

'You've just driven us over four hundred miles. That's some favour.'

'Not really, son. I've got a brother in Newcastle, I haven't seen him in years. I'm going to stop off on the way back.' He turned to Roisin. 'You look after my son,' he said.

Roisin nodded.

Jeff switched his light back on and parked up at the station's taxi rank.

Princes Street was full of Saturday morning shoppers. We headed away from them, towards the Old Town. We were so tired we booked into the first hotel we found, a little Georgian number in Cockburn Street.

Roisin insisted we take a double room. The concierge was delighted to give us the one that had an hour earlier been vacated by Eddie Izzard.

We feigned a stunned silence. You could have heard a name drop.

'Mr Izzard played the Gilded Balloon last night,' he added, handing me the hallowed key.

The room was comfortable, if a little unspectacular. I suppose I had expected something more ostentatious, given its previous incumbent.

'Let's go to bed,' said Roisin.

It caught me off guard. I had never suspected she could be so forward. I whipped off my cords.

'To sleep,' she added. 'You're not going to have sex with me.'

'Of course not,' I said, quickly pulling my boxers back up. 'I didn't want to have sex with you.'

'Oh cheers. Do you not find me attractive?'

'No, I didn't mean . . . that is . . .'

I was suffering from a bad dose of foot in mouth.

'Shut up and get in,' she said. She took her T-shirt off, but only when she was safely under the covers.

We lay together, two spoons. I stroked her to sleep.

Roisin was so beautiful, but something was missing. She reminded me of a butterfly that I had once given birth to.

As a boy, I found a chrysalis that had stuck itself to a tall blade of grass. It was hanging on for dear life as the wind blew it about. I decided that it was in danger and that I had to operate. So I cut the chrysalis open, a Caesarean of sorts. A butterfly emerged, all wet and new. Only it was premature, so the colours on its wings hadn't developed. I had ushered this colourless butterfly into the world.

It would have been at around the same time that a car bomb blasted the colour from Roisin's wings.

Twenty-One

Sam needn't have worn her puffa jacket. She had never come down to the market this early and she had anticipated that it would be much colder. But this morning it was mild enough to turn your milk.

'Hurry up, Bic,' she said. But there was no-one around to hear it. She felt like she did when she stood at her kettle and asked it to hurry up. It didn't make it boil any quicker.

She switched her mobile on, to check the time. The screen went momentarily black. Then it displayed Sam's name and the time: 6.41.

Where the hell was Bic?

The phone emitted two short sharp bleeps. A little envelope appeared in the top left-hand corner of the display. Sam had a message. She read it:

Am off 2 Ednbr.
2 tired 2 talk.
Got U some

help 4 2day –
Kev & James.
Pay U £200.
C U soon. Bic

Great, she thought.

But she couldn't argue. The trauma of seeing his dog killed must have been too much for Bic. Actually, when she thought about it, he'd been acting all moody for the last week or so, ever since he set eyes on that Roisin girl. It was probably best that he got away from the market for a while.

Sam should have been annoyed, but instead she was excited. She was going to make a real go of the day. She didn't know who Kev or James were, but she would make sure they knew she was the boss. This was the closest Sam had ever come to running her own business. She was determined to enjoy it.

Then she remembered she didn't have the stall keys. Bic must have given them to the hired help. If they had the keys, did that mean he wanted them to take charge? Surely not. Bic wouldn't do that to her, not after all the work she had put in – the new menu, the specials, the coffee percolator. The extra two hundred quid would be useful but, for the first time in her life, Sam wasn't as interested in the money. She wanted power. She wanted to rule the roost.

Sam heard the sound of wheels on gravel and a green transit van pulled up. Two men sat in the front. She wondered whether she could guess which one was Kev and which one was James just by looking at them. The pale redhead in the driver's seat had to be a Kevin. The good-looking passenger with the spiky black hair would be James. She hadn't expected them to be driving a van. But they were hired caterers and she supposed they had a lot of fancy equipment in the back.

Kevin and James got out. Sam introduced herself.

'Morning, lads. Samantha Gold. Bic's left me in charge.'

The two men blanked her and walked round the back of their van.

Sam followed them. 'Hello? I don't bite, you know,' she said.

They opened the back doors. The van didn't contain any catering equipment as such. It contained a barrel of batter and a small, ratty man. Ratman had one other distinguishing feature. He held a gun.

'What is this?' asked Sam.

Derm climbed out of the van. He pressed his gun into Sam's crotch. That way, no-one could see it. He stood tight against her, forcing her to walk backwards. 'Where's Bic?' he demanded.

Cathal and Eamon unloaded the barrel from the van.

'I don't know,' said Sam. The gun felt cold between her legs.

'Bollocks. You knew we were coming, so you did.'

'Bic sent me a text message.'

'I told you Roisin wouldn't let us down,' said Eamon.

'Aye, but where the fuck is she then?' shouted Derm.

'Maybe if you took your gun out of the wee girl's twat and checked her mobile, we might find out,' said Cathal. He used the keys, the ones his sister had given him, to unlock the stall.

The gun was now on Sam's chin. It didn't feel any warmer. Derm frisked her with his free hand. He ran the hand all over her, dwelling on her breast a little longer than was necessary.

'My phone's in my top left pocket,' she said, in an effort to curb his assault.

Derm read the text message. He was confused. He turned to the others. 'This message says he's gone to Ednbr. Where the fuck is Ednbr?'

'Edinburgh, you prick,' said Cathal.

'Jesus, Cathal, your sister's spelling is terrible,' said Derm.

But the two brothers were deep in discussion.

'Shit, Cathal. Roach has bottled it,' said Eamon. 'Do you think she'll say anything to Bic?'

'For fuck's sake, Eamon. Roisin trusts us. She won't want to jeopardize it for us. She won't want to see me back in prison.'

'What if she sees the news this afternoon? She'll know what we've really been up to.'

'Are you deaf as well as stupid? She trusts us, Eamon. Completely and utterly. She doesn't think we're capable of something like this. She doesn't know how deep we're involved.'

'I'm not so sure. Maybe it's nerves, I dunno, I just think this Bic fella is bad news. He's bound to put two and two together. We've got to get to Edinburgh before he does his sums.'

'You want us to take him out?' Cathal ripped off his gloves.

'Is there another option?' asked Eamon. 'If we get out of here before seven, we can beat the traffic. We could be in Edinburgh after lunch.'

'Well quit fuckin' talkin' then, and let's do this,' said Cathal.

Sam was still obeying a gun. Derm slipped his hand down the front of her jeans.

'Please don't,' said Sam.

'Have you never let a man touch you there before?'

Sam shook her head. The gun moved with it, from side to side.

'You don't look like a good Catholic girl,' said Derm.

'Jewish,' said Sam. The less she spoke the less chance of accidentally triggering the gun. Each syllable could be her last.

'Jewish, eh? We don't get many Jews in Ireland. What are you, a Protestant Jew or a Catholic Jew?' Derm fought with her underwear.

'What the fuck are you doing?' shouted Cathal. He smacked Derm's hand away.

'I'm only having a wee feel.'

'Well stop it.'

'Come on Cathal, I've been inside a long time,' said Derm. 'Or rather, I haven't been inside in a long time.'

'And you don't want to go back in the Maze, so shut the fuck up and do your job,' said Eamon. 'I need you to keep that gun on her while I put her to sleep.'

'What do you mean, put me to sleep?' asked Sam. Like she was some sort of cancerous pet.

Eamon had already retrieved his little green box from under the passenger seat of the van. 'I'm going to dispose of you the same way I disposed of that black bastard who wouldn't sell me his stall,' he said. 'Cathal, take her shoes and socks off.'

'Eamon, do we need to kill her?' asked Cathal.

'No Cathal, we don't. Sure we can just let her go, now that she knows our real names, now that she's seen our faces and heard our accents. Tell you what, why don't I give her a lift to the police station?'

'OK, OK. Just make it quick.' Cathal knelt down. He started to undo one of Sam's laces, but Sam still had Loz in her head. She kicked Cathal full in the face.

'Fuck.' His nose was pissing blood.

Derm inserted the gun into Sam's nostril. He pushed it upwards, forcing her onto tiptoes. 'Take your fucking shoes off, wee doll,' he said. He stood back from her. He let the gun follow her as she sat on the gravel.

Eamon tore off a fresh swab of cotton wool and handed it to Cathal. He told him to tilt his head back and pinch the top of his nose. He filled a syringe with morphine – more than enough to kill Cathal's pain. More than enough to kill Sam.

Sam removed her trainers.

'Cathal, Derm, I want you to stand here and screen me. I don't want anyone to see this.' Eamon turned to Sam. 'Give me your right foot,' he said. 'Slowly,' he added, fearing a repeat of her kung fu.

Sam winced. Her toes had splayed with cramp.

'You should feel a little prick,' said Eamon.

'Yes, she should,' said Derm. 'Mine.'

Eamon slapped the arch of her foot. Her veins came up like a road map. He jabbed the needle into a big blue motorway.

Sam couldn't describe the pain. Morphine had rushed from her foot to her head and seized control of her mouth. Pain gave way to pleasure. Vodka and Red

268

Bull doesn't even come close, she thought, just before her eyelids fluttered and she passed out.

'What'll we do with her?' asked Cathal.

'Leave her to me,' said Derm. 'I've a few ideas.'

'Just get her into the fuckin' van will you, before we're seen. It may be early but you can bet this place is crawling,' said Eamon. 'We'll dump her upriver.'

Quickly and without ceremony, Cathal and Derm loaded Sam's body into the back of the van, like they were smuggling an illegal slab of bush meat.

Eamon rolled the barrel over to Bic's stall. He returned it to the same place he and Cathal had stolen it from. The 20 lb container now weighed closer to 80 lbs. Eamon opened up the lid. He set the timer to ten a.m.

Twenty-Two

There were exactly 35 days, 7 hours, 32 minutes and 16 seconds to go until the Edinburgh Festival 1999.

I knew this because the large electric clock erected outside St Giles Cathedral was engaged in the countdown. It also told me it had gone noon. Roisin was still sleeping in the hotel room. I had wanted to lie in too, but hunger had got the better of me. The last time I had eaten, my dog was alive.

I reacquainted myself with Edinburgh. I walked the narrow wynds and closes, the high 'lands' and many-storeyed tenements enclosed by the King's, Flodden and Telfer walls. I walked past an abundance of cafés, their smells as idiosyncratic as their names: The Electric Frog, Tempting Tattie, Creeler's, Bann's and Igg's. Fly-posters informed me that the Scottish Colourists were exhibiting at the Dean Gallery.

I stopped at a makeshift stall on the Royal Mile. It

270

reminded me of Loz's in that it sold all manner of useless junk. The most bizarre item on sale was a stuffed rabbit with varnished pebbles for eyes. I made the mistake of lifting it. The woman running the stall was onto me in a flash.

'My ex-husband used to do a bit of shooting. Grouse mainly. Unfortunately that rabbit was the wrong animal in the wrong place at the wrong time. Rather like I was when I first met my husband.'

I declined the rabbit and continued walking until my nostrils were once again filled with baked bread and bacon. I had resisted temptation long enough. I bought a copy of the *Herald* and took a table in a colourful little café that went by the name of the Elephant's Sufficiency.

I ordered a plate of stovies. I was served an island of beef and sausage stew floating on a loch of cooking oil. This wasn't the traditional Scottish dish I remembered, but I was too hungry to quibble.

I cracked open the pages of my paper and amused myself with a reader's letter that dismissed England as 'the neighbouring southern peninsula'. Not that the English could give two hoots what *Herald* readers thought. The Scots had reckoned that by devolving, the English would finally sit up and take notice of them. Quite the opposite had happened. The Scots now barely register on an Englishman's radar. In fact, the English perceive the north/south divide as one contained within their own borders. The Irish, on the other hand, find England's imagined north/south partition a laughable one. Name me one 'northerner' who ever got shot trying to sneak across Leicestershire to bury guns in

Bucks. The Irish know what a north/south divide really is.

My thoughts turned to Roisin. She had initially tried to draw such a line of entrenchment between herself and me. Now here we were, together in Edinburgh, like it was some sort of neutral territory. We were beyond all jurisdiction. No-one could touch us. We were unstoppable.

I cannot begin to tell you how happy that made me feel.

As if to emphasize the cross-cultural point, my ears were drawn to a debate being conducted on the café's radio:

'*The phones are red-hot this morning. We're discussing Monday's Twelfth of July marches. So whether your band is making its way across the Irish Sea for the bank holiday festivities, or you're opposed to the marching season, get that call in to Radio Scotland. We'd love to hear from you. I'm going to take another caller now, a Mrs Dolores O'Neill from Kilmarnock. Dolores, from your name I'm guessing you're opposed to the marches. What point would you like to make?*'

'*Well Alex, it's just in response to an earlier caller who complained about the lack of toilet facilities for all the thousands of Orange marchers. I think I may have a solution.*'

'*Fascinating, Dolores, and what solution would that be?*'

'*You can tell the Orangemen to go piss in their bowler hats.*'

'*Quickly to line two. Hello, you're on Radio Scotland—*'

Undeterred by my stovies, I ordered a coffee and a slice of banana cake. The coffee, when it eventually arrived, was a peculiar colour. Earl Grey, judging by the small bag bobbing in the cup. The banana cake looked and tasted like loft insulation. I was about to complain when the radio broadcast was interrupted by news:

'This is BBC Radio Scotland. We can now bring you more on that massive explosion that occurred at around ten o'clock this morning on London's Greenwich dock. A police spokesman has said that it has all the hall-marks of a terrorist bombing, although no organization has yet claimed responsibility. The number of dead has risen to nine. Admiral James Sutherland, a cousin to Her Majesty the Queen, has been confirmed as among the fatalities. Buckingham Palace has said that the Queen will issue a statement at two thirty. Greenwich was today hosting the annual Cutty Sark Tall Ships Regatta. Several crewmen are feared to have died and many are reported injured. An incident room has been set up, and police have issued a telephone number for anyone concerned about friends or relat—'

I left a twenty-pound note, an unread *Herald*, a coffee and a slice of loft insulation in the Elephant's Sufficiency.

I ran like my tail was on fire. I had to find some space to make a phone call. There were too many people about. They spilled down from the castle like they were floodwater. I was swept downstream towards the Mound. I found an alley behind a disused gallery.

I called Sam.

'Come on Sam, for fuck's sake answer.'

She did. Except she spoke with a man's voice and an

273

Irish accent. 'Hello . . . Roisin? Is that you, Roach?' he asked. He sounded like he was speaking from inside a moving car.

'No, this isn't Roisin. It's Bic. Who the fuck are you?'

The line went dead.

Nothing in the world made sense.

I called Jambo.

'Bic, it's fuckin' chaos down here. Where are you?' His voice fought against sirens, helicopters, and car alarms.

'Edinburgh. But never mind that, where's Sam?'

'I'm sorry, Bic. Sam's in hospital. She's in a coma. She's no looking good.'

'I knew I shouldn't have left her. Shit man, the radio said it was terrorists. Are her injuries bad?'

'Sam wasnae hurt in the blast. The explosion happened at around ten. Sam was already in hospital by then. She was picked up by the coastguard at half seven this morning.'

'The coastguard?'

'Aye. They found her lying on the riverbank. She was near drowned. Fucked out of her head on something. Bic, tell me straight, did you do this?'

'Are you serious?'

'The polis are asking questions. Their boys have already pinpointed your stall as the source of the blast. You're the only one wi' keys.'

'Jesus, Jambo, my stall was broken into the night before last. There'd been a theft. Anyone could have got in and planted something.'

'Did you report the theft?'

'No. I meant to, but . . . other things . . . Duncan . . . you know.'

'Relax. I believe you, cuz. But it's only fair tae warn you, Joe Carlin's already told the polis you had some grudge wi'him. Something tae do wi'Loz. He reckons you could've planted some device tae destroy his market and get back at him. It's bollocks I know, but it's all the polis have got tae go on fae now. But the fact that you didnae show this morning isnae goin' tae help. They'll think you're on the run.'

'This is crazy. I can explain everything. Roisin suggested I get out of London. Jeff drove us up here, to Edinburgh. He had me in the back of his cab all night and most of this morning. He's my alibi.'

'Well I hope tae Christ he is, mate. Coz this is fuckin' serious shit. They've been pulling corpses out of here all morning.'

'Tell the police to speak to Jeff.'

'Jeff will be more concerned about his daughter, Bic. She jumped into the fuckin' Thames. She must have been off her tits.'

'No. I know Sam. She doesn't do drugs. And even if she did, she wouldn't do them the night before such an important day. She was really up for this regatta. She'd put too much work into it.'

'Listen Bic, I have tae go. They want tae stick a cordon round the market. I'd keep my head down for a wee while, if I was you. Save yourself a night in the cells. If terrorists have caused this explosion, they'll claim responsibility. That's your best hope. I won't tell anyone where you are.'

'OK, but promise me you'll call me when there's word on Sam.'

'I will, cuz.'

I felt sick.

I felt like a dyspraxic mathematician. Nothing seemed to add up.

Sam wouldn't waste her money on drugs. She was saving. She needed the cash from the regatta. And why did some Irish guy have her mobile? Why did he think I was Roisin? When he received my call, Sam's phone would have displayed my name. Why would he think I was Roisin?

Then I remembered Loz. They had found him dead, stoked full of all sorts. He did a lot of dope and a lot of rum but I had found it difficult to believe that he was any more hardcore than that. Had someone spiked him? Had the same person got to Sam? Did he now have her phone? If he did, he clearly knew Roisin. And he expected her to answer my mobile.

I noticed another fly-poster on the gallery wall. The paste was still wet. It advertised an Irish band due to play the Ceilidh Bar at the forthcoming Edinburgh Festival. Lughnasa, they were called. I looked a little closer at their fiddle player.

I felt sick.

Twenty-Three

Roisin woke up with a man on her bed and a hand on her throat.

'Bitch. You scheming bitch,' he shouted.

Roisin couldn't breath, never mind talk.

'I knew it,' he said. 'I knew I shouldn't have trusted you. I knew something wasn't quite right. Jesus, I really pick them, don't I.'

'I cadth breedth,' she said.

He relaxed his grip.

Roisin rolled off the bed and ran to the dresser. She lifted the stool and threw it at him. He put an arm out to protect himself. She heard a crack. He fell to the bed, clutching his hand.

'Shit,' he winced.

'I'm calling security. You're out of your mind,' she shouted.

She grabbed the phone and ran backwards, pulling it

into the en-suite bathroom. She slammed the door. She bolted it. She dialled '0'.

The phone went dead.

I twirled the phone jack between my thumb and finger. My good thumb, that is. My other one was broken.

'Since when did your brother want to open a themed restaurant?' I asked.

'Bic, I don't know what you're on about,' said Roisin. Her voice echoed off the bathroom tiles.

'Your murdering bastard of a brother is what I'm on about,' I said.

'My brother wouldn't hurt a fly.'

'No? Well, he managed to persuade one of my friends to fly, high as a kite, and crash-land on a boat.'

'Bic, you're not making any sense.'

'Make sense of this for me, then. The man I saw you kiss that day at the dock, that was your brother, right?'

'Eamon. What of it?'

'He was the guy that tried to buy Loz's stall. Your stall. It was definitely him, I've just seen his ugly bake on a poster outside. I didn't recognize him before, without his white coat. That is what he wears at the Greenwich Apothecary, isn't it? Don't try and tell me otherwise, the same guy sold me a bottle of TCP.'

'Bic, I told you, he's a pharmacist. And yes, Eamon bought me a three-month tenure on the stall. He paid Joe Carlin. It's all above board. He's done nothing wrong.'

I couldn't believe what I was hearing. I couldn't believe the audacity of her. How could she still lie to

278

me? This woman had allowed me to invest such feelings in her and now she revealed herself as a clinical, calculating cow. I suspected it ran in the genes. Her brother was a murderer, after all.

'Why did Eamon want the stall so much? He was prepared to give Loz a grand for a load of junk and a grand for his stall. Two grand for a three-month lease, don't you think that's just a tad extravagant?'

'He was doing it for me. I didn't ask him how much it cost,' said Roisin.

'Two grand so you can flog all your Celtic shite. I mean, it's hardly a boom fucking industry, is it? How did he expect to recoup his investment? Were you selling bits of the original fucking Blarney Stone?'

'Bic, you don't know what you're saying. You're still upset. You've had very little sleep.'

'You're right. But Loz is sleeping well. He's in a coffin. The same day your brother tried to buy his stall, Loz was left for dead on the *Cutty Sark*, pumped full of chemicals. Do you not think that's just a little suspicious, given that your brother is a fucking pharmacist?'

'Sam told me that this Loz fella was a drug addict,' said Roisin.

'Ah, Sam . . . that wouldn't be the Sam who's now lying in a London hospital in a drug-induced coma?'

There was a long silence from the bathroom. Roisin was plotting her next move. Either that or she was shaving her legs.

'OK, Bic. Let's do this properly. I'm going to unlock the door and come out. Then we're going to sit on the bed and talk about it calmly.'

279

The bolt cracked. I was already on the bed when Roisin came into the room. I had a pillow in my good hand in case she threw anything at me. I expected a volley of hotel soap, sewing kits and monogrammed bathrobes.

Her hands were empty. She looked terrified. She looked beautiful and terrified. When she spoke her eyes filled. They were like two varnished pebbles.

'Bic, I haven't been honest with you.'

'You don't say.'

'Cut the sarcasm and let me speak.' Roisin positioned herself on the corner of the bed. 'Eamon did want that stall badly. But no, not for any restaurant. He needed me to work there and gather information on the regatta. I had hoped to make some money to fund a campaign to free Cathal, but Eamon had other ideas. This morning they kidnapped Admiral Sutherland. They're going to use him as a bargaining tool to free Republican prisoners.'

'They?'

'Cathal escaped last week. He's been staying with us in Kilburn. There's another guy, Derm. The three of them are holed up with the admiral as we speak.'

'I don't think so,' I said.

She must have seen something funny in my face.

'What's happened, Bic?'

'There's been an explosion. People are dead, Roisin. People are fucking dead.'

Roisin emitted a watery heave like she'd flooded her engine. 'No. No, that can't be right. Tell me my brothers are OK,' she said.

'Uch, spare me the tears, Roisin. You know very well

that they're OK. You know they planted the bomb. That's why you were in such a hurry to get me out of the way. You're working with them. What is it we're doing here, you and I? Is it some kind of honey trap? Shit, I wouldn't have minded if there'd at least been a little honey. It's more like an ice trap—'

I felt the full heat of her hand as it smacked my face.

'He tried to rape me,' she howled. 'He tried to rape me and you say something like that. You're an asshole, Bic.'

Roisin had been too tired to unpack her rucksack when we'd first checked in. She now gathered her few effects from the dresser and threw them in with her clothes.

'Where are you going?' I asked.

'I'm going back to London to find my brothers.'

My cheek felt like nettles. My thumb was up like a tenpin. The woman I loved had done this to me and now she was packing her bag. She was leaving me. It was like I had grabbed a handful of the softest, whitest Antrim sand and was now watching it disappear just as quickly through my fingers.

The woman I loved. God. Why was this happening to me? Amid all this mayhem – this horrific, ungovernable mayhem – I decide that I love her. And then, when it happens, when I finally allow my emotions to fully attach themselves to a woman, she turns out to be a terrorist? Some sort of Mata Hari? Surely not.

I had to focus. If I was going to hold onto her, I had to trust her. And fast.

Maybe Loz's death was just a tragic accident. We all have secrets. Perhaps Loz had a few Class A secrets of his own. I had never seen needle marks on his arms.

Then again, he always kept them covered under the long yellow sleeves of a Jamaica football shirt. Did he have something to hide?

And I thought I knew Sam, but she did have a wild streak, the capacity to do something violent and unpredictable. Sure, hadn't I sat and watched her cut someone's ear off? And last night was a Friday night. Sam went clubbing on Friday nights. She was only a teenager. They experiment with all sorts of shit at that age. What if someone had spiked her vodka? Rohypnol was becoming a big problem in London and Sam was an attractive young thing.

Maybe I was wrong about Roisin and her brothers. At least she'd been honest with me. At least she'd told me about Cathal and the kidnap. What if they *had* got caught in the explosion? Maybe I'd jumped to the wrong conclusions, the same way the police were forming their own mistaken conclusions about me. Her brothers could be dead. Someone had tried to rape her. She needed me.

I needed her.

'He tried to rape you. Who tried to rape you?'

'That fucker, Derm. Not that you care. By the sound of it, Bic, you had the same thought on your mind.'

'I'm an asshole, Roisin. I'm not a rapist. Now put that bag down and tell me about it. I don't want you to go.'

She set the rucksack down. By the door. Ambiguous, I thought.

She lifted the stool that had broken my thumb. I flinched. She sat on it.

'Derm . . . he's a psycho. My brothers left me alone

282

with him the other night, you know, after Eamon's gig. He tried to rape me. If they hadn't come home when they did I . . .'

The varnish fell off the pebbles.

Roisin ran into the bathroom. I heard retching. I heard the toilet flushing. When she came out again, her mouth was hidden by a tissue. She held it to her nose like she was sniffing a large white rose.

'Sorry,' she said. She tucked the tissue into her sleeve. 'If anyone's planted a bomb, it's this Derm guy,' she continued. 'He knows a lot of heavies back home. IRA. My brothers aren't bombers. They couldn't do something like that. Someone would have to hold a gun to their heads. Even then, I would've known about it. They would've told me. They've never kept anything from me. We're too close. They know the pain bombs cause. Look at our family, all blown apart. They'd never put another family through that.'

'Roisin,' I said. I waited until she looked me in the eye. 'I believe you, Roisin. But I need to know what happened to Sam. You said you phoned her last night, to tell her we were leaving. What time was this? What did she sound like? Was she in a club?'

'I didn't speak to her, Bic.'

'You mean you lied to me?'

'No. I text-messaged her. I told her we were coming to Edinburgh.'

'But you let her think you were me.'

'I had to, Bic. I had to do it for my brothers. I had to get your keys and arrange for them to go to the stall to help Sam out. They needed to get close to the admiral. If they

283

don't carry out the kidnapping, Cathal is as good as dead. Sam was in no danger, my brothers promised no-one would get hurt.'

'But you had to get me out of the way.'

'I did all this for you. Last night I was supposed to give you something to make you sleep, to keep you out of the way. But I didn't. Then I was supposed to join my brothers and Sam this morning, to work the stall. But I couldn't go through with it. Yes, I had to get away from Derm, but I wanted to be with you. Don't you see, if I'd done what they told me I would never have been able to see you again.'

Roisin walked to the door and picked up her rucksack.

This was it. She was off. There was nothing I could do to stop her.

'I'm going,' she said, '. . . to take a soak.'

She locked herself in the bathroom. I heard the reassuring judder of the bath taps emptying themselves.

I grabbed the remote control and searched Ceefax for news of the bomb. I had forgotten that our hotel sat in the shadow of Edinburgh Castle. The weak signal constructed its own language only loosely based on English. Words like: ex6l8si%n, tw3lv&, and d£7d.

I switched it off.

I checked my mobile for news, but until they invented a Wireless Applications Protocol all I could do was play Snake.

And then I remembered my phone call to Sam. To the man purporting to be Sam. The Irishman in the car. Only I bet myself that it wasn't a car, that it was a transit van. And if the Irishman had checked Sam's messages, the van would be well on its way to Edinburgh.

I knocked on the bathroom door.

'Are you going to be long in there?' I asked.

'A wee while. Why, do you need to pee?'

'No, I can hold on till we get to Stranraer.'

Twenty-Four

Detective Inspector Jackie McMullan's face and hands were covered in masonry dust. He looked like a grey bonbon. He had spent the last two hours hauling bodies from the wreck around the *Cutty Sark*. He was monochrome.

He washed himself at a sink in the Scotland Yard toilets. He dried off using fistfuls of paper towels. He smelt of stale soap.

Jackie had been due to attend the regatta at ten thirty that morning. He was a guest at the admiral's garden party. He'd been promised a good spread. But he had decided to go down a little earlier to catch the Tall Ships. He wanted to see what all the fuss was about. Sure, they were only boats.

So Jackie got himself there at ten to ten and *wham* – he had an international incident on his hands. He had already counted two Danes, one Finn and one American

286

among the dead. The American alone would be enough to trigger World War Three. If this was the work of the IRA, they had cocked it up big time with the American. The IRA were virtually bankrolled from the States. Noraid's war chest could soon be very empty. And that's before you even considered the deaths of four Irish schoolgirls.

Jackie took his leg off. He lowered himself onto the toilet. His timing had never been good.

On his first and only night on patrol with an RUC unit in South Armagh – Ulster's bandit country – a rocket was fired into Jackie's car. How was that for timing? He remembered lying on the tarmac and seeing an ambulance draw up. They ran over with a red blanket and a grey blanket and he knew he was in a bad way. The grey blankets only came out when they were scooping you up.

He lost a leg, but at least he survived. His colleague, Hilary Denny, wasn't so lucky. Jackie missed her funeral. He was too heavily sedated, blitzed on painkillers. They had waited a week to tell him Hilary had died. It had taken him almost as long again to remember who Hilary was. As soon as he checked himself out of Musgrave Hospital, Jackie checked himself out of the province. He came to London in '87 and was given a desk job at the Yard. He was also given a prosthetic limb. The boys called him Plastic Paddy.

He married his physiotherapist – a Cornish lass named Rachel, hair the colour of clotted cream. They tried for children. They tried and failed. They thought it was Jackie. The rocket had taken one of his testicles along with his leg. Plastic balls weren't an option. They both took the test. It emerged that it was Rachel who needed fertility treatment.

She was ecstatic.

Unlike Jackie, Rachel's timing was impeccable. She was twelve weeks pregnant. The baby was due on 01/01/2000. Rachel had planned it that way. Somehow she had managed to synchronize her ovaries with the big clock up at the Old Royal Observatory. Rachel had wanted to conceive their child at zero degrees longitude, on the line of the prime meridian. She believed it would increase their chances of getting the millennium baby she craved. It would've required them sneaking into Greenwich Park on a night in early April.

Jackie was against it, for a number of reasons. How was he going to climb over the park fence? Rachel would have to give him a leg up. Then she'd have to throw his plastic one over the railings – a real passion-killer. If he managed to get into the park, nights in early April were notoriously cold. Jackie couldn't see how that would increase his chances of siring a child. And even if he managed to rise to the occasion, having sex in a public place was illegal. He'd be duty bound to arrest himself and his wife as soon as he caught themselves in the act.

His reasoning was persuasive. In the end they conceived with the aid of a natal clock, a bottle of Rioja, Ricky Martin, and the living-room sofa.

Jackie wiped his arse with a swollen and cracked hand. This morning had been a close call. People were running so hard away from the bomb, their feet left their shoes. Jackie was just glad he was still alive to welcome his baby into the world on whatever day it was born.

Jackie's office was a mess. He would've said that it looked like a bomb had hit it, but he knew all too well that it didn't. The office had been hastily converted into an incident room. In fact, Jackie could only be sure it was his office when he picked up a framed photo that was lying face down on top of a pile of files stuffed into a cardboard box on the floor. It was a scan of his son to be. He returned it to its rightful place on his desk.

A young officer had to ask him twice to get his attention: 'Sir, can you come downstairs? We've got something on Bickmore.'

Jackie followed the junior down to one of the interview rooms. 'Is there any more news on the girl they pulled out of the Thames this morning?' he asked.

'Yes, Sir. We know she worked for Bickmore. We still haven't managed to get hold of her father, though. He works for a cab company. They say he hasn't radioed in. Not last night or this morning. The hospital needs his consent to switch off her life support.'

'Jesus. What a decision.' Jackie pictured his wife's gestating belly.

He thumped open the door to the interview room.

'Right, who have we got?' he asked.

'Not *who*, Jackie. *What*.' A detective was holding a cassette. 'Listen to this.' He popped it into a tape machine normally used for recording, rather than playing. 'This was taken at Greenwich yesterday afternoon. It aired this morning on Radio Two, on *Frost Bites*. It's Bickmore.'

Jackie listened to a ten-second loop of his prime suspect, repeating over and over: *'Tomorrow will be a great day. I'll make a killing. The race? It should go off with a bang.'*

Jackie recognized a bit of Ulster in the Scots accent.

The detective stopped the tape. 'A Mr Joe Carlin has told us that Bickmore grew up in Stranraer, but he was born in Northern Ireland,' he said. 'The boys are running a profile on him as we speak.'

Jackie spoke. 'I want you to mobilize every unit in Dumfries and Galloway. Get our anti-terrorism boys up there. I want that radio clip on every channel – digital, terrestrial, extraterrestrial if you have to. Stick it on the Net, pipe it into supermarkets, pin a transcript to every fucking tree in Britain. I want this bastard caught.'

Twenty-Five

They drove past a floral clock.

'OK, so we're in Edinburgh, what now?' asked Eamon.

'We wait for Roach to get in touch with us,' said Cathal.

'What makes you think she'll call us?'

'She's bound to have heard about the bomb by now. She'll want to check that we're OK. She'll know that we have the wee girl's mobile. Bic will have told her that he called it and we answered.'

'We could try calling Bic,' said Eamon.

'Yeah, sure. Hi Bic, we're the guys who murdered a couple of your friends and blew your stall to smithereens. Can you pass us over to our sister?'

'What if she doesn't call?'

'She'll call,' said Cathal.

'What are we supposed to do with ourselves until then?'

'I don't know, do I. We could go visit the Camera Obscura, buy a couple deep-fried Mars bars, whatever.'

Cathal switched on the car's radio.

It told them they had achieved their target. Admiral James Sutherland was dead. But, at the latest count, they had taken eleven innocents with him. They included Britain's oldest resident, Collette Breen, 106; a lottery winner, Liam McAlindon; and four pupils from Belfast's Sacred Heart of St Mary primary school, the youngest of whom – Siobhan Cullen – was only nine years of age.

'Jesus Holy Fuck,' said Cathal. 'It's over. We're dead men.'

'Calm down, Cathal.'

'Christ, how did we manage to kill four Catholic schoolgirls? I thought you and Roach were getting us information, so we'd know exactly who was on that stage with the admiral.'

'How were we to know?'

'Jesus, Eamon, we're as good as dead. They're going to kill us. You don't know these boys as well as I do. IRA Continuity Council won't want to claim responsibility for this one. It would be the end of them. They're going to have to bring us down. You, Derm and I are all walking fucking corpses. Wait'll you see, I bet you Derm doesn't make his plane to Perth. Or if he does, it'll hit a fucking mountain. Wait'll you see. The word will have already been given.'

'Shut the fuck up, will you,' said Eamon.

He turned the volume up:

'*Police are intensifying their search for Ulsterman Anthony Bickmore. He was the owner of the stall in which they believe the Greenwich bomb was planted. In an interview conducted yesterday with Sir David Frost, Bickmore gave a chilling portent of this morning's events: "I'll make a killing. The race? It should go off with a bang."*

Scotland Yard believe Bickmore is on the run. He may be headed for the Stranraer area, where he is known to have family. A London taxi driver has come forward to say that Bickmore has taken a hostage, a young Irishwoman. An emotional Jeff Gold told reporters, "He got me to drive them north of the border. I would've done anything for Bic. He was like a son to me. Then I find out he's put my daughter in hospital. I hope he burns in hell."

Police describe Bickmore as being in his late twenties, slim, with short brown hair. Detective Inspector Jackie McMullan had this to say: "On no account should any member of the public approach this man. We could be dealing with one of the biggest killers in the recent history of these islands."

Police have provided a phone number for anyone seeking information on loved ones—'

Eamon switched the radio off.

'I think we may just have found a way out of this,' he said.

'What are you thinking?' asked Cathal.

'Continuity Council aren't going to claim responsibility for this. But they don't need to. The police are already pinning it on this Bic fella. They think our sister's a hostage. If we can find Bic, stick a bullet in him, and convince Roisin to tell the police that she shot him in self-defence, then we're off the hook. It's perfect. The police will look good for getting their man. The public will have their demon.'

Eamon was laughing. He reached over to the back seat and found his road atlas. He threw it onto Cathal's lap.

'Look up Stranraer,' he said.

Cathal wasn't convinced. He knew what the IRA did to punish people like him. And they weren't going to ask him to write a hundred lines: *I must not murder innocent Irish schoolgirls.*

'What makes you think Roisin will co-operate?' he asked.

'Because if she doesn't, Cathal, she'll have to bury us both.'

Twenty-Six

'Hey mister, I'm driving da poo poo shrain.'

A kid tugged at my arm. I couldn't work out if it was a boy or a girl. It was still at that indeterminate age. It made train noises, showering me in spittle. Then it ran down the narrow channel that bisected the seats in our carriage.

The journey had been a nightmare but at least Roisin and I had managed to secure seats. Our carriage was so packed, one guy was even sleeping on the baggage rack. He wore a purple and orange suit. A can of Tennent's fell out of his hand. We were sharing the carriage with a Protestant marching band – The Sons of Dunfermline Houl Yer Whisht Defenders. Three hours of 'The Sash' and the 'Lily O'. A Lambeg drum blocked one of the exits. God help us if our train fell off the rails like they did in England.

I was relieved to look out the window and see

the tiny, whitewashed cottages welcoming us into Stranraer. They sat against the dark hills, like chips of icing at the foot of a last moist slice of wedding cake. There was a small hole in my window spinning out a cracked web of light, the spiritual effect of which belied the hand that threw the brick that struck the glass. We decelerated into the station and watched life on the loch flicker through the fence-posts like old cinema.

Loch Ryan was so calm you wouldn't have known it was there. It attached itself to the town like a sheet of cling film. We hadn't been able to talk on the crowded train. It all came out as Roisin and I walked along the Cairnryan road.

She told me that Cathal had twice tried to take his own life inside the Maze. She reiterated his innocence. She told me how much Eamon loved his Irish music. She used to perform with him at a pub called the Lurig Inn, back in Cushendun. She would dance while he played his fiddle. They used to make a few quid, but Roisin reckoned that was less to do with the music or the dancing, and more to do with the fact that they'd been recently orphaned. The community had rallied round her family. She told me about Rory. He was the reason she didn't drink. He was the reason she was about to lose the family farm.

It wasn't a one-way conversation. I managed to chip in that I was the most wanted man in Britain.

I also told her we had to lie low until some organization claimed responsibility for the bomb. We could stay the night at my Aunt Sylvia's and work something out from there. Under no circumstances was she to contact her brothers. I knew they were already on their way to Edinburgh, but I didn't tell her that. Derm would be with them. I was sure it was he who had answered Sam's phone. Derm must have attacked Sam. Roisin told me he was a loose cannon. She said he had killed a girl before.

We walked past the old people's home in Bayview Road. I had always hated walking past that building. The Steam, the kids called it, because of the tall chimneys at its rear that continually billowed the stuff. I used to walk past the Steam and dip my head down to peer under a crooked rowan tree that tapped against one of its windows. Behind this window there used to sit an old woman with an inane smile, the sort you see stitched on dolls. She sat there every day, smiling and crying. Always crying. This dipping of my head had become an involuntary tic as I walked past the home. Six years on and I did it again.

'Are you all right?' asked Roisin.

'Oh, it's nothing. I thought I saw someone I knew,' I said.

The old woman with the stitched-on smile wasn't there. She must have passed away. At least her crying had stopped. I imagined that the steam coming from the chimneys must be the very souls of these old people being boiled away. My mother preferred to bake potatoes because she said that boiling sucked out all the good in them. I was so glad the old woman's crying had stopped.

And then we saw Anchorage. Or so read the badly painted sign that swung in the sea breeze outside my aunt's guest house. Anchorage was one of those grand, rather camp old buildings that you see on British

297

seafronts. Its architect had never heard of the right angle, or possibly believed it imposed too many constraints, abandoning it from his blueprint. Thirty-nine steps (I kid you not) had to be climbed to reach the porch. When you stood at the foot of the steps and looked up to the roof, the whole building seemed to rock backwards and forwards. Jambo and I didn't have a rocking horse, we had a rocking house.

'Who owns the car?' asked Roisin. She fixed her hair in its chrome.

'It's Sylvia's. It used to belong to her fiancé. It's a Bentley.'

'It's beautiful,' said Roisin.

'Sylvia can't drive,' I said. 'But she looks after it, should the need ever arise. She likes to sit in it and listen to the engine.'

I pulled Roisin away from the old car. The car that never moved.

It had been years since I'd walked up these steps. The nostalgia was soon replaced by sadness. For Anchorage stood with all the resignation of a one-time prizefighter, broad-shouldered and battered, having pawned belts and memories of more glorious days.

I stopped Roisin at the door.

'Roisin, if you don't mind, I'll call you Roach in front of Sylvia.'

'Why?'

'You've heard of Orange Lil. Prepare to meet Orange Syl.'

'Are you ashamed of me, Bic?'

'No.'

'Well, sorry for being papist scum. I'll try not to do it again,' she said.

'It's not that. Just trust me on this one. Sylvia lost her fiancé to *the other lot*.' I used my fingers as quotation marks. 'Jambo never knew his dad.'

'Ah,' said Roisin.

'One more thing. Sylvia may have heard about the explosion on the news. As far as she's concerned, you and I have been in Edinburgh since Thursday.'

'Anthony? Is that you, my boy?'

A ruddy face met us at the door. It wasn't Sylvia. I knew this because Sylvia didn't have a ruddy face. Nor did she have a thick white moustache. The figure that greeted us was my Uncle Tam. He wasn't a real uncle of course, just one of those pretend ones. He had been a permanent, paying guest at Anchorage long before I was dumped there.

'I see you've brought Sylvia a wee drop of the widow's ruin,' he said. He was referring to the bottle of Gordon's in my hand.

'You know Sylvia and her gin,' I said. Sylvia loved gin. I had considered fixing a teat to the top of the bottle.

'And who's this lovely young creature?' asked Tam.

'Rois—'

'Roach,' interrupted Roisin.

Tam carried an orange rectangle of plastic fishing line decorated with many gleaming hooks.

'Where are you off to?' I asked.

'I'm just nipping across the road for a few hours. Over to the pier. I'm going to catch some crabs for supper. Maybe you two will join me later?'

'Sure,' I said.

We watched him go. He paused to steady the Anchorage sign. He shouted, 'Anthony, if you're stopping for a while, you can help me fix this blasted thing. It's been swinging like a toilet door on a prawn trawler.'

When he had crossed the road, Roisin punched my arm.

'We're not really going to eat crabs, are we?' she asked.

'Of course we are,' I lied. In all the years I had known Uncle Tam, he had never caught a crab. At least, he'd never caught an edible one. He'd caught a few condoms and several rusty cans of Irn-Bru, though.

Sylvia wasn't in the hall when we entered. But that was no surprise. It was easy to disappear in this building. It was a warren of split-levels, nooks and adjuncts. As I said, not a right angle in sight. The hall was heavy with mildew. The place was in decay. All the silverware on show had long since turned brown. Sylvia rarely had cause to impress guests. Her guest book was so slim, if you flicked back a few pages you'd find yourself transported back to the seventies.

We eventually found Sylvia putting her face on in the kitchen mirror. It was a sight I had seen often – the familiar flurry of pads, powders, brushes and sprays – Sylvia on autopilot, all polo neck and pearls. When she spoke, she acted like she hadn't seen us coming up the steps.

'Uch Anthony, you gave me an awful fright there. Forgive me doing my make-up. I've got to get my glad rags on. I'm supposed to be going out with some of the girls tonight.'

Sylvia never went out. There were no 'girls'.

'Come here and give your auntie a hug,' she said.

When I put my arms round her, the kitchen's familiar pot-pourri of sausage fat, cat food and Vim was replaced by the headier aroma of Anais Anais.

'Sylvia, I want you to meet Roach.'

'Roach?'

'It's short for Rochelle,' said Roisin, quick as a fox.

I felt another pang of uncertainty. She was a good liar. No. Trust her, Bic. You've got to trust her.

'Why don't you two sit yourselves down in the living room, and I'll wet a pot.'

God love Sylvia, she always made a fuss.

The living room was lit by an impressive bay window. Two zebra finches *twerped* in their bell-shaped cage, tossing sunflower seeds onto the piano below. An onyx duck led her ornamental brood along the piano top. If it was onyx, it was in Sylvia's living room – ducks, dolphins, cats, eggs.

I tapped out a few notes on the old joanna – Chopin's Mazurka in A minus (the piano was missing some keys). I closed its walnut lid. The commemorative Charles and Di engagement plate almost toppled off it as I did so.

Roisin seemed uncomfortable. 'I feel like this is our fifth date and you're finally taking me to meet the parents,' she said.

'Here we go,' said Sylvia.

From nowhere she had conjured a pot of coffee, a cheese board and an array of biscuits. Sylvia always made proper coffee. She wouldn't touch that granulated, vacuum-sealed, freeze-dried muck that they put in jars.

'Suggestive?' she offered.

Roisin accepted a digestive biscuit from a newly opened packet.

'I see Angus Neill's died. Heart attack. He was the purser on my first ferry over here. He was only forty-eight.'

Sylvia had reached that stage of life when she opened newspapers and immediately scanned the 'Deaths' columns for dearly departed friends.

'I don't know,' she added, 'they're dropping like flies.'

Roisin looked at me. I knew what she was thinking.

Sylvia threw a menthol number into her red lips and struggled with the weight of an onyx lighter, sucking its flame into the small white rod.

'You shouldn't smoke those things,' I said.

'Would you listen to him. Is he like that with you, Rochelle?'

Roisin nodded her head. I couldn't believe it, they'd only just met each other and already they were ganging up on me.

'Those things are killers,' I countered.

'Listen Bic, he's devoured my ovaries and done away with my breasts. Mr Melanoma can take my lungs and complete the set, for all I care. But he's not getting his hands on my cigarettes. It's my one pleasure in life. That and black coffee.' She turned to Roisin. 'Is yours OK, darling? I can get you more milk. Anthony, get Rochelle more milk.'

'I'm fine. Honestly,' said Roisin.

I walked over to the finches and rubbed some biscuit crumbs in through their bars.

'I got a letter from your father today. Sounds like he's having the time of it,' said Sylvia.

'Oh,' I said.

My only memory of the day my dad left me with Sylvia was not one of anger or sadness. I just remember thinking that Sylvia was the best woman ever. Sylvia had crisps and nuts and home-made jam, not bought jam, and drinks with big curly straws in them, and a large egg timer with purple sand inside that she allowed me to turn upside down when she was cooking. She even let me listen to her records. I would spend hours locked in my bedroom with Gene Pitney and Neil Diamond, the empty record sleeves strewn across the floor like big square Polo mints. I never remembered my mum listening to music.

'Look at him,' said Sylvia. She was conspiring with Roisin again. 'He's always been difficult. Did he tell you he was expelled from Stranraer Boys?'

'No,' said Roisin. She smiled at me.

'Anthony, tell Rochelle about your argument with the history master. He wrote an essay entitled "Jack the Ripper was a Fenian". Didn't you, Anthony?'

Sylvia was trying to embarrass me. I thought I'd better explain before Roisin got the wrong idea.

'He *was* a Fenian. Francis J. Tumblety, an Irish–American. He was part of the Irish Republican Brotherhood in 1888 and, when he died, the Sisters of Mercy found two cheap rings in his inventory. The same two rings had been cut from the fingers of one of the Ripper's victims. The history teacher thought I was making it up. He said I had an overactive imagination and it would get me into trouble. The same way he didn't believe me when I told him about Paddy Hitler, Adolf's nephew.'

Roisin folded her arms.

'It's true. Hitler's half-brother Alois worked as a waiter in the Shelbourne Hotel in Dublin. He married one of the local girls and together they had a son – Paddy.'

'God, it's no wonder they expelled you,' said Roisin.

'No, dear,' said Sylvia. 'Anthony was expelled because he got himself in the school photograph twice. He ran round the back of the other boys with the camera snapping him at both ends.'

I had to shut her up before she really dropped me in it. But Sylvia was first in again. 'So how's Jamie, my one and only? He told me they stopped work on that god-forsaken Dome.'

Sylvia hadn't heard the news about the bomb. How would I break it to her?

'Aye,' I said. 'You know Jamie. A lad of leisure.'

'What about you, Anthony? Anything strange or startling?'

'I haven't been up to much,' I said. 'Listen, Sylvia, do you mind if I stick the telly on?'

'Go ahead,' she said. She tapped Roisin's knee. 'Anthony used to love his wildlife programmes. He takes after my brother Ken. Have you ever seen Anthony's dad?'

'I haven't,' said Roisin.

'That's him on the telly – oh my . . .' said Sylvia.

My dad was on the screen, being interviewed by Moira Stewart via a live satellite link.

'So what would you like to say to your son?' asked Moira.

'Anthony, I know about the lies. I know you're not at university, and I know you cashed my money to fund the organization you represent. But you're still my son. Please, let the girl go and give yourself up. We can work something out. Please, son. Don't do anything stupid.'

'That was Kenneth Bickmore, the father of the suspected bomber, speaking live from our Johannesburg studio. Police this morning released a recording of Anthony Bickmore speaking yesterday on Radio Two. In it, he claimed he would kill and, he added, the Tall Ships race would go off with a bang. Following this interview, the BBC managed to capture exclusive footage of Bickmore attacking Culture Secretary Chris Smith. Our reporter, Matthew Williams, witnessed the assault –'

'At around two o'clock yesterday afternoon, our cameras were following Chris Smith as he toured the Greenwich Dock. Mr Smith had earlier announced another handout of twenty-five million pounds to the Millennium Commission, to help speed up work on the Dome. It was supposed to be a routine publicity exercise, but it ended with an attempt on his life. As our footage clearly shows, Bickmore first tries to smash the window of the Culture Secretary's car. Mr Smith, fearing for his safety, makes a desperate bid for freedom, only to be thwarted by a ferocious onslaught from Bickmore, slamming the car door against him. Mr Smith was later admitted to the Kensington Royal Infirmary with a broken wrist. He is said to be both shocked and saddened at this morning's events. Moira –'

'Police say the attack was politically motivated. Anthony Bickmore is believed to be working for a dissident Republican splinter group, unhappy with the terms of the Good Friday Agreement. Although no organization has yet claimed responsibility for the bombing, Detective Inspector Jackie McMullan of Scotland Yard had this to say –'

'Bickmore was arrested only last week in Hyde Park. He was protesting against Monday's upcoming marches by the Orange Order. He was also distributing Sinn Fein newsletters. We believe he could be commanding a new and particularly militant IRA cell on the British mainland. It is imperative that we catch this man.'

'Sinn Fein claim they know nothing about Anthony Bickmore. But, in a carefully worded statement, they did not condemn the bombing.'

I pressed the 'mute' button. It seemed to affect not only the TV, but my own powers of communication. The shock of seeing my father had robbed me of the ability to speak.

'So,' said Sylvia. 'You haven't been up to much?'

'It's all rubbish,' I said.

'Of course it is. I mean, it's not as if they've got a shred of evidence against you.'

Twenty-Seven

A searing white light infiltrated the bay window like cheap science fiction. Anchorage was surrounded by squad cars.

'Right Anthony, you and Rochelle get up to the attic room. I'll deal with this,' said Sylvia.

She could hear the bell from the reception desk. She waited till Bic and Rochelle had grabbed their bags and mounted the stairs before she made her way through, head held high, forever the matriarch. She counted a dozen police officers.

'Good evening, gentlemen. Twelve of you, is it? I can do you six doubles,' she said.

One of the two officers not in uniform flashed his ID: 'Jackie McMullan, Scotland Yard. Are you Sylvia Bickmore?'

'I *was* Sylvia Bickmore. I am now Sylvia Jameson.'

'That's odd,' he said. 'We have no record of you having married.'

'That's because I never married.'

The officer didn't pursue the matter. 'Sylvia, I'm looking for one Anthony Bickmore in connection with a very serious incident. I believe he's your nephew.'

'That's correct. One out of two, you're doing well.'

'Has Anthony contacted you recently?' he asked.

'No, I haven't seen hide nor hair of him. He did send me a card with a robin on it. Now let me see, when was that? Christmas, I think.'

'So you don't mind if we search the premises?'

'No, but you won't find it. I threw it out. It's unlucky to keep your Christmas cards up.'

'Please co-operate, Missus . . . Miss . . . Sylvia. We just want to take a quick look round.'

'Be my guest,' she said. 'And when you're done, you can put your comments in the guest book.'

Roisin and I ran up every flight bar the last. We walked that one. There was a time when I could conquer all seven storeys of Anchorage in thirty seconds. And my lungs were a lot smaller back then.

Roisin quietly clicked the door behind us. We were in the attic. We weren't alone. The bodies of three women had been left to rot in the room.

They were Sylvia's mannequins. She once used them for her dressmaking. They stood round a double bed like King Lear's daughters, waiting for the old fella to die.

'Get naked,' said Roisin. In two well-rehearsed movements, she removed all her clothes. She climbed into

308

the bed. 'Come on. This is no time to be going all coy on me. Get them off and get in here.'

I did as I was told. I could hear a commotion on the stairs. The door opened. Roisin pushed my head under the covers, between her legs. She started to writhe and make the sort of noises more commonly associated with wolves.

Someone entered the room.

'Who the fuck are you?' shouted Roisin. In a Scottish accent.

I felt her slapping my back. 'Alasdair, git up here, there's a man in oor room,' she screamed.

Before I had a chance to surface, I heard the man apologizing. He closed the door behind him.

'Jesus, Roach, that was inspired.'

She looked flushed, but proud of herself.

'I figured that if they're looking for a murderer and his hostage, they're unlikely to think that the two of them are shagging each other.'

I could feel her soft belly move against my cheek as she spoke. I could also feel myself hardening against her leg. I rolled away from her before she snapped it off.

'Oi,' she said. 'You're going nowhere.'

She pulled me back into the bed. She kissed me. Tongues.

I broke away from her. 'But I don't have condoms,' I said.

'I'm a Catholic, Bic. I don't believe in contraception. Just be careful.'

Finally we had something in common. I didn't believe in condoms either. Well, you wouldn't wear a comedy nose to a job interview.

We made love. We were careful.

We were also great. As we lay post-coitus, I expected our mannequin audience to hold up marks for artistic impression.

'Bic,' said Roisin. She was stroking my neck. 'What am I going to do about my brothers?'

'You mustn't contact them, Roach. Not until someone claims responsibility for this bomb.'

'But no-one has.'

'It only happened this morning. It's early days. Let's be patient. We're OK as long as we don't tell anyone we're here. I won't even tell Jambo. We'll just have to stick it out. I can't leave the house. My face will be everywhere.'

There was a knock at the door. I knew the drill. I was between Roisin's legs like a shot.

'Oh dear. I am sorry.'

It was Sylvia.

I surfaced again. 'It's OK. Come in. We thought you were the police.'

'They're long gone. I got rid of them. Nice boys, though. A few of them said they'd come back here for their annual golf weekend. I said I'd do them a special rate, full breakfast thrown in.'

'Thanks, Sylvia. We'll have to hide here for a day or two, till this mess sorts itself out,' I said.

'No problem. But you might want to tidy this room up a bit. Get rid of those dummies. Rochelle, did Anthony ever tell you about the time he got the Social Services onto me?'

Sylvia told her tale. I was only ten at the time. I had gone into school on a Monday. We were asked to write that familiar composition: 'My Weekend'. I wrote that my aunt had been sticking needles into a lady's boobs. I was referring to her mannequins, but my teachers didn't read it that way. They wanted to put me into care.

'Anthony, you start clearing the room and I'll bring you a cuppa,' said Sylvia. 'I just have to nip out and buy a carton of milk. I wasn't expecting guests.'

'No Sylvia, I'll go,' said Roisin. 'It's the least I can do.'

'That's awful nice of you, love. Just make sure it's full fat. That skimmed stuff is a waste of my time.'

They left me alone to make sense of the room.

I moved the mannequins out to the landing. I stood them outside the door like a praetorian guard.

I filled four cardboard boxes with junk, including a corked glass ball that held bath salts, numerous swatches of fabric, a Bell's bottle with a bellyful of half-pennies, and a broken clock whose hands hung limp, flinching for eternity round the half past six.

I cleared the last item from under the bed. It was a tin box with a picture of a matador and the word Madeira painted onto it. I recognized this tin. Sylvia used to keep her pins and needles in it. I remembered her tin because I once thought it was made by the paramilitaries – Made ira. I thought Sylvia was a terrorist.

The tin weighed almost nothing. I shook it. I couldn't hear any pins and needles. It must be empty. I opened it. The tin was stuffed with letters. They sprang out like a cheap trick when I removed the lid. I lifted one of the envelopes. It was postmarked Bangor – 28th June 1982.

I recognized my father's handwriting. I had seen it enough on the blue airmail envelopes he sent me. I opened the envelope, but there was no letter inside. It contained four press cuttings – *Ulster Newsletter*, *Belfast Telegraph*, *Irish News*, *County Down Spectator* – all referring to the same story. I read the clipping from the *Belly Telly* first:

FOUR ORPHANED IN HORSE TRAGEDY

Michael Patrick McKay, 38, and his wife Dympna Mary, 35, were killed yesterday afternoon when their car was hit by a runaway horse.

The freak accident leaves four children without parents.

The tragedy happened on the coast road just two miles from the family's home in Cushendun, Co. Antrim. Roisin McKay, the couple's daughter, was also travelling in the vehicle when it was hit. She suffered a broken leg, but staff at Ballymena Hospital say she is recovering well.

The horse belonged to the stable of Kenneth Bickmore from Bangor, Co. Down. His son Anthony was riding it when the accident happened.

'We come up here every Twelfth fortnight for a holiday,' said Mr Bickmore. 'My wife likes to bring a couple of the horses with us, to run them along the beach. My son was riding our youngest mare, Gracy, when she just took off. Something must have spooked her.'

Young Anthony Bickmore is believed to

have suffered a head injury in the collision. His father extended the family's deepest sympathies to the McKay children.

Mr Bickmore, a trained vet, destroyed the horse at the scene.

Twenty-Eight

Roisin paid for full fat milk and menthol cigarettes. She couldn't remember what brand Sylvia smoked, but the woman in the shop said she knew Anthony's aunt and handed Roisin twenty Consulate. Roisin let her keep the change. She set the coins down on Bic's face – his picture was on the late edition of the local rag.

A young man entered the shop. Roisin recognized him as the officer who had burst into the attic. As she passed him, she waved the cigarettes.

'I only smoke after sex,' she said, adopting her Scots lilt. 'I'm a twenty a day girl.'

The officer didn't know where to put himself.

Roisin didn't go back to Sylvia's straight away. She crossed to the docks.

The wind had got up and the loch was choppy. The Larne ferry was cutting through the waves. It towed a

314

white 'V' in its wake, like the train on a wedding gown. Appropriate, she thought, for wasn't Larne married to Stranraer.

She lifted Bic's mobile out of her pocket and checked that the battery was still powered up. She had taken the phone from the pile of Bic's clothes by the bed. He had been otherwise engaged between her legs.

She selected Sam's name. Her blood was racing.

The phone clicked.

'Cathal?'

'Roisin?'

'Oh thank God, Cathal. You don't know how good it is to hear your voice. Is Eamon with you?'

'Aye, do you want to speak to him?'

'No. I just— God, Cathal, I thought youse were dead, so I did.'

'Well, I'm alive. I'm not sure about Eamon, though. He looks like death warmed up. Then again, he's always been a pale bugger.'

'And Derm?' asked Roisin.

'Sadly Dermot is alive.'

'Is Derm with you?'

'No. He'll be on a Qantas jet by now, travelling under an assumed name.'

'The bomb. What happened?' asked Roisin.

'INLA. The bastards killed a load of wee girls. It's sick. We were at the dock this morning when we got a tip-off. Our boys called off the kidnapping, told us to get the fuck out of London. It was too late to stop them. Scum, they are.'

'I knew you weren't involved.'

315

'Us? Jesus, Roisin, what do you think we are? We're your brothers. We're not monsters. The bomb was big-league stuff.'

'I told Bic. I told him it wasn't you.'

'Has he touched you, Roach?'

'No. Why would he?' she asked.

'We heard on the radio that he's wanted in connection with the bomb. I know he's not INLA, he doesn't look like he has the wit. But some taxi driver's claiming that Bic killed his daughter, you know, that Sam girl. We found her coat at the stall before we got the order to pull out. We took her phone. It was the only way we could get hold of you. We tried to call you this morning, to warn you about the bomb, in case you showed up. When Bic didn't answer, we thought he'd taken you.'

'Bic's harmless. I've been with him since last night. It was my idea to bring him up here. I'm sorry, Cathal. I couldn't go through with it, the regatta, the presentation, any of it. I had to get out of the way.'

'That's OK, sis. At least you're safe. You did what you thought was right.'

'So where are you?' asked Roisin.

'We're staying with Eamon's mates in Watford. I was going to ask you the same question.'

'OK, but you mustn't tell anyone.'

'I won't.'

'Promise me, Cathal.'

'Roisin, when have I ever lied to you?'

'True. OK, I'm in Stranraer. We're holed up at a guest house. It's a bit grotty, but we're fine. Bic's aunt runs it. She's a funny critter. You should see the car she's got parked outside. It's an old Bewley, you know, like the

316

coffee. You'll have to tell Eamon. He'll be dead jealous.'

'Oh I'll tell him, don't you worry about that.'

'Cathal, I'd better go. They'll be expecting me back.'

'See you soon, Roach.'

Cathal put Sam's phone back in the glove compartment.

'Here we are,' said Eamon. 'Fish & Ships. The finest fish suppers in Stranraer.'

'I know where they're staying,' said Cathal. 'And the police are looking for Bickmore, so we'll be able to stroll right in.'

'Aye, but it can wait five minutes. I'm going to grab myself a Scotch pie and a can of Vimto. I'm not about to kill someone on an empty stomach.'

Twenty-Nine

I had killed her parents.

I read all four news clippings, just in case the *Belfast Telegraph* had got any of their facts wrong, say, the name of the kid on the horse. But they all said the same thing.

I had killed her parents.

There was no car bomb. Roisin's brothers had been lying to her all these years. They had brought her up to believe her parents had died at the hands of loyalist paramilitaries. They had brought her up to hate.

Why would they do such a thing? Why hadn't they told her it was all a tragic accident?

They would've been angry. But you couldn't hate a wee lad on a horse. Perhaps they needed another focus for their anger. They would've known I came from an affluent Protestant family. They would've read the papers. It would've been easy to resent us. It would've

318

been easy to hate us and all those like us. We were *the other lot*. The injustice of it. The brothers would have united themselves in their hatred towards *the other lot*. Their sister would hate *the other lot* too. The McKays would be stronger because of it. They would have a cause.

I closed the tin that the IRA hadn't made.

I now knew that Roisin's brothers were liars. And if they were liars, I was certain they were bombers and murderers. Roisin would have to believe me. I had the proof. But if I showed it to her, I would lose her. *Say looky here Roisin, your brothers are lying, murdering scum, and while we're at it, I killed your mum and dad.* It wasn't the basis for a long and fruitful relationship.

I had to tell her. And I had to go to the police with what I knew. It was my only way out of this. But what would that achieve? I would come out of it without her. I didn't want that. I wanted us to stay on the run for ever.

I felt the bump on the back of my head. I could remember nothing about that day, the Worst of Days. Why had my father never told me the full implications of my accident? Why hadn't Sylvia said anything?

I found her in the kitchen. She had her hands in a basin of white water and potato peel. She was rinsing the starch from some spuds.

'I'm only cutting spuds for Rochelle, yourself and me. It seems roast chicken and mash isn't good enough for Uncle Tam. He's away into the town for haggis and neeps.'

I set the tin on the worktop.

'Uch Anthony, where did you find that old thing? I meant to chuck that out years ago.' She gazed affectionately at the matador. 'Course, I can't sew any more, not with hands like these. I can barely peel a King Edward.' She cut the spuds into fours.

I threw the tin in the bin. But not before I had removed the envelope with the press cuttings. I unfolded one of the news stories and read its headline. Aloud.

A potato shucked across the worktop like a wet soap. Sylvia dropped her knife. She didn't bother to pick it up. She looked like she'd aged ten years in as many seconds.

'OK, sit down,' she said. She wiped her hands on a tea towel. She sparked up the gas hob and relit her half-smoked fag from the blue ring. She sat down opposite me, setting a heavy onyx ashtray between us. When she talked, her lips burst open like a wound that hadn't healed.

'Your father sent me the cuttings. He always kept in touch. I think he was too upset to write about what happened, so he sent me the news reports. Your parents didn't want you to know, Anthony. They didn't want you growing up with a thing like that on your conscience. You can't blame them for that.'

I said nothing.

'It wasn't your fault. Gracy, the horse that is, she saw a dog on the beach. She wasn't used to dogs. Your father wouldn't have dogs on the farm. Gracy just took off with you on the back of her. It wasn't your fault. Course at first your mum, well, she blamed your father. If you'd kept a dog on the farm, Gracy wouldn't have been spooked by them. None of it would've happened. Your mother didn't mean it, of course. She was at her wits' end. She and your father hadn't been getting on. Ken had been spending too much time away from you two, with his work. He knows that, Anthony. Don't think he doesn't regret it, because he does. I get letters from him all the time and in every one of them he says it. He thought he was providing for the two of you, earning enough money to get you the things you wanted. Your mother loved her horses. It costs a lot of money to keep horses.'

'But Dad got rid of them,' I said.

'He had to. You had become so terrified of them. I suppose that was the beginning of the end. The horses were all your mother had. She didn't have a husband. At least, not one that was there for her. And she didn't think she could be a mother to you. She had nearly lost you. She hated herself for that. So what was left? She couldn't ride her horses. She couldn't love her husband. And she couldn't be a mother to her son. She couldn't go on and that was that.'

Sylvia stuck the end of her cigarette against the cold stone of the ashtray and squeezed the life out of it.

'Are you saying it's my fault that Mum killed herself?'

'Love, it's nobody's fault. Not yours, not your father's. Sometimes there's just a sad inevitability about these things. It wasn't your fault that your mother loved you to bits. It was sad that she thought you deserved better.'

We heard the front door.

I quickly pocketed the news clippings.

Sylvia dabbed at her eyes with the tea towel, then blew her nose into it.

'There you go, two pints of full fat and a wee present for you Sylvia, just to say thanks,' said Roisin. She handed Sylvia a packet of cigarettes.

'Uch, you shouldn't have bothered. That's awfully kind of you, love. Sit yourself down there, I'm making some gunpowder.'

Sylvia plopped her potatoes into a pot of bubbling water.

I put Roisin straight. 'Gunpowder. It's Sylvia's mustard mash.'

'It's getting quite blustery out there. The wind would cut you in two,' said Roisin.

'Welcome to Stranraer,' said Sylvia.

It should have been so easy. All I had to do was take one of the clippings from my back pocket and set it on the table in front of Roisin. I could tell her it was time to stop hating. If she was to hate anyone, it should be me. But I couldn't do it. I just couldn't bring myself to let go of someone that meant so much to me. I couldn't allow the sand to slip through my fingers. Not again. Not after Mum.

The bell rang from reception.

'Shit, you don't think that's the police again?' I asked.

Sylvia had her hands full, basting a chicken.

'I'll walk through to the hall and check,' said Roisin. 'They think I'm a guest.'

'Tell them I'll be with them in a second,' said Sylvia. She donned her oven gloves, put the chicken back and closed the door on the bird. She threw the gloves off and rinsed her hands. 'Do I look presentable?' she asked.

I nodded.

She piled her hair on top of her head and clipped it in place. She needn't have bothered, for Roisin had already escorted the two officers into the kitchen.

'Bic . . . Sylvia,' she said. 'I'd like you to meet my two brothers, Eamon and Cathal.'

One of them set a green toolbox and a can of Vimto onto the table. The other offered me his hand. And I might have taken it, if it hadn't been holding a gun.

Thirty

'Cathal, what's going on?'

'This doesn't concern you, Roisin.'

He didn't take his eyes, or his gun, off me.

'Who's Roisin?' asked Sylvia.

'Shut the fuck up, lady,' said Eamon.

'Excuse me, this is my kitchen. I won't have someone using that sort of lang—'

'Did you not hear him? Put a sock in it before I put a bullet in it,' spat Cathal. He forced Sylvia backwards till her back arched over the cooker, perilously close to the flaming hob.

Roisin stood behind her younger brother. 'Cathal, don't do this. You can't go back to prison.'

'I knew it, Roisin,' I said, 'I knew at least one of your brothers was behind the bomb.'

'Who's Roisin?' repeated Sylvia.

'Would everyone just shut their mouths. Jesus fuckin'

Christ, I'm trying to think here. Eamon, I'm going to have to shoot the both of them. The old girl will blab about the bomb.'

'Less of the old,' said Sylvia.

'No, Cathal. You couldn't have,' said Roisin. She looked at her brothers, seeking even the slightest reassurance that they weren't behind the attack. But they couldn't give it to her.

'Derm put you up to it, didn't he?' she asked. 'You had no choice.' She was panicking. Like a cornered animal, she didn't know which way to turn.

'You're right, Roach,' said Eamon. 'We had no choice. We're fighting a war. We did what we had to do to defend our nation.'

He put a hand on his sister's shoulder. She beat it away.

'Don't be like that, sis. We can still get out of this. You can still come with us to Boston. With these two out of the way, nobody can trace us to the bomb. Bic is as good as guilty in the nation's eyes. They'll find him dead, case closed.'

Roisin's eyes seemed unusually large. It was like her brain was on overload, too much going in at once. So much information it was forcing her eyes out of their sockets.

'How could you kill all those people?' she asked.

'The cause,' said Eamon. 'The cause is bigger than all of us. It's too important. It's certainly more important than some scrawny Brit bastard that you've got a bit of a crush on.'

I assumed he was referring to me. I couldn't see any other scrawny Brit bastard in the kitchen.

'But you killed schoolgirls. Cathal told me four schoolgirls died,' said Roisin.

'What, you've been in contact with them?' I asked.

Roisin took something out of her coat pocket and set it on the table. My mobile. She couldn't look at me.

'See that, Bickmore. Your girlfriend's already cheating on you,' said Cathal. He jabbed at me with his gun.

'Cathal, leave him alone. If you kill him, you'll have to kill me.'

'Don't be ridiculous, Roach. You'll get over him. There'll be plenty guys in the States. And they're all loaded over there. They'll be able to offer you a lot more than a fucking pancake stall,' said Cathal. 'Or what's left of it.'

'I'm not going with you. You're . . . *evil* . . . the both of you,' she said.

'Roisin, how can we be evil? We did this for you.' Eamon tried to hold his sister. She wriggled out of his hands like a raw liver coated in oil.

'We did this so we could be a family again,' he explained. 'So all those brave Irish soldiers in British prisons could be free to join their families. And we did it for Mammy and Da. The Brits had to pay for taking them from us.'

'What makes you so sure the horse was a Brit?' I asked.

'Nobody asked you to talk,' said Cathal. His gun brushed my forehead when his hand shook. Which was often.

'I'm just asking. How did you know the horse was a loyalist? Did he have FTP tattooed on his hooves?'

'Bic, keep quiet. I can make them see sense,' said Roisin.

'Go on, Eamon. Tell her,' I said.

'You're talking out your blowhole, sunshine,' said Eamon.

'Oh yeah?' I reached into my back pocket.

'Jesus, he's got a gun,' said Cathal. He grabbed my hair and slammed me flat onto the table.

'I don't have a gun,' I protested.

'Bring your arms up slowly and put them on the table,' said Cathal.

'My aunt always told me it's bad manners to put your elbows on the table,' I said. 'Didn't you, Sylvia?'

'Elbows off table, don't pick at your food, no dessert till you've eaten your greens,' said Sylvia. From my position on the table, I could only see her feet. Her sharp potato knife lay between them, on the tiled floor.

'Well, your Uncle Cathal allows you,' he said. His gun kissed the lump on the back of my head.

I raised my arms. I opened my hands. Four pieces of newsprint fluttered onto the table. Roisin got to them before her brothers.

'What's this, Eamon?' she asked.

He didn't answer.

I was about to die. I thought it as good a time as any to tell her.

'Roisin. I killed your parents. It was an accident.'

'That was you, you fucker,' said Cathal.

'What are you going to do, boys, kill me even more?'

'I don't understand,' said Roisin. 'I remember a horse. I remember the young girl who was riding it. It can't have been you, Bic.'

'It was the Eighties, Roisin. I was only twelve. I had a long mullet. It was an accident.'

'Why . . . did you mean to get a short back and sides?' asked Cathal.

Roisin was still reading.

'Why didn't you tell me?' she asked. 'Any of you?'

'I only just found out,' I said. 'What was I supposed to say?'

'That you killed my parents.'

'That's right, Roach,' said Eamon. 'He killed Mammy and Da. And now he's got to die.'

'You killed my parents,' repeated Roisin. This time it was more of an accusation.

'Well, you were an accessory to the murder of one, possibly two of my friends,' I said.

'What do you want to do, call it quits?' said Roisin.

'What have we here, a lover's tiff?' asked Cathal.

'Excuse me,' said Sylvia. She brought her feet in front of the potato knife, hiding it. 'This has been lovely, but I've a bird drying up to nothing in the oven and a guest house to run. I'd love to stay and chat, but—'

'You're going nowhere,' said Cathal. He rested his gun on the table and bent down to pick up the knife with his free hand.

Roisin made a grab for the gun. 'Sick bastards!'

The gun fired.

My hands became raspberry ripple. They were spattered in Sylvia's blood.

Cathal pointed the gun at his sister.

'Go on then,' she said. Her face was hot with tears.

'No Cathal,' said Eamon. 'Not like this.'

Sylvia was still breathing. It was a thick, rasping staccato, the sound bits of cardboard used to make on my bicycle spokes. I tried to get to her, but Cathal forced

328

me back onto the table. He was too strong for me. Did the Maze have a gym?

Eamon opened his green toolbox.

'Let me guess,' I said. 'That box wouldn't happen to contain drugs, would it?'

'Eamon, please don't do this,' begged Roisin, all sticky-faced. A bubble popped in her nostril. I wanted to give her a tissue, but they were in my back pocket. I knew what would happen if I reached for my tissues. Cathal would blow my nose for me. He'd blow it right off my face.

Eamon prepared an injection.

'Is that for my hay fever?' I asked.

'This is a little something to mimic the effects of alcohol in your bloodstream,' he said.

'Could you not have just bought me a carry-out?' I asked.

'Trust me. This will get you blocked much quicker.'

'I dunno, Eamon. I haven't eaten in a while. A bottle of Thunderbird might do the trick.'

'You're funny,' said Cathal.

'You're not,' I replied.

'Eamon, I'm not going with you,' said Roisin.

'That's right, sis. You're not coming with us. But I will always be proud of you. The Irish people will be proud of you. You'll be a martyr to the cause,' he said.

I felt a little prick at the back of my neck. And it wasn't Cathal.

'What are you on about?' asked Roisin.

'We're all going to take a wee drive in that nice old car outside. Only, Cathal and I will be getting out before we push it into the loch, with you in the passenger seat, the old girl in the boot and Bic here at the wheel. You can see the front pages. The tabloids will really lap it up. Bic, the psychotic bomber, the child-killer, fuelled on alcohol, driving his innocent hostage into the sea. They'll find his aunt's body in the boot and the gun that shot her in his hand. They'll think the poor defenceless woman tried to turn him in. And you, Roisin, you'll become the biggest martyr Ireland's ever had.'

I don't remember much after that.

Thirty-One

Roisin pushed Bic into the back seat. Her brothers had forced her to walk him out to the Bentley. He was as drunk as a skunk, and he smelt as bad. He reminded her of Rory. The times she'd had to put him to bed. Surely Rory wasn't involved in all of this. Her mind was racing. It was tripping over itself. There had to be a way out of this. She got into the front passenger seat and pretended to click her seat belt closed. She left it loose, hiding it with her forearm.

'Did you get the old girl's keys?' asked Cathal.

'Aye,' said Eamon.

'Good, I can close this boot then.' He slammed the door on the still-breathing Sylvia. He climbed into the back seat beside Bic.

Eamon drove.

The Larne ferry had docked. It held its mouth wide open to accept the cars and lorries, but nothing was moving. The long queues of traffic tailed out of the port and back along Cairnryan road. Roisin quickly realized the delay was due to the bad weather. The loch looked as angry as the drivers waiting to board. The only people who didn't look angry were the coachloads of bandsmen. The delay gave them more drinking time.

Roisin noted lorries from Dumfries, Leighton Buzzard, Torquay and Ostend. She saw others returning to Cookstown, Finaghy, Enniskillen and Coleraine. She cried, because she knew she would never have the opportunity to return to Cushendun. She couldn't bring herself to look at her brothers, never mind speak to them. She gagged. She felt as if her stomach was in her throat, like she'd just hit some big, giddy bump in the road.

'I don't like this,' said Eamon. 'There's too many people about.'

'If you double back, we can cut round to the east side of the port. We'll be screened by those shipping containers.' He pointed them out to his brother.

Eamon followed his directions and drove the car a good distance from the ferry. He parked the Bentley on a redundant jetty that had been blackened by the rough licks of the sea. He kept the handbrake off.

'Right Cathal, we've got to be quick. We need to get Bic into the driver's seat,' he said.

Cathal opened his door and stepped out into the rain. Bic fell across the back seat as he did so.

'I know you understand, Roach,' said Eamon. 'If our organization took responsibility for this, the damage would be irreparable. Wee Irish schoolgirls, Roach. It would put us back years. Cathal and I . . . they'd kill us.

We have no choice. We're soldiers, we have to fight on. We have to fight for Ireland. I had hoped you could see it that way and come with us.'

Roisin said nothing. She didn't recognize her brothers any more than she recognized their rhetoric.

'Shit, someone's coming,' shouted Cathal. He dropped Bic onto the wet jetty. Bic's head cracked on the concrete. There was no life in his body. 'Eamon, help me lift him back in.'

A man was approaching the car. He wore a red white and blue uniform. A flute peeped out of his breast pocket.

The brothers slid Bic back into the seat. They jumped into the car.

'What'll we do?' asked Cathal. 'I think Bic's dead.'

The bandsman stopped about twenty feet from them. He took out his dick. He took a leak behind one of the corrugated containers.

'We're OK, he's only having a pish,' said Eamon.

'What if he checks us out?' asked Cathal.

'Let me think,' said Eamon. 'Right, Cathal, you pretend to be asleep on Bic's shoulder. Roisin, start kissing me.'

Roisin felt her brother's lips on her face. She tried to beat him back. He tucked a gun under her ribs.

'Give us a fucking kiss, sis.'

The bandsman zipped up his fly. He walked back towards the ferry.

'Thank fuck for that,' said Eamon.

The bandsman turned round. He eyed the Bentley. He started towards them again. He looked hammered.

'Shit, he's coming back.'

Roisin had Eamon's gun in her belly and his tongue in her mouth.

The bandsman rapped on the driver's window.

'Fuck off, mate,' shouted Eamon.

The bandsman slapped the window again.

Eamon wound it down. 'I said fuck off pal, I'm getting my oats.'

The bandsman fixed his drunken eyes on Roisin.

'She's a ride,' he said. 'Give us a crack at her when you're finished, mate.'

Eamon aimed his gun at the drunk.

A shot.

The bullet flew out the back of Eamon's head and shattered the passenger window. Roisin had her head in her knees. She had bits of Eamon's head in her jumper. She had seen the bandsman pull a gun.

'Police,' he shouted.

He checked the two in the back. They hadn't flinched when he fired. They must be dead. He opened the car door. He reached a hand out to Roisin. 'It's all over, love. Sam told us everything. She's going to be fine—'

'Get back,' shouted Roisin.

Cathal sprang up. He wound the seat belt round the policeman's neck and pulled hard.

Roisin got out. She opened the back door.

'Bic. Wake up.' Nothing. She grabbed his arms.

Cathal couldn't prevent his sister from dragging Bic from the car. He needed both his hands on the seat belt. The more the guy struggled, the tighter Cathal pulled the belt around his neck. He held on till the policeman started to impersonate his bandsman's uniform. His face turned red, then white, then blue.

Roisin supported Bic as best she could, guiding him across the wet dock towards the ferry terminal. The driving rain had begun to resuscitate him. He started to show some signs of life, occasionally throwing out a foot in an attempt at walking. Some bandsmen cheered as she walked him past. They raised their tins of Harp, toasting Bic's admirable drunkenness and Roisin's even more admirable ass.

Where were the police, thought Roisin. Surely they'd have the dock surrounded? Surely they wouldn't have just one guy covering such a big area? But what if the cop that discovered them had stumbled upon the Bentley by accident? What if he really had walked across to their side of the dock to take a leak behind the containers? He hadn't radioed for back-up. Cathal had wound a seat belt round his neck before he had time.

Roisin knew she had to be quick. She saw one of the bandsmen puking his ring behind a coach. She told Bic to stand where he was. She approached the vomiting man and feigned concern for his health.

'I'm fuckin' spannered,' he complained, like it wasn't obvious.

'This should sort you out,' said Roisin. She kicked him in the shin. He started to hop. He was so drunk, she was able to push him over with little difficulty. As he lay prostrate, she removed his jacket and hat.

Roisin forced Bic's arms into the tight sleeves of the jacket. It was about three sizes too small and orange, definitely not Bic's colour. She stuck the orange hat on her head and walked him to the footbridge, to board the boat.

The rusted iron steps felt like they were giving way

under her feet. She was knackered by the time she hauled Bic to the top of them. The ferry smelt of diesel and fish. She was soaked through. The last thing she needed was confrontation. She was stopped by one of the crew. He lifted Bic's chin.

'Christ, yer man's going to wake up with a sore head,' he said.

'Aye, and he has to play the Lambeg drum tomorrow,' said Roisin. 'He's been drinking for God and Ulster.'

'Jesus. His skull will be split.'

Roisin smiled and made to walk past the steward, but he stopped her with a firm hand.

'I'll need to see your tickets, love.'

'They're on the coach,' said Roisin. 'I had to come on ahead with this one before he threw up over the lot of us. These uniforms are a bitch to clean.'

The steward immediately recoiled from Bic. 'On you go then. You might want to get yer man into a toilet. You'll find them either end of the Stena Globetrotter lounge.'

'You're a darling,' said Roisin. She gave him a wet peck on the cheek.

Roisin got Bic into the ladies. She sat him upright on one of the toilets. She put a wad of paper towels behind his head and steadied him against the back wall of the cubicle.

'Can you hear me, Bic? It's Roisin. We're safe. I got us onto the ferry. The police know about Eamon and Cathal. Sam told them. Do you hear me, Bic? Sam's OK.'

Bic was mumbling. At least he's trying, thought Roisin.

'Bic, listen to me. I'm going to get you a coffee. I'll be

336

right back. You sit there. Don't move a muscle.' Not that he was capable, she thought.

Roisin left him in the glory hole.

When she returned, an elderly lady, clad head to toe in tartan, was drying her hands. She was staring at Bic with evident disgust. Roisin ignored her. She set the coffee down at Bic's feet. She slapped his cheek, trying to get a response.

'Why didn't I think of that,' said the tartan lady. She walked over and smacked Bic twice round the head. 'Pride of Penicuik, indeed. You've nothing to be proud of, sonny.'

It seemed to do the trick.

'Roisin,' he said. 'I need some air.'

I smelt salts. The sea was bringing me round.

Roisin and I walked to the front of the ferry. I felt drunk. I kept pitching to one side then the other. Roisin assured me it was just the boat listing. Loch Ryan had got all crotchety with us. It would stay rankled for another hour before spitting us out into the Irish Sea.

'Eamon's dead,' said Roisin. She was shivering. For some stupid reason she had dispensed with her jumper.

I took off my orange jacket and insisted she put it on. Why was I wearing an orange jacket?

'And Sylvia's dead,' I said.

'You don't know that, Bic. Cathal shot her in the shoulder. The police will have picked up the car by now. They'll find her in the boot and get her to hospital.'

'She's in the boot of a car? What car?' I couldn't remember a thing. 'And what about Cathal?' I asked.

'He doesn't know we're on the boat. I doubt he'll make

it out of Stranraer. He'll be back in a cell before we hit Larne. He can rot in hell, for all I care.'

'And us? Do you care about us?' I asked.

Roisin took a deep breath.

'It's hard for me, Bic. You killed my parents. I know it was an accident, I'm not blaming you. It's just, all these years I believed they were killed by terrorists. I've tried not to hate, I really have. But it's so hard. Countless times I pictured my mammy and da on that sunny day in the car. I've replayed it over and over – Da with his wisecracks, driving with no hands just to put the wind up us, and Mammy tearing strips off him for crunching his barley sugar instead of sucking it. It makes me sad, but my grief has always given way to bitterness and anger and hate. I *hated* the people who murdered them. And now I find that my hatred has been misplaced and I have to learn to grieve for my parents all over again. It's going to take a bit of time.'

'Well, isn't it as well I don't wear a watch,' I said.

I put my arms round her and shielded her from the elements.

The gulls were laughing. A band on the upper deck was in full drunken song. They thumped out a reel. We stood immediately below them and stared out to sea as 'Aghalee Heroes' echoed off the hills on both sides of the loch.

'What the fuck is this . . . *Titanic* meets the Twelfth?'

We turned to see Cathal, gun raised.

Roisin's nails dug into my wrists. I guessed it was the shock but, almost as quickly, her grip relaxed. She peeled my arms from her waist. 'It's over, Cathal,' she said. She took three slow strides towards him and stopped. There was a new determination about her. 'Larne harbour will be crawling with RUC. They know everything. There's nowhere to go.'

Cathal wiped his neck with his hand. A purple welt had formed on his palm. 'Yes there is, Roach. I've got hostages. You two are my ticket to the States.'

'So you're going to re-route this ferry to the U S of A?' I asked. 'It'll take months. If madness doesn't claim us, scurvy will.'

'I've got a good mind to shoot you now, pal,' screamed Cathal. 'I don't think I could stick you for another couple of hours. In fact, I can't. You're going overboard.' He looked mad. He shooed me away with his gun. He didn't give a damn that it could be seen from the deck above.

'You're making a big mistake,' I said. 'I'm a good swimmer. I could retrieve a brick from the bottom of that loch if I wanted, while wearing my pyjamas.'

'Go on. Get yourself up on the handrail.'

I refused to budge.

Cathal grabbed Roisin's arm and reeled her in to his chest. He put the gun to her head.

'Bic,' she screamed. She crunched her eyes shut as the gun bored into her temple.

'Don't make me do this,' said Cathal.

I wasn't about to. I climbed onto the handrail, the way I used to mount horses, throwing my right leg over the side.

'Let Roisin go,' I said.

'Jump,' he said.

'Not until you let her go.' I wanted to take one last

339

look at Roisin before I died. I didn't want to see her with a gun to her head. I didn't want to take her terror with me, under the seething water.

Cathal let her go, but forced her to watch.

'Now jump,' he said.

I brought my left leg across, so there was nothing between me and my death. I hooked my feet under the bars of the handrail and stood tall, just like they do in Acapulco. Only this was Loch Ryan. It was cold and wet and the sea was as black as a bin-liner.

I set myself. I heard Roisin cry as I jumped.

'Bic!'

The boat listed badly. One of my feet had stayed hooked to the railings and I was catapulted backwards onto the deck. There was a sound from below, like we'd hit an iceberg. The ferry was putting out its stabilizers. I saw Cathal getting to his feet. I couldn't get up, my ankle had snapped. He came towards me waving the gun.

There was an almighty bang.

A Lambeg drum rolled off the upper level and dispensed its full weight on top of Cathal.

He fell forward, smacking the metal deck.

He didn't move.

He lay on his chest and looked directly up at us.

His head was the wrong way round.

Thirty-two

The sound of barking.

My dad panicked. Two Alsatians were already upon him. A policeman came at him with something hard and metallic.

The policeman stopped. He presented my father with the pewter figurine, a miniature beagle. Engraved underneath it were the words: *Kenneth Bickmore, Life Patron, Battersea Dogs' Home*. Dad held a pretend handshake with the Chief Constable for the benefit of the cameras; a frozen handshake, as though both men were petrified. The Alsatians sat obediently either side of them. Dad *was* petrified. The cameras captured his grimace as he reluctantly accepted the award for five years' generous patronage to the famous dogs' home. His donations had topped the £20,000 mark. There was talk of them opening the Kenneth Bickmore Wing.

Roisin and I applauded. Sylvia was unable to join in.

She sat between us with her arm heavily strapped to her shoulder. The bullet had passed through the muscle and shattered her oven door. It had lodged in the breast of her roast chicken. Sadly, the bird was beyond resuscitation.

Sylvia's doctors had only allowed her down to London for the day on the condition that she saw a Harley Street specialist. He had delivered some bad news: the worst news a woman like Sylvia could hear. He had told her to quit smoking.

Sylvia tapped my knee. She asked me to rummage in her bag and light her a fag.

Jambo was unable to join us. Work had recommenced on the Millennium Dome. The black redstarts had not been seen in the fortnight since the bomb. Like the Tory politicians who had originally approved the Dome, they had taken flight and now distanced themselves from the building. If these bomb birds were true to their alias, they would now be constructing a nest from slivers of teak deckboard and burnt rope blasted from the *Cutty Sark*.

We lunched in a chain Italian in Victoria Station. Sylvia, Roisin and I finished our gnocchi while Dad talked. His plate was taken away half-full. He just couldn't stop talking. He waved a cold slice of garlic bread in the air, not once stopping to take a bite, and told his tales.

He told us the one about the honey badger, that most tenacious of creatures, how it could bring down an adult wildebeest by biting onto its balls and locking its jaw. Pound for pound the honey badger was Africa's most fearless animal, or so Dad claimed.

342

He told us how he was nearly killed while artificially inseminating a rhino. 'The vaginal canal contracted and my inseminating gun got stuck inside the poor old girl . . . she just took off with me still attached.'

Sylvia and Roisin shifted uncomfortably in their seats at that one.

We listened to the sad tale of the springbok that fell out of the sky. Dad had been airlifting the creature in his helicopter when its harness slipped. The animal went into free fall, crashing onto telephone wires and cutting off communications to half the Orange Free State.

When he went to the toilet, I apologized to Roisin. She told me to leave him alone. She thought he was 'a hoot'.

We finished our cappuccinos. Dad left a tip – 50 rand – and we sought the Gatwick Express. He and Sylvia were flying back up to Scotland that afternoon.

We made our way across the Victoria station concourse, but our progress was slow. My ankle remained in plaster and I still hadn't got the hang of my crutches. Sylvia insisted on staying back with Roisin and letting me hobble ahead with my father. She knew we had some talking to do.

Resolution Number Three: I had to start talking to my father again. Trouble was, you couldn't get a word in.

'So, Dad,' I said, 'when do you fly back to Jo'burg?'

Nice one, Bic. The first opportunity you've had in thirteen years to initiate a one-to-one conversation with your father, and you ask him when he plans to bugger off again.

'I don't know, Anthony. I'll stay till Syllie recuperates, I suppose. I'm not so sure I'll go back at all.'

'But what about the animal hospital? What about all

those things in your letters . . . the African sunshine, the cheap booze, the mountain golf, Sun City, the rich divorcees?'

'Uch, Anthony. You get tired of all that.'

I didn't believe him.

'What about you, son?' he asked. 'Now that we know you're not a Doctor of Botany and that you're no longer destined for a lucrative career on the payroll of some drugs multinational.'

He had it all planned out, didn't he.

'Dad, have I disappointed you?' I asked.

He stopped walking. A few paces behind, Sylvia feigned a pain in her shoulder, ensuring that the girls didn't catch us up.

'Son, you've disappointed nobody. Your mother would be proud of you.' He smiled, but it quickly fizzled away. 'Sarah's death hit me hard,' he said. 'She suffered from depression, but back then it wasn't considered an illness. Nobody thought to treat it. You were supposed to put up with it, to *thole* it. You were told to stop feeling sorry for yourself. You had to catch yourself on. And there was me, a vet, able to diagnose the most subtle and rare malady in animals, but incapable of spotting the decline in my own wife. I couldn't live with myself, Anthony. So I ran away. I ran away from my wife, my home, my country and, ultimately, my son. No, I'm the big disappointment in all of this.'

He looked as if he was about to hug me. He tentatively raised his arms, like he was on page one of *Teach Yourself Ballroom Dancing*, but his hands fell back into his blazer pockets.

'I don't know you, Anthony. Jesus Christ, when

344

Reuters got hold of me in the Drakensberg and told me about the bomb and the disappearing university money, I honestly thought you could have done it. I thought my running away had left you so screwed up that . . . you know . . . well, you read about these kids in the States, who walk into McDonald's with automatic weapons.'

Dad put himself between Sylvia and me. He didn't want his sister to see his eyes.

I forced a smile. I made sure that he registered it, before I said, 'Don't torture yourself, Dad. I turned out OK. Or, as Mum would say, I turned out *proper*.'

He nodded.

Roisin and I saw the two of them onto the train, a more difficult task than it sounds. Before he boarded, Dad chose to interrogate the platform guard about the make of the train, the year it was built, the yard it was built in, the materials it was built from and what proportion of his ticket price went directly into the pockets of Mr Branson. I pitied the pilot of their Glasgow-bound plane. Dad had every intention of visiting the cockpit.

Jewish Jeff was waiting out at the taxi rank, engine running. We drew huffs and tuts from the long queue, as we appeared to jump it and hop into his cab.

'Are you sure you want to do this, son?' he asked.

'Yes, Jeff. I need to see it.'

Jeff typed *Greenwich* into his new Sat Nav Route Master. It was so new the protective cellophane remained stuck to the screen, making it bubble. Jeff hadn't yet mastered its operation. He punched some keys and waited. The Route Master spat back that Greenwich was 1,164 miles away, with a predicted journey time of 18 hrs 43 mins. He switched it off.

'How's Sam?' asked Roisin.

'Fine, love. Sam's fine. Great hospital she's in. St George's, down in Tooting. Finest bed baths south of the river. I was thinking of checking myself in till I realized they had male nurses as well. Sam's had all her blood changed. I says to her, if it's good enough for Tina Turner, it's good enough for my daughter.'

In the end, Greenwich was only 6 miles and 25 mins away. It was 25 mins too far. Jeff sang 'Simply the best' for most of it.

Jeff parked up. He waited while I did what I had to do.

Roisin handed me my crutches and walked patiently beside me. We made our way into the market. Only the market was no longer there. The stalls and half the *Cutty Sark* had evaporated with it. There was just a waste-land of bricks and wood, fenced off on three sides and open on one (but the river prevented access from that side). The fencing was in full bloom. Still-wrapped bouquets sprouted out from every available gap. Lilies, carnations, tulips, gyp, orchids and irises panicled this way and that. They were tagged with cards handwritten by, among others, Americans, Danes, Germans, Japanese, Swedes, Spaniards and Canadians. There were a lot of cards from Irish people, many of whom also claimed to be Londoners. An Irish football scarf was tied to the very top of the fence. One end had been set on fire. The scarf read: *Republic of Ire*.

We stood in silence. It was a silence that the Thames did its level best to respect. I counted sixty elephants and then, like a referee's whistle, I broke the peace.

'What next, Roach?'

'I'm not sure. I'm going to wait till Eamon and Cathal

346

are buried before I go back to Northern Ireland. I'll visit their graves in my own time, but I want nothing to do with the funeral. Black gloves on the coffins, shots fired over their bodies . . . I won't be a part of that carry-on.'

'And what about the farm?'

'I'll have to sell up to pay off Rory's debts. I'll go and see him in prison but I can't say I'll welcome him back when he gets out. *If* he ever gets out. I had no idea Rory could be so deeply involved. Prison's probably the best thing for him. It might be the one thing that can stop his drinking.'

I wanted to take her for a last drink in the Seagull's Arms, but its windows were boarded up. Police incident posters were stuck to the boards. Some of them had my face on them – a still, culled from television pictures.

It was all too much for Roach. Those beautiful black eyebrows fell over her eyes and she cried into her sleeve.

'I've lost everything, Bic. And all because of some stupid war that started before I was born. I should leave that bloody country behind, get a plane ticket to JFK and take my chances from there. But I don't know how I'll cope without the farm. What am I going to do?'

'Sell it to me.'

'Bic, where would you find that sort of money?' She sniffed hard and wiped her cheeks from bottom to top, as though she was trying to push the tears back in.

'I have some savings tucked away. I was going to start a new business. I'll be due some insurance on the stall, Joe included a premium in the rent. And I own a flat in Crouch End. It may be a burnt-out shit-hole, but this is London, some idiot will still pay six figures for it.'

'I appreciate it, Bic, but you shouldn't feel sorry for me. You've been through enough yourself. You have your own life to be getting on with.'

But she said it like she wanted me to disagree.

'Don't be an eejit, Roach. You *are* my life now.'

As we walked back to the taxi, my ears caught some words lilting on the breeze. Roach was singing to herself:

'When yer man gets the ball, Non Iron beat them all—'

'Non iron?' I interrupted.

'It's the non-iron song,' she explained.

I must have looked at her like she was nuts, for she then swapped her broad Ulster accent for plummy BBC RP: 'The *Northern Ireland* song.'

'Ah,' I said.

'Honestly Bic, if you're going to live in Cushendun, you'll have to learn the lingo.'

Non Iron. How appropriate. For doesn't its border run across the island of Ireland like a crumpled crease. A crease that refuses to be ironed out.

1st January, 2000

A Tipperary teacher once avoided the lash and a lengthy spell in jail by persuading an Islamic court that drinking poteen was an act of worship. Judging by the size of my hangover, my place in heaven was assured.

Roach, on the other hand, was full of vim. And I don't mean we'd run out of whisky and she'd drunk whatever she'd found under the sink. I had to admire her energy. Only four hours previously, she had been dancing her legs off in the Lurig Inn.

Roach rubbed the sleep from her eyes. She looked tired but beautiful, dressed in nightie and wellies. She grabbed a big zinc bucket and walked out to the fields.

The kitchen needed a good clean, but at that moment the scouring pads would have been better applied to the inside of my head. The cleaning could wait.

Thankfully, I knew a good cure for a hangover. I rooted round our cupboards.

While Roach fed the horses I fixed the two of us an Ulster Fry: bacon, sausage, fried egg, grilled tomato, soda bread, potato bread and ostrich.

THE END

Remembering
Charlie & Dora Radcliffe, Elsie Carlisle, and D.H.

A SELECTED LIST OF FINE WRITING AVAILABLE FROM BLACK SWAN

☐	99860 5	IDIOGLOSSIA	*Eleanor Bailey*	£6.99
☐	99914 8	GALLOWAY STREET	*John Boyle*	£6.99
☐	77097 3	I LIKE IT LIKE THAT	*Claire Calman*	£6.99
☐	99979 2	GATES OF EDEN	*Ethan Coen*	£7.99
☐	99836 2	A HEART OF STONE	*Renate Dorrestein*	£6.99
☐	99925 3	THE BOOK OF THE HEATHEN	*Robert Edric*	£6.99
☐	99945 8	DEAD FAMOUS	*Ben Elton*	£6.99
☐	99759 5	DOG DAYS, GLENN MILLER NIGHTS	*Laurie Graham*	£6.99
☐	99987 3	NO ONE THINKS OF GREENLAND	*John Griesemer*	£6.99
☐	99966 0	WHILE THE SUN SHINES	*John Harding*	£6.99
☐	77082 5	THE WISDOM OF CROCODILES	*Paul Hoffman*	£7.99
☐	99916 4	AMERICAN BY BLOOD	*Andrew Huebner*	£6.99
☐	77109 0	THE FOURTH HAND	*John Irving*	£6.99
☐	99936 9	SOMEWHERE SOUTH OF HERE	*William Kowalski*	£6.99
☐	99984 9	STICKLEBACK	*John McCabe*	£6.99
☐	99907 5	DUBLIN	*Seán Moncrieff*	£6.99
☐	99901 6	WHITE MALE HEART	*Ruaridh Nicoll*	£6.99
☐	99919 9	NEEDLE IN THE GROOVE	*Jeff Noon*	£6.99
☐	99959 8	BACK ROADS	*Tawni O'Dell*	£6.99
☐	99844 3	THE BEST A MAN CAN GET	*John O'Farrell*	£6.99
☐	77096 5	BIG JESSIE	*Zane Radcliffe*	£6.99
☐	99645 9	THE WRONG BOY	*Willy Russell*	£6.99
☐	99952 0	LIFE ISN'T ALL HA HA HEE HEE	*Meera Syal*	£6.99
☐	99902 4	TO BE SOMEONE	*Louise Voss*	£6.99
☐	77000 0	A SCIENTIFIC ROMANCE	*Ronald Wright*	£6.99